NORTH
SEA

GREAT

DENMARK

BALTIC SEA

Belfast

IRELAND

BRITAIN

ATLANTIC

OCEAN

Portsmouth   London

NETH.

Calais

GERMANY

Cherbourg

Le Havre

FRANCE

SWITZ.

AUSTRIA

PORTUGAL

Marseilles

Toulon

ADRIATIC SEA

ITALY

SPAIN

Naples

Gibraltar

MEDITERRANEAN SEA

SP. MOROCCO

MOROCCO

Oran

ALGERIA

SICILY

NORMANDY

NORMANDY

a novel by
VICE ADMIRAL WILLIAM P. MACK

The Nautical & Aviation Publishing
Company of America

Library of Congress Catalog Card Number: 95-70665

ISBN: 1-877853-38-0

Printed in the United States of America
Library of Congress Cataloging-In-Publication Data

Mack, William P., 1915
Normandy: a novel / by William P. Mack.

CHAPTER ONE

Just before dawn on the 1st of May 1944, the four slim 1,630-ton Benson-class American destroyers of Destroyer Division 32 steamed north past the city of Boulogne on the northern coast of France along the Pas-de-Calais. The darkness of night still covered them as the ghostly column turned northeast after rounding Cape Griz-Nez. The ships' intended course led them parallel to the French coast, but far enough offshore to be outside the range of German artillery emplaced in the low-lying dunes and hills.

On board the USS *Lawrence*, eighteen officers and three hundred enlisted men stood at their battle stations, manning the ship's guns and operating her powerful propulsion machinery. Lieutenant Commander Robert Brosnan could feel the sweat starting on his chest under the weight of the kapok life jacket he was wearing, and even the short brown hair under his steel helmet was damp. The morning was cool, and a stream of salt air came in through the open pilothouse door. The moisture on his taut muscular body came from nervousness. Brosnan, as Executive Officer and Navigator of the Division's flagship, was responsible for the safe navigation of the *Lawrence* and also for the three ships astern of her. Safe navigation meant keeping the *Lawrence* in a position outside the one hundred-fathom curve. Six hundred feet was considered to be the maximum depth in which the Germans could place moored mines and still have them explode by contact with passing ships.

Brosnan finished a plot of a radar bearing and range to Cape Griz-Nez on the German-occupied coast of the Pas-de-Calais and looked at it nervously. It seemed to lie on the pencilled safe track he previously had drawn on the chart, and he straightened up, drew a deep breath, and stretched his aching shoulder muscles. Hours of bending over the chart of the English Channel had brought on fatigue.

Brosnan's shoulders were heavily muscled by years of intercollegiate wrestling, so much so that his uniform jackets bulged away from his uniform shirts at the back of his thick neck. Even the efforts of an expensive British tailor had failed to correct the problem. His shipmates still called him "Beetler," because of the section of jacket collar gaping at the back of his neck.

The Captain of the *Lawrence*, Commander Pete Fannon, came up behind Brosnan, leaned over the chart, and squinted at the latest pencilled position. He had difficulty making it out in the subdued glow of the red light over the chart desk. As he leaned closer, the light reflected off of his new commander's insignia and outlined his pencil-thin mustache and angular Oklahoma cowhand's face. "Jesus, Beetle, don't cut it too close. One of these Jerry mines going off could land us in downtown London without using a taxicab."

Brosnan laughed, his teeth glowing an odd cherry-red in the light. "Don't worry, Captain, I'll be careful. Much as I want to go back to London, I'm not in that much of a hurry."

Fannon was obviously jittery, "Come on, Beetle, let's take a look outside on the wing. The waters ahead are clear on the radar."

Before leaving the pilothouse, Brosnan checked the round glass surface of the surface search radar repeater, called a Plan Position Indicator, or PPI for short. Its blackness was lit by a small pencil of green light with one end anchored at the center and the rest of it rotating endlessly around its surface. To the south it traced the low, regular coast of the Pas-de-Calais.

Behind them glowing pips showed the other three ships of the division, the *Grayston*, *Hanly*, and *Thatcher*, all sister ships, following in column at intervals of one thousand yards. Brosnan laughed. "Never saw them keep such good station."

Fannon nodded as he walked away. "Damned right! They won't hit any mine that we hit first."

Brosnan handed his pencil to Quartermaster First Class Jack Benson, his assistant. "Keep the plot going, Benson. I'm going to see what the Captain wants."

As Brosnan stepped outside the pilothouse door onto the wing of the open bridge, he could see in the faint light of the coming dawn Captain Fannon standing next to the Commodore of the squadron, Captain Horace Phelps. Phelps was tall and slender and spoke with a slight British accent he had acquired during two tours of duty in the U.S. Embassy in London. Phelps said, "I don't see anything, but then I don't expect to since you reported the radar was clear."

Brosnan could hear Fannon, his eyes also glued to his binoculars, say, "Could be some wooden fishing boats out here. The radar wouldn't pick them up."

Phelps let his binoculars fall on their straps. "Bloody—I mean damned—hands are getting tired." Phelps seemed to be making a conscious effort to rid himself of the British expressions he had acquired in London.

Brosnan grinned. Phelps was married to the former Lady Claudia Staggers, and although not entitled to the honor, she was still called Lady Claudia. Fannon was engaged to her younger sister, Cornelia.

"Good morning, Commodore," Brosnan said.

Phelps nodded to him. "Good morning, Beetle."

The Captain turned to Brosnan, "Beetle, are the boat crews ready?"

"Yes, sir, they're in the boats, but they are curious as hell as to what we're really here for."

Phelps took a deep breath. "I don't like this silly business either, but orders are orders. Brosnan, please tell Lieutenant Kuberski to come out here."

Brosnan said, "Aye, aye, sir. I'll call him. He's looking at the PPI."

Brosnan stepped into the pilothouse and tapped the bulky Kuberski on the shoulder. "Stanley, your boss wants to see you out on the wing."

Kuberski looked up, his broad face reflecting the pale light of the PPI. "What do you think he wants?"

"Probably wants to start the operation. You'd better take a pencil and scratch pad with you."

Kuberski nodded. "Yeah, thanks. I'm still new to this damned staff job. I wish I were back up in the gun director." Kuberski was now the Commodore's Chief Staff Officer. In a long chain of reliefs two months ago, Lieutenant (junior grade) Severn Aronson had relieved Kuberski as the ship's gunnery officer, Kuberski had taken over from Brosnan as the Commodore's Chief Staff Officer, and Brosnan had relieved Fannon as the ship's Executive Officer. Captain Fannon's predecessor had assumed command of DesDiv 22 now working up in the Norfolk area. Kuberski picked up a pencil and pad and went out to the open bridge.

* * *

On the bridge wing, Commodore Phelps listened to the faint hum of the hydraulic motors of the 5-inch gun director above him and the deeper growl of the motors of the two 5-inch mounts on the forecastle below. Now and then their sounds became louder as the gun mounts moved faster, automatically following the electronic orders of the 5-inch gun director operators above. He grinned. "The kids up there are getting nervous." Phelps scratched his almost horse-like jaw which had long ago earned him the nickname "Horse" at the U.S. Naval Academy.

Fannon looked at him. "So am I. I don't like this business of being the bait on the hook."

Kuberski came out on the open bridge and stood next to the Commodore. "You wanted to see me, sir?"

Phelps sighed. "Yes, Stanley, send out an order on TBS: Immediate execute; commence Plan Charlie."

Kuberski scribbled hastily on his pad and left for the pilothouse.

"Now we begin," Phelps said.

* * *

In a few seconds Fannon could hear Kuberski's booming voice over the bridge speaker, and the officer of the deck poked his head out of the pilothouse door and said, "Captain, Plan Charlie has been executed. Request permission to stop the ship and lower the boats."

In a resigned voice, Fannon replied, "Permission granted. When they're clear, go to five knots and tell the gunnery officer to be alert. It will be daylight in a few minutes."

Fannon leaned over the starboard side and watched the boat being lowered. Astern of the *Lawrence*, the other ships stopped obediently and began to lower their boats as well. The *Lawrence*'s boat crew was in full battle dress. A signalman and a quartermaster sat in the stern compartment together with the boat officer, Lieutenant (junior grade) Tubby Raymond. Raymond's rotund form appeared stuffed into his restraining kapok life jacket.

Fannon walked over to the port side and watched the second boat being lowered under the command of Lieutenant (junior grade) Michael Farraday, the *Lawrence*'s torpedo and communications officer. Quickly both boats headed toward the distant coast of the Pas-de-Calais. In the new light, Fannon could see the combination of curiosity and anxiety in the faces of the crews looking back toward the ship, and he cursed silently at the thought of having to send them on a dangerous mission without explaining the reason behind the risk.

As the boats of the four ships faded into the distance, Fannon heard the officer of the deck order, "All ahead one-third." Below, the vibration of the ship's propulsive machinery started again.

Above the bridge, the 5-inch director was pointed toward the shore, now becoming increasingly visible in the morning light. Fannon clenched his fists, "Come on out, you bastards, and get this over with," he muttered.

Phelps heard him. "It may not be so soon. Maybe not until tomorrow. We have to make certain they know we're here."

* * *

In the *Lawrence*'s number-one whaleboat, Signalman Third Class Buster Acton said, "Just what the hell are we doing, Mister Raymond? This doesn't make sense."

Raymond shrugged, secretly admiring Acton's slim blond California surfer good looks and wondering why his own body insisted on putting on weight in spite of how much he dieted. "I can't tell you exactly myself. We just have to carry out our orders. Keep a good lookout on the ship for signals. Swenson will take soundings when we reach our assigned area, and I'll record them on the chart."

Swenson was carefully checking the coils of line attached to his heavy sounding lead. "Jesus, Mister Raymond, I've got fifty fathoms of line here. That's a helluva lot, and I'll never get it to the bottom."

Raymond said patiently, "Get it down as far as you can. If you don't hit bottom by thirty fathoms, pull it up, report no bottom at thirty fathoms, and heave it again. We'll keep moving in closer."

"Don't make sense. What are we suppose to do? Pretend to take soundings?"

Raymond sighed. "Maybe that's just what we're supposed to be doing. Now get on with it."

* * *

Raymond looked back at the column of four ships, paralleling the coast of France at about five knots. Even at such a slow speed, he thought, they looked fast. Their graceful twin stacks raked back at a slight angle, and the four 5-inch guns in square steel mounts looked powerful and ready. Filling the gaps aft of mount 52 and forward of mount 53 were 40- and 20-millimeter machine guns. A single quintuple torpedo tube mount was poised on the raised torpedo deck running aft from the forecastle to the after deck house.

The young Lieutenant was proud of his ship, her skipper, and her crew. He had served in her for more than a year in the campaign in the Mediterranean to take Sicily and Southern Italy. The ship had fought well, and he had every confidence that she could continue the fight.

Still, the briefing he had been given by the Captain troubled him. Fannon was normally frank and straightforward in his dealings with his officers. This time Raymond knew he was holding back. The chart Fannon had given him, for instance, already had more and better soundings on it than the *Lawrence*'s crew could take. But Fannon only mumbled something about checking them, evaded Raymond's questions, and wouldn't tell him the purpose of the mission.

Raymond looked down at the chart perched on his lap and shifted his thick thighs so it wouldn't fall off. "Jesus!" he said. "This line on the chart we're supposed to traverse shows depths of more than fifty fathoms." The Lieutenant remembered that he had asked the Captain about the danger of mines, and Fannon had told him not to worry about it. "Your boat," he said, "only draws about two feet, and the mines will be riding at least ten feet under the surface."

Raymond sighed, regretting the words he said next. "Captain, I think this mission is a lot of bull."

Fannon had turned red, and his hands had clasped and unclasped, but he regained his composure before he responded. "Tubby, don't say any more. I can't answer you now. Just do the best you can."

*   *   *

Raymond's thoughts were interrupted by the coxswain of the boat who leaned over the side and thrust his hand in the passing water. "Mister Raymond, this stuff is cold as hell. What do you want us to do if the Germans come out here and strafe us?"

Raymond shrugged. "The Exec gave us two choices: stop the boat and go over the side and hold on, or keep moving and get down behind the engine."

The coxswain was silent for a moment. Then he said, "I don't think we want to be in that damned water. I vote for the engine bit."

Raymond nodded; then he grinned. "Somebody will have to stay back here and steer the boat."

The coxswain shrugged. "I lose either way."

Raymond shook his head. "No you don't. I'm the boat officer and I'll steer it. You head for the engine."

Raymond looked at his watch, made a rapid mental calculation, and pencilled a mark on the chart on his lap. "Coxswain," he said, "turn west and slow to half speed.

Then he turned to Swenson, who was standing in the bow holding the heavy sounding lead and several bights of line in his hands. "Swenson, start your soundings."

Acton was watching the *Lawrence*'s signal bridge. Raymond said, "Acton, watch the ship for signals, but spend half your time looking toward the shore for signs of air attack. The boat engineer will help you."

Acton's face paled, and he turned away. Raymond suddenly felt sorry for the young Californian and tried to cheer him up. "Acton, just imagine you're looking at the beach in Southern California."

Acton laughed. "Not the same, Mister Raymond, those Nazi bastards over there mean business."

CHAPTER TWO

Commodore Phelps paced the open bridge nervously, the leather heels on his British Wellington half boots clicking in a regular pattern on the bridge deck. He shifted his gaze alternately as he reached the end of his pacing, watching the slow progress of the eight motor whaleboats toward the distant shore while scanning the sky for German aircraft.

For the tenth time since dawn, he asked his chief staff officer, Lieutenant Kuberski, if there had been any aircraft contacts on the air search radar. As with each time before, Kuberski nodded patiently and said, "Nothing yet, sir."

At 1200, with the sun at its highest and Phelps starting his sixth cup of coffee, Kuberski stuck his head out of the pilothouse door. In his booming voice, he said, "Com-modore, single air contact on the air search radar headed west. Must be a Jerry patrolling along the coast. He hasn't changed course so he must not have seen us."

Phelps was relieved. "Thank you, Stanley, but next time not so loud. You're scaring the director crew up there."

Kuberski looked up at the gunnery officer, Lieutenant Aronson, and his trainer, who were standing up in the director with their heads out of the top hatches. Aronson grinned and waved a hand at Kuberski.

Kuberski grinned back, nodded toward the director, and said to the Commodore, "Good crew up there. I trained them well, and I hated to leave them."

Phelps nodded patiently. "I know, Stanley, but I needed you down here."

Kuberski tried to hide his disappointment. "Sir, if the German aircraft has sighted us, shouldn't we get some action any minute now?"

"You're probably right, Stanley, although not from him. I'm hoping he will report us to his base and other aircraft will be sent out to investigate us." Phelps cleared his throat. "Ask Captain Fannon to come out here a minute."

Kuberski disappeared. Soon Fannon stepped over the raised door coaming, catching his toe on it and cursing as he regained his balance.

Phelps laughed. "I think we're all getting tired, but I think this deception plan is about to pay off. I want the German command to make an overt move toward us so we'll be sure they know we're here."

Fannon gripped the bridge bulwark with his left hand, and his caloused knuckles whitened as if he were gripping the reins of a stallion on his quarter-horse ranch back in Oklahoma. The Captain sounded edgy as he spoke to the Commodore, "Sir, you told all the skippers what we're doing, and we understand, but it's hard not to be able to tell our officers and men. They're going to bear the brunt of the German reaction to our movement, and they don't know why they've been put at risk."

Phelps said gravely, "I know, but General Eisenhower insisted on the utmost secrecy. General Patton's elaborate plan to make the Germans think the Allies are going to land on the beaches along the Pas-de-Calais has to succeed, and our part is designed to make the Germans think we are taking soundings in preparation for a landing. One loose remark about what we've been doing by one of our men in a bar later, might destroy the whole deception and result in unnecessary deaths. Our men must think we're taking soundings for a landing." Fannon shivered slightly, put his hands in his jacket pockets, and stared at the deck without saying more.

*   *   *

After a hurried lunch on a tray, the Captain returned to scanning the sky over the beach, but the sky above the narrow band of haze hanging over the coast stayed clear.

About 1400, Kuberski burst out of the bridge door, closely followed by Brosnan. Kuberski shouted in his fog-horn voice, "Sir, CIC reports multiple contacts on air search radar headed toward us at low altitude. They've got to be what we've been waiting for."

Fannon hurriedly lifted his binoculars and scanned the shore. Phelps and Brosnan, standing beside him, did the same. The tension grew as they held their breath and moved their binoculars back and forth over the coast. Brosnan was the first to spot the aircraft as they came out of the haze. "Eight Heinkels!" he shouted. "Starboard beam! Low! Spread out in two lines!"

Fannon studied the approaching formation. Then he said, "They'll put one Heinkel from the first group on each destroyer, and the other four will leave the formation and strafe the whaleboats."

Phelps rubbed his long jaw and said, "I agree." He turned to Kuberski. "Stanley, send out on TBS: Immediate execute; maneuver independently!"

Kuberski dashed for the TBS transmitter in the pilothouse, nearly tackling two signalmen rushing for the signal bags.

Fannon didn't wait to hear the signal come over the loudspeaker. He turned to Brill, the red-headed Chief Yeoman, wearing a telephone headset, who was standing next to him. "Gun Control, commence firing when aircraft are in range! Be careful not to hit our boats!"

Chief Brill nodded, mashed down on his transmitter button, and relayed the message.

Fannon stuck his head in the pilothouse. "I have the conn. All ahead full."

The deck began to vibrate as the ship's turbines gulped the steam blasting from the the wide-open throttles. The wind coming across the *Lawrence* began to fill out the colors flying from the gaff, and the signal halyards started to thrum loudly. Fannon faced into the wind, felt the increasing pressure, and took a deep breath as he felt a surge of adrenalin. It had been several months since the *Lawrence*'s last battles with the Germans in the Mediterranean off the coast of Italy. During those battles, he had served as the ship's Executive Officer and had only limited responsibilities. Now, he was in command, and this would be his first experience with the full responsibility for his ship and her superb crew. Fannon's thoughts momentarily returned to his quarterhorse racing days in Oklahoma. The excitement he felt before taking a spirited horse through a race was not unlike this moment on his surging ship. He wanted the action to begin.

The guns jittered back and forth under the control of the 5-inch director and then steadied as the gunnery officer coached the director trainer onto the Heinkel approaching on the left and headed directly for them. Fannon wondered why Aronson was taking so long to open fire. Then he realized the young gunnery officer was waiting for the lead Heinkel in the forward line of the formation to pass clear of the boats, so shrapnel from the antiaircraft bursts would not fall on them.

Fannon gripped the bulkhead exultantly, and just when he thought he could stand the suspense no longer, he heard Aronson's calm command, "Commence firing!"

Almost immediately the four guns spoke. For a moment Fannon was blinded by the smokeless powder residue flying across the bridge from the forward guns. Though the small particles stung his eyes, he forced them open in time to see the Heinkel coming directly at them, a large bomb slung under its belly. The aircraft closed, with its propellers whirling ominously, and Fannon braced himself for the attack. Then, suddenly, as the pilot prepared to pull up and release his bomb, a projectile ripped into the aircraft, squarely at its left wing root. The left wing peeled back like a stripped banana skin, and the aircraft rolled sharply to its left and plunged into the water. When the nose broke the surface, the rest of the silver fuselage twisted forward, and the wreckage disintegrated.

Fannon's elation quickly faded to concern as he searched for the three remaining Heinkels. Two, he saw, had crashed in the water amid pools of burning fuel, shot down by the gunfire of the other ships; but the fourth had pulled away without dropping its bomb. All four destroyers started firing at it. Phelps, inside the pilothouse, grabbed the TBS transmitter from Kuberski and yelled into it, "Fantastic, this is Barracuda, cease firing at retreating aircraft! Let the bastard go! Commence firing on aircraft strafing our boats!"

Fannon suddenly realized he had neglected the whaleboats, and he cursed himself silently. Brosnan, who saw the boats turning to avoid the attacking aircraft, shouted, "Captain, our boats need help! They're catching hell!"

The other four Heinkels were strafing the distant line of boats in looping shallow dives. When the aircraft began their firing runs, gouts of water rose from the marching lines of bullets where they hit the surface. Fannon shouted to Chief Brill, "Tell Gun Control to shift fire to the Heinkels that are shooting at our boats!"

Fannon leaned in the pilothouse door and shouted to Benson, who had taken the helm, "Head for our boats; to hell with the mines!"

Benson spun the wheel, and the *Lawrence*'s bow swung toward the helpless craft.

"Damn!" Fannon muttered "I hope we're in time."

Already the forward guns were blasting away, but the ship's superstructure prevented the after guns from firing. Bursts of fire exploded around the diving Heinkels, as all four ships began to fire at them. Fannon gritted his teeth, hoping that the gunfire would drive them away before it was too late.

*   *   *

In the number-one whaleboat, Tubby Raymond had seen the Heinkels approaching in two parallel lines low over the lead-gray water. He glanced over his shoulder and noted that the destroyers were beginning to manuever independently, but they were too far away to offer much help.

Raymond shouted to the coxswain, "Head toward the ship at full speed!"

In the bow, Swenson yelled, "But, sir, I've got thirty fathoms of line over the side!"

Raymond scanned the other boats. Most were headed for their parent ships, white water bubbling under their pointed bows. Two had stopped, and their crews were over the side. The operation was definitely over.

Raymond turned to Swenson, "Throw the rest of the line over the side! We're not taking this lying down, or at least I'm not. The rest of you get down in the bottom of the boat and keep your heads down."

The coxswain gratefully relinquished the tiller and joined the others crouched on the bottom of the boat next to the heavy steel engine. Raymond took over the tiller and hunched down in the after compartment as far as he could. Overhead, the first line of four German aircraft screamed by and headed for the destroyers. Raymond felt the aircrafts' propeller wash beat the water as the Heinkels skimmed over at low altitude. He could see the swastikas under the wings of the nearest Heinkel and an ugly bomb hanging under the fuselage. The Lieutenant made out the black helmeted face of the pilot, but the German ignored them and Raymond raised a middle finger in salute.

When the gunfire from the ships began, Raymond ducked instinctively. The boom of exploding projectiles filled the air just ahead of their speeding boat. On the third salvo, the big Heinkel lost its port wing, cartwheeled, and crashed, scattering debris over a wide area. The boat crew cheered, but the boat engineer, keeping a good lookout aft, cursed over the din and pointed at the second line of approaching aircraft. One was coming directly at their laboring boat. Raymond followed the engineer's pointing arm and anticipated disaster. "Holy Christ!" he muttered, and he jammed the tiller over full so that the engine would be between the oncoming aircraft and the crew huddled on the other side of it. He knew he would have no protection, and for a moment he felt sure of death.

When the two machine guns in the Heinkel's wings began to blink, parallel rows of splashes raced toward the boat. But, apparently, Raymond's course change threw off the pilot's aim, and the speeding lines of splashes passed close astern. Raymond let out his breath and watched as the Heinkel circled for another run. This time the pilot anticipated Raymond's turn. The Lieutenant heard the rows of splashes coming, but then they seemed to stop just short of the boat, and for a split second Raymond thought the pilot had ceased firing. Then he realized projectiles were thudding into the side of the boat, and one clanged loudly as it hit the metal engine.

Something struck Raymond's lifejacket and pushed him to the deck. Tubby knew he had been hit, but he felt little pain. Pulling himself up to the tiller, he felt around his midsection with his free hand. Reaching under a huge tear in the kapok section of his lifejacket, he saw that his hand was covered with blood. A swell of fear and pain began to spread across his chest, but he knew he still was able to function.

While he was pulling himself up, a 5-inch projectile struck the attacker, and the boat engineer, who was still bold enough to raise his head over the side of the boat, pointed forward. "They got the bastard!" he yelled.

Raymond looked up in time to see parts of the Heinkel raining into the sea and puddles of gasoline beginning to burn. Other German aircraft were either burning or trying to escape from the curtain of fire hanging in front of the boats.

Raymond grinned at the boat engineer, a first class machinist named Frenchy Bennaret, who had volunteered to take the place of the regular engineer. "Sorry you came?"

Bennaret's bushy mustache quivered. "Hell no, Mister Raymond; best show I've seen since I left the China Station, but you're bleeding. Can I help?"

Raymond took a deep breath. All his limbs seemed to work, although the pain around his midsection was increasing. "No," he said. He looked down at the other men crowded behind the engine. "You guys can get up now. It's all over."

The four destroyers were now speeding toward their boats like mother hens looking for their chicks. Bennaret looked over his shoulder at the oncoming ships. "Look at the bastards come!" He bent over the boat engine and nudged the throttle, "Sorry, sir, this is as fast as she'll go."

Lights began to blink on the *Lawrence*'s signal bridge. Acton watched them intently, his blond hair blowing in the wind. "Sir," he said, "They're recalling us."

"Hell!" Bennaret growled. "They couldn't keep us away."

Raymond, beginning to feel faint, gave up the tiller to the coxswain. "I've got to sit down," he said in a weakened voice. "Take her in."

* * *

Fannon came out on the bridge wing and watched the approaching boats. He shook his head. "Those boat crews had a helluva scare out there."

Brosnan agreed. "I'm sure they'll be glad to get back aboard and to know this is over."

Fannon nodded grimly. "Not half as glad as I'll be when this operation is over."

Phelps, standing nearby, shook his head. "Sorry, gentlemen, it isn't over yet. Come down to my cabin when the boats are all safely aboard and we're back in formation headed away from France. There'll be more of this operation, but I think you'll like the rest of it."

Fannon snorted. "I haven't seen anything about it I've liked yet."

Phelps grinned, "Be patient, Captain."

* * *

Alongside, crewmen watched the *Lawrence*'s two whaleboats rise slowly under their davits. From one of the boats, Tubby Raymond could see the chief boatswain's mate and the chief pharmacist's mate waiting expectantly.

Raymond grinned. "You two look like a couple of ghosts."

The chief pharmacist's mate said, "The executive officer said you may be wounded."

The boat was stopped at deck level and Raymond stepped on to the deck. The chief boatswain's mate untied his kapok lifejacket and gently removed it. "You sure tore up my life-jacket," he said glumly.

Raymond laughed. "Don't knock it. It probably saved my life."

The chief pharmacist's mate ripped Raymond's shirt aside and looked at his wound. "Well, I'll be damned. You lost some blood, but it isn't serious. Come with me to the wardroom and I'll get the doctor to sew you up."

Raymond asked hopefully. "I'll be laid up for a few days?"

"Naw, you'll be back to duty by breakfast."

CHAPTER THREE

Fannon, Brosnan, and Kuberski joined the Commodore in his cabin. Stevenson, the Commodore's steward, served coffee and a large plate of cookies and then left, closing the door firmly. Kuberski bent over the plate of cookies and chose two of the larger ones. "Stevenson is one hell of a good cook," he said.

Phelps smiled as he watched the first cookies disappear. "Well, if the rest of us want any cookies we'll have to get the jump on Stanley," he said, reaching for a sugar cookie.

Kuberski colored slightly. "Sorry, sir, but I didn't get much dinner."

Phelps grinned. "I know, and I'm glad you liked these. Now the rest of you sit down and listen carefully. I know you think we've finished our part of General Patton's deception."

Fannon fidgeted. "Yes, sir, it could have been worse. Can't we leave now?"

Phelps rubbed his jaw. "We could, but I think our men deserve a chance to do something positive, and to get a little revenge."

Brosnan pulled the plate of cookies away from Kuberski. He took his eyes off of the plate, and Kuberski pulled it back. Brosnan gave up and said to the Commodore, "Sir, do you have something specific in mind?"

Phelps looked at the overhead. "As a horse race lover, nothing I would bet much on, but I'll lay odds that the Germans will send a pack of E-boats out from Ostend, Belgium, looking for us tomorrow morning."

Kuberski beamed. "And we'll be there?"

"Oh, no, we'll be there long before they get there. I figure about 0200."

Fannon grinned. "What we westerners would call dry-gulching 'em."

Phelps nodded. "Thanks. Somehow I couldn't remember the American word."

Fannon was beaming. "Hot damn! That'll cheer up the troops, and they need something."

Phelps got up and stretched his long arms. "I thought you'd like the plan. Now you and I can turn in and our two bloody-er-stellar assistants can go up to CIC and concoct a battle plan. The plan should call for the division to approach the area we were in today about 0200 in a line of bearing at 25 knots. Reverse course tonight and put the plan together to make that possible. The *Hanly* should be prepared to fire a starshell spread on command, and all ships should all be prepared to open fire at about six thousand yards."

Kuberski scooped up the remainder of the cookies. "Aye, aye, sir. Let's go, Beetle."

*   *   *

Brosnan and Kuberski went to the darkened combat information center. Several men sat at consoles or stood at plots around the compartment. The operators at the consoles watched the air and surface search radar beams rotate endlessly around the screens. A huge air plotting board covered one side of the room. Behind a transparent plexiglass screen a man wearing earphones conferred with the air search radar operator and plotted contacts with a grease pencil. The plots were written backwards so that the writing appeared readable to those working in front of the screen. In one corner, Lieutenant (junior grade) Sean O'Grady, the staff operations officer in charge of the CIC watch, was sitting at a small desk. Although he was on the Commodore's staff, the Commodore had ordered him to stand watch in CIC until a replacement for the CIC officer of the ship arrived from the States.

O'Grady looked expectantly at Kuberski's handful of cookies. "Do I get some of those?"

Kuberski laughed. "Why not?" He handed O'Grady half of the cookies. "But you'll have to let us use the dead reckoning tracer top for a desk while we're putting this plan together. Beetle and I have a lot of work to do."

O'Grady said, "Sure, the DRT is all yours. Just don't drop any crumbs in the works. We need it badly."

Brosnan spread out a chart of the area on the DRT and placed some blank dispatch forms on top of it. Kuberski bent over the chart next to him. "Ostend is over here to the southeast," Brosnan said. "The E-boats will be coming from there. We need to approach the area on a southeasterly course in a line of bearing, but enough off line from the direction of the enemy so that all four guns of each ship will bear on them. That means about 20 degrees."

Kuberski made some marks on the chart and said, "Got it. Approach course one seven zero, speed two five."

Brosnan said, "Write all this down on a dispatch form. Start with the words, 'Battle Plan X ray. Expected action against German E-boats.' "

Kuberski scribbled furiously. "What next?"

Brosnan rubbed his tired eyes. "Put in the expected enemy force, six to ten E-Boats."

"What next?"

Brosnan was now more awake. "On making contact and when directed, *Hanly* fire four-gun starshell spread. On identification of the enemy, *Lawrence* assigned leading target. Others assigned targets in sequence from the left. After destruction of initial targets, shift to secondary targets. Expect to open fire about 0100 on signal or following motions of the flagship at about six thousand yards."

Kuberski finished the dispatch. "This is pretty simple. Is it enough?"

Brosnan yawned. "Sure. The simplest plans are best. The Commodore will like it. Take it to him. I'm going below for a little rest."

Kuberski looked at the clock. "The Commodore said to reverse course at midnight. It's 2350. You won't have much time to sleep."

Brosnan shrugged. "Any rest is better than none. I'll be ready."

*　*　*

On the signal bridge, Chief Rosco Barley, signalman, stirred the black brew in his mug with a pencil.

Acton, standing nearby, was finishing his own mug of coffee and thinking about getting another.

Barley watched him by the light of a first quarter moon and grinned in the partial darkness. "Better get another mug. You haven't been too steady since you got back from that boat trip yesterday."

Acton shrugged. "That was a bad time. I thought the prop from that damned Heinkel was going to cut off my head when it went over us."

Barley laughed. "You ought to cut your hair shorter. That yellow mop sticks up like a signal flag."

Acton was not impressed. "Don't be funny. It was very serious. I owe my life to Mister Raymond."

"I hear he got tagged."

"Yeah, but he'll be all right."

Barley put down his coffee mug. "I'm sorry I kidded you. I know it was tough, and you did fine."

"Thanks, but it all seemed so useless."

"Yeah, but from what I heard a little while ago we're on our way to get a little revenge."

Acton sighed. "I'd like that, but please don't send me out on that boat again any time soon."

*　*　*

Kuberski went to see the Commodore, and Brosnan headed below to his room. Ordinarily Brosnan, as Executive officer, would have been entitled to a room of his own, but the Commodore's staff crowded the ship, and when he became Executive Officer he remained in the room he had previously shared with ship's doctor, Braxton Taylor.

He pushed open the door and looked across the room at Doc Taylor. His long form was curled into a ball. Taylor got seasick in the slightest sea, and tonight was no exception. Brosnan groaned. Two hours listening to the Doctor retch wouldn't be worth it. He shook Taylor, who was only sleeping lightly. "How's Tubby Raymond?"

Taylor yawned. "Good condition, generally. Lost some blood. Five stitches in his belly. But his kapok lifejacket bought the farm. He was very lucky."

Brosnan sighed with relief. "Thanks. Go back to sleep, and try not to barf on the deck."

On his way out, Brosnan moved a bucket next to Taylor's bunk and closed the door. He went aft to the wardroom and arranged his tired body on some cool leather cushions. Sleep came quickly, but was soon interrupted by the strident tones of the general alarm, calling the crew to battle stations. Instinctively, Brosnan swung his feet down to the deck and headed for the bridge. It would be another long day, but he looked forward to it.

*   *   *

By 0130, the four ships were at general quarters, speeding through the channel chop in the darkness. Brosnan could plainly see the bows of the other ships on the *Lawrence*'s starboard beam in the moonlight, their forecastles rising and falling as bow waves curled back from the sharp stems.

It was easy to recognize American destroyers in the Atlantic. All of them were of the *Benson* or *Livermore* classes, almost identical, except for the shape of their stacks. The Navy still had a few old four-stackers, but these were assigned primarily to escort duties.

Phelps and Fannon were glued to the surface search PPIs, and Brosnan knew he would have little chance of seeing much of the surface radar picture over their hunched shoulders and bulky lifejackets.

Suddenly, Phelps shouted, "There they are!" and he dashed out on the port bridge wing. Almost simultaneously the bridge talker, Chief Brill, said, "Sir, CIC reports six surface targets in column headed toward us."

Now Brosnan could get at the PPI, and he leaned over it in the space Phelps had vacated. Fannon, still watching, pounded the edge of the console. "Damn! This is perfect! We're crossing the Tee."

Brosnan nodded in the dark and looked closely at the column of tiny dots. "They'll make a great target."

Phelps came back into the pilothouse. "What's the range?"

Chief Brill replied, "Twenty thousand yards, sir."

"Great!" Phelps shouted. "We'll let them come in to six thousand and then fire a starshell spread."

Fannon said, "Why should we fire starshells, sir? We know who they are."

"We're ninety percent sure, but I want to make it one hundred. They can't get away."

Brosnan watched the column on the PPI inch its way toward their onrushing formation. Chief Brill called off the ranges. "Sixteen thousand, twelve thousand," and then he said, "six thousand." Brosnan let out his breath. Now they would make up for yesterday.

The Commodore shouted, "Stanley, execute battle plan X ray! *Hanly* fire star shell spread!"

Instantly, the *Hanly*'s four guns flashed on the starboard beam. Brosnan, the Commodore, and the Captain raised their binoculars, and in a few seconds, four brilliant green stars formed above and behind the column of approaching ships. The points of light began to descend, swaying back and forth on parachutes, trailing white smoke.

Brosnan shouted, "They're E-Boats!"

"And German!" Fannon added.

"That's all I wanted to know." Phelps said. "Stanley, on TBS, commence firing."

Almost before the acknowledgements came back on TBS, sixteen guns fired, each ship taking a separate target in accordance with the battle plan Brosnan and Kuberski had labored over the previous night.

After the third salvo, Chief Brill reported, "Gun Control says the first E-Boats have exploded and are sinking rapidly. They are shifting to secondary targets."

Brosnan raised his binoculars. The first four E-Boats were burning and the next two were zigzagging wildly to avoid the fire of the relentless destroyers. Evasion was a hopeless task, and in minutes the targets were stopped and burning.

In the faint, pale green light of the expiring starshells, Brosnan could see relief on Fannon's face. Brosnan was happy for him; he knew what a burden the Captain had been carrying and he thought some day, if he were lucky, he might be shouldering a similar responsibility.

"Looks like a clean sweep," Phelps said.

Brosnan shifted his study to the PPI. "Sir, there's something fishy about the surface radar picture. There's another surface target about five miles to the east of where the E-Boats were. It's a little bigger on the PPI than the E-Boats were, and it's heading slowly toward France."

Phelps leaned over the PPI. "Oh, my; we may have another customer."

CHAPTER FOUR

Phelps raised his binoculars toward the contact Brosnan had described and studied the darkness intently, as if hoping to penetrate it by force of will. Finally, he gave up and lowered the glasses hanging about his tired neck. He said patiently, "What do you think it is, Skipper?"

Fannon shrugged and turned to Chief Brill. "Ask CIC if they have another target to the east of the E-Boat location."

Chief Brill relayed the message. Fannon waited impatiently, pacing the deck. Just as he was about to send another message to CIC, Brill said, "Sir, CIC says it has him and has been tracking the contact. It is bigger than an E-Boat but not as big as a destroyer. His course is one eight zero. His speed is eight knots."

"Must be a fishing boat," Phelps said. "Fannon, when the situation calms down, please have CIC report contacts more promptly. If that had been a German cruiser we'd have been in trouble."

Fannon nodded grimly. "Aye, aye, sir. I'll put on some heat. Brosnan, go below when this is over and find out what happened down there."

Brosnan, not liking what he would have to do, said, "Aye, aye, sir. I'll take care of it."

"Good," Fannon said. "Commodore, I apologize."

Phelps shrugged. "Everybody makes a mistake sometimes. Over the months your CIC has been superb."

Fannon said, "Thank you for your understanding. They're getting careless because they've been away from combat too long."

Phelps, studying the PPI, said, "I agree with CIC. It's too big for a fishing boat and too small for a cruiser."

Fannon said, "Sir, I recommend we close and illuminate in order to find out just what it is."

Phelps nodded. "I agree. Stanley, on TBS, tell the division to form column. Change course to head 20 degrees right of the contact."

Fannon changed course to the left without waiting for the execute, and Brosnan watched the other ships change course and fall in astern of the flagship.

Phelps looked at the PPI closely. "I make the range to be about ten thousand yards. Stanley, tell *Hanly* to fire a starshell spread."

Again the four guns on the *Hanly* boomed, and those standing on the flagship bridge watched tensely. When the brilliant stars appeared and floated down, Brosnan searched quickly and was the first to spot the target. "Looks like a large trawler," he reported.

Phelps had trouble locating the contact, but finally found the faint dot on the horizon and studied it carefully. "You're right, Brosnan. Fannon, fire a shot across her bow."

The Captain turned to Chief Brill, who relayed his order to gun control. Mount 51 fired a round, and soon a single geyser of water welled up in front of the trawler.

Phelps and Fannon watched impatiently. Brosnan started to say something, but Phelps interrupted, "She's not stopping. Sink her, Fannon."

The Captain gave the order to sink the trawler, and 5-inch projectiles from the *Lawrence*'s four mounts converged on the trawler, now only about four thousand yards away. Projectiles burst all around her, and red glows showed where some were hitting her steel upperworks and hull. Still she stood on, a faint blue haze coming up the stack from her laboring engines. Three more salvos produced more hits, and then a violent explosion blew off her upper works and stopped her in a cloud of steam and smoke. In the glare of the fire, Brosnan could see men running about her slanting deck and jumping over the side. Brosnan said, "She's going down, Captain, shall I get our boats ready to rescue survivors?"

Fannon thought for a minute. "No, too much danger from submarines. We'll pick them up over the forecastle with a cargo net. Secure the crew of mount 51 and tell them to get the net ready and to stand by."

*　　*　　*

In the closed-up steel box of mount 51 the crew had been laboring to keep the 5-inch gun firing as the *Lawrence* approached the trawler. Only the pointer, Seaman First Class Larry Swenson, and the trainer, looking through their telescopes, could see the action. For the rest of the mount crew, loading and firing the gun was monotonous and demanding repetition. Each man had to repeat flawlessly a simple action he had been trained for months to do. The projectile man had his hands around the projectile, held vertically in the fuzesetter. When the order was received to fire, he picked up the projectile and slammed it into the breech area. The powderman then placed a brass casing, filled with propellant powder, in the breech area behind the projectile and the spademan rammed the load into the barrel. The breech block was then closed and the round was ready. After firing, the breech block was opened and the spademan lifted the gate-like spade at the back of the breech area. The brass powder casing slid backward into the arms of the waiting hot shell-man. He, in turn, grabbed the casing, upended it, and shoved it down an opening in the deck known as a scuttle. The cases then rolled around the deck until the crew could gather them during a lull in the firing. The mount was set on automatic with the director controlling the mount's movements, and Swenson had nothing to do but watch the action. "Ha!," he shouted. "That one really got her."

Gunner's mate First Class Merle Bronski, the mount captain, said, "Swenson, tell us what's going on."

Swenson laughed. "You're not supposed to know. Just load and fire the damned gun."

Bronski bristled. "Swenson, I'll lose your liberty card if you don't make more sense than that. Just tell us what you see through your telescope."

Swenson sighed loudly. "Okay, okay, don't get mad. We're sinking some little spit kit. The last round did the job."

Bronski said, "You must be right. We just got the order to cease firing."

There was a loud pounding on the mount door. Bronski said, "Swenson, see who that is and tell him we don't want any unless it's chow."

Swenson put down the telephones and headed for the mount door.

*   *   *

On the bridge, Brosnan put down his binoculars and ran down the ladder and up the forecastle. He banged on the mount door of mount 51. Swenson opened it. Brosnan said, "Secure the mount crew. We've got a job to do."

Swenson turned back to Bronski and relayed the order. The crew hung up their telephone sets and piled out the mount door to join Brosnan on the forecastle.

As the *Lawrence* neared the scene of the sinking, Brosnan could see about fifty bobbing heads in the light of the burning trawler. "Damn!" he said. "That's too many men for a trawler crew. There's something wrong here."

Lieutenant Raymond was standing nearby. Brosnan turned to him. "Tubby, go up to the director and relieve Aronson. Tell him to come down here and that I may need him to interpret."

CHAPTER FIVE

On the forecastle, in the light from the burning remnants of the trawler, Bronski and his mount crew unlashed the cargo net kept secured to the lifelines used for rescuing men in the water. Bronski also brought along a red-lensed flashlight from the mount.

On an impulse, Brosnan had Bronski send two men below to bring back two Thompson submachine guns to supplement the .45-caliber pistol he carried on his belt when the ship was at battle stations. Brosnan took a look around the forecastle and decided all was in readiness. He turned to Swenson, who had brought his telephone set from the mount. "Swenson, report to the bridge that we're ready up here."

Swenson transmitted the message to the bridge and then called out, "Sir, we're just about there."

The ship began to tremble as the Captain backed the engines, and Brosnan, looking over the starboard side, could see a few dozen men clustered around life rafts in the water.

In that latitude in May the long period of daybreak was beginning, and as the first men climbed slowly up the cargo net, Brosnan could make out their faces in the dim light of the early dawn. There was something about them that Brosnan didn't like, and he called out to Lieutenant Aronson, who had joined him. "Don't let these men leave the forecastle, and tell the machine gunners to keep them together. I don't think these guys are just a trawler crew."

Some of the men were wounded and had to be assisted up the cargo net. By the time the last swimmer was on board, there was enough daylight to see the survivors plainly. Brosnan searched the water carefully to make sure there were no more swimmers, and then sent word to the bridge that all survivors were aboard and that the ship could proceed.

Brosnan heard Fannon, obviously thinking about submarines, give the order to come to full speed.

Brosnan turned to the survivors. He noticed that they had separated into two groups. The smaller group of about fifteen had longer hair and were more tanned. The larger group of about forty were short-haired and pale-skinned. Brosnan walked over to the smaller group and picked out one of the older men. In French, he said, "Does anyone here speak English?"

The man he had addressed pointed to an even older man with a heavy mustache. Brosnan turned to him and asked, "If you speak English, who's the Captain?"

A huge smile lifted the man's mustache. "I am, mate, or at least I was before you sank my ship."

Brosnan asked, "Are you French?"

"Sure am, Mate, Captain Marcel Evian of the late trawler *Elvira May* at your service."

"Where did you learn such good English?"

"Lived in London for thirty years. My wife, Elvira May, is British. We ran a fish and chips chain. I caught 'em. She cooked 'em. But the Germans captured my ship, my crew, and me when we were ferrying troops from Dunkirk back to England. They've been using us ever since."

"Who are the rest of these men?"

"Well, as you can see, they are not like us. Five of them took us out to sea to take the crew off a U-Boat that was disabled and couldn't submerge. It was off Northern Scotland. Most of them are the crew of the sub. They're all a bunch of horrid Nazi bastards."

Brosnan grinned. "Don't worry. We'll keep you well separated." He turned to Aronson. "See what you can get out of the other group. They're all Germans. When you've finished, come up to the bridge and brief the Captain. When you take them aft, keep the Germans under heavy guard using the crew of mount 51 and the repair parties. We'll be securing from general quarters soon, and I'll send you more men as soon as I can. I'm going up to the bridge."

*   *   *

Phelps and Fannon watched the scene on the forecastle from the bridge. When the last man was up and over the lifelines, Fannon quickly gave the order to go to 20 knots. He turned to Phelps. "Commodore, may I secure from general quarters and head down the Channel toward Portsmouth?"

Phelps scratched his jaw, "Ah, I don't think so yet. Let's see what Brosnan comes up with."

Brosnan pounded up to the bridge and trotted over to Phelps and Fannon.

"Well?" Phelps asked.

Brosnan said, "We've got the crew of a U-Boat up there. Aronson is interrogating them now and will brief you as soon as he's finished."

Phelps turned to Fannon. "That answers your question. We've got to get these German blighters—er-crewmen— into the hands of the intelligence boffins as soon as possible. Head for the Thames Estuary. I'll send a message asking for a berth and telling them why we need it."

Phelps turned to Kuberski. "Stanley, send to the *Hanly* by flashing light 'Take charge and proceed Portsmouth. *Lawrence* will proceed independently.' "

Kuberski went off to find Chief Barley, and soon the *Lawrence*'s signal light was blinking.

Brosnan went into the pilothouse to break out charts for the Thames Estuary, and Phelps sat down in his bridge chair to write a message to the shore authorities. By the time Brosnan had plotted a course up the Thames, Phelps had completed his dispatch and had sent Lieutenant O'Grady off to code it for transmission.

"Let's all get some breakfast while the wheels of progress turn," Phelps said.

Brosnan looked up from the chart, "It's about 80 miles to Gravesend where they'll probably put us. We ought to be able to add a shower and shave to breakfast."

*   *   *

Barley and Acton finished sending the dispatch to the *Hanly* and headed for the signal bridge coffee pot. Acton filled two of the cracked white mugs and handed one to the Chief.

Acton leaned back against the flag bag, "Barley, what's this place like we're going to?"

Barley shrugged. "I've never been there, but I hear it isn't much of a liberty port."

Acton put down his mug and ran his hand through his thick blond hair. "Do you think we'll get ashore?"

"Damned if I know. But I do know that the Commodore will get us liberty if it's possible."

CHAPTER SIX

About 0800 the *Lawrence* steamed up the Thames Estuary with Brosnan navigating and Phelps looking over his shoulder at the chart. Phelps knew the area thoroughly. "Beetle, those two bridges ahead will give you a good fix. The channel is deep and well marked."

Brosnan nodded nervously. Phelps realized he was being overly helpful and went out on the port wing to join Fannon. Fannon was scanning the Gravesend Docking Area ahead and the approaches to it through his binoculars. "A helluva lot of British LSTs secured there," he said.

Phelps raised his binoculars and scanned the piers. "There," he said, "Just this side of the near nest of LSTs is a large clear space. I can see some seamen waving at us. That must be our berth."

Fannon acknowledged, "I see them. There are four British trucks and several sedans parked on the pier. They must be there to take off our prisoners."

"Right," Phelps said. "I knew they'd want them badly."

Fannon, who had the conn, said to Brosnan, "I have our berth in sight, and I'm heading for it."

Brosnan looked relieved and said, "Aye, aye, sir. There's good water all the way."

Fannon brought the ship slightly left and headed for the vacant section of the pier. As they neared it, Phelps studied the people on the pier through his binoculars. "Ha!" he shouted, "There's old Brigadier Tweety Terwilliger. I'd know that mustache anywhere."

Fannon followed the direction of Phelps' binoculars and saw a meaty-faced British Army Brigadier General with a large drooping mustache standing in front of a group of junior officers and a platoon of British Military police. "You mean him?" he asked, pointing at the Brigadier.

Phelps cleared his throat. "By Jove—er-I mean hell, yes. I spent many an hour pumping him when I visited the British Admiralty on my last tour. It took at least three martinis to get anything out of him. He's an intelligence expert and a very skilled interrogator. He'll give those bloody Jerries hell and they won't know what's happening to them."

Fannon looked aft. The forty Germans were standing in ranks at attention, while the French trawler crew lounged on the rail. Fannon sighed. "They may be bastards, but at least they're military bastards."

Twenty minutes later Fannon brought the *Lawrence* alongside, and Phelps leaned over the bridge rail. The Brigadier grinned broadly and waved his riding crop at Phelps. Phelps returned his wave and shouted, "Got some live ones for you, Twiggy."

The Brigadier saluted with his riding crop and said in a high-pitched voice, "Thank you, Horse. Can you have dinner with me tonight at my club?"

Fannon said, "I see where he gets that name, Tweety. He sounds just like a bird."

"Ah, yes," Phelps said, "But a very smart one."

Phelps leaned over the side again and said to Terwilliger, "With pleasure. We're not leaving until dawn. Come aboard and have some coffee while the prisoners are being unloaded."

The Brigadier brightened. "Thought you'd never ask. Can't stand the tea we're getting now. Mostly hedge clippings and maybe a little horse manure."

Phelps laughed and went below to meet him.

*   *   *

Brosnan moved out on the bridge wing to watch Aronson and Raymond below on the main deck supervising the turnover of the German prisoners to the British MPs. He looked longingly toward the distant London skyline. Fannon, watching him, said, "Beetle, I suppose you think your fiancee, Annette, is over there."

Brosnan grinned. "I'm sure she is."

Fannon frowned. "Sorry you won't get to see her. It's too long a trip for you to get up there and back in the short time we'll be here."

Brosnan shrugged. "Maybe I can get some leave when we get to Portsmouth."

Fannon was playing with him. "On the other hand, you could take some leave now."

Brosnan brightened. "Could you spare me, sir?"

Fannon looked away to hide a grin. "I don't know. It will be a tough trip to Portsmouth."

Now Brosnan realized he was being conned. "Aw, come on, Captain, it's less then a day. Chief Benson can do the navigation in a breeze."

Fannon finally smiled slightly and turned back to Brosnan. "I guess you can have five days leave."

Brosnan said, "But if you're not sure about Benson and the navigation?"

Fannon snorted. "Get below and pack. After all, I was the navigator of this bucket just two months ago. Before you go, Beetle, turn your job over to Lieutenant Kelly. The engineering plant is in good shape, and he needs a little executive officer experience. Tell him to give each watch four hours liberty starting at 1000. All hands are to be aboard at 2100; we're sailing at dawn. Give Annette my love."

* * *

Brosnan ran below, packed, and had Chief Brill make out his leave papers. Then he called a reluctant Lieutenant Kelly up to his room to turn over the job of executive officer.

Lieutenant Gerald Kelly graduated from the Massachusetts Institute of Techchnology with a degree in marine engineering design. He knew all there was to know about designing steam engineering plants, but he had been slow in picking up the more practical aspects of running steam engineering plants on ships. His face was open and showed his intelligence, but even his slightly floppy mustache failed to hide his lack of self-confidence. During his time on board the *Lawrence* he had concentrated his attention on learning the duties of chief engineer, and had carefully avoided trying to qualify himself for the next step up the career ladder, the position of executive officer.

Brosnan liked Kelly and tried to raise his self-esteem, but it was a tough task.

Kelly knocked on Brosnan's door and entered when Brosnan said, "Come in."

"You wanted to see me?"

Brosnan nodded. "I'm off on five days leave, and you're to relieve me for the period as executive officer. There isn't anything unusual about the ship's routine for the next few days that you don't know about. Chief Brill will make out the plan of the day and check in all the returning liberty party. I'll rejoin the ship in Portsmouth. I'm sure you can handle everything without any trouble."

Kelly cleared his throat nervously and asked, "But what if all the men aren't back on time?"

"Send Chief Barley over to round them up. He'll have discovered every pub within taxi range."

Kelly was still hesitant. "But what will I do if I have to navigate?"

"You won't. The Captain and Chief Benson will take care of it. But if you ever want to make lieutenant commander, I suggest you show up on the bridge and take an interest in it. You might even volunteer to try it. You know enough technically to do it just fine."

*   *   *

After the officers left the bridge, Chief Barley went over to the large signalman's telescope and trained it on the line of buildings across the fence enclosing Gravesend. Barley was wiry and spare, with a New Englander's thin lips and pinched nose. Acton joined him, carrying a cup of coffee he had just poured from the signal bridge coffee pot. He nudged Barley, "What's over there?"

Barley sighed. "Paradise. I see a line of at least twenty-five pubs— the 'King George,' the 'Three Barrels. . . .' "

Chief Benson came out of the pilothouse in time to hear Barley's list. "I guess you'll be ashore soon. I put your name at the head of the 1000 liberty list."

Barley laughed. "Damn right. I hope to de-flower a couple of barmaids by lunch time."

Benson shook his head. "You're dreaming. Look at all the British LSTs over there. They've already chased every virgin within fifty miles back into the hills."

Barley sighed. "Yeah, I know, but's it's nice to dream."

Acton took off his white hat, smoothed his blond hair, and jammed his hat back on. "I guess my name is on the late liberty list."

Benson picked up the coffee pot and looked inside. He shuddered. "Acton, this thing hasn't been washed out for a week. You can see why I put you on the late list. These limey swabs will have drunk up the pub's daily ration of beer by the time you get there."

Acton frowned and looked pleadingly at Barley.

Barley looked at Benson and raised his eyebrows. "Could you put him on the early list so I can look out for him? He did a great job in the boat yesterday."

Benson grinned. "I guess so. I'll stand by for him, and I want him to look after you."

"Me? I won't need any help."

"Not with the broads, but I need you back here on time."

* * *

Fifteen minutes later Brosnan flagged down a cruising cab and flung his bag on the front seat.

"Where to, Mate?" the cabby asked.

"Trafalgar Square," Brosnan said.

"You Navy gents are all the same. You head for the girls every time."

Brosnan laughed. "Not me. I'm heading for a telephone box there."

Two hours and a slow trip in the battered taxi later, Brosnan paid the taxi driver and stepped into a telephone booth. He took a well-worn piece of paper out of his wallet, put some change in the box, and dialed the number of Emile Piccard, the Free French intelligence agent he had met through Annette in North Africa. Brosnan had used Emile to get in touch with Annette when she was in London several months before.

"Piccard *ici*," came Piccard's well-modulated voice.

Brosnan said in French, "Lieutenant Robert Brosnan here. May I speak with Annette?"

Piccard clucked doubtfully. "Brosnan, you know you can't talk to her directly. Where are you?"

"Trafalgar Square."

"I'll be there in ten minutes. I'll walk right by you. Follow me for at least a block, and when I'm sure we aren't being followed, I'll take you to her. Incidentally, your French has improved."

"Thank you, I've been working on it."

Piccard, ever correct, hesitated, and then said, "Brosnan?"

"Yes?"

"Annette will be glad to see you."

CHAPTER SEVEN

Brosnan leaned against a piece of the marble wall of the Trafalgar Monument and watched the crowd go by. At any other time he would have enjoyed the lunch-time scene, but today he was impatient to see Annette. He looked out of the corner of his eye trying to see Piccard approaching, but he knew Piccard would not approve if he seemed too obvious, so he tried to concentrate on the passing parade. They were an interesting lot, he thought: British sailors and American soldiers on leave; prostitutes and their escorting pimps; lawyers in nearly uniform dark suits, bowlers, tightly rolled umbrellas, and slim leather brief cases. Interspersed were a few average British citizens mostly dressed in threadbare but clean clothes and intent on their business. No one paid the slightest attention to him except the prostitutes, and they soon lost interest when he failed to respond to their raised eyebrows, wiggling hips, and eager smiles.

He thought about how he had met Annette Duchamp at a sidewalk cafe in Oran when the *Lawrence* had been waiting in port to begin the Sicily invasion, and how the chance meeting had grown into love. Then later he had discovered that Annette was a Free French intelligence agent working also for the Allied governments. Soon after their first meeting, she left for London to prepare for an intelligence-gathering visit to France. After her visit, he saw her again, briefly, during a trip to London, and he remembered the few but wonderful days they had spent together while she was waiting to leave again for France.

Annette owned a large chateau in the middle of a vast wine-growing plantation, and Brosnan knew that they could live quite contently after the war, if they both survived. It was this chance of not surviving that kept them from getting married. Brosnan sighed and tried to push the memories of his times with Annette to the back of his mind. After all, he would see her soon.

After a long fifteen minutes, a middle-aged Frenchman with a small mustache, rimless spectacles, and a soft black fedora passed in front of Brosnan trying to give the impression that he did not know him. It was Piccard, of the Free French Intelligence Service, and Brosnan tried not to stare at him.

After a suitable interval, Brosnan looked casually at his watch, yawned, and slowly turned and followed Piccard. Piccard crossed to Wardour Street, and walked slowly along the narrow way, pausing occasionally to look in the shop windows. Brosnan followed, carefully staying at least fifty yards behind the cautious Frenchman. Three blocks up Wardour, Piccard entered the wrought iron gates of a small public garden.

As Brosnan walked slowly up the block, he could see Piccard peering out of the iron fence. When he was abreast of Piccard, he said without turning his head, "Come on out, Emile. There's nobody else in the whole damned block."

Piccard moved to the gate, looked both ways, and joined Brosnan. "Brosnan," he said in French, "I'm glad to see you. Let's go." He started up the street at a brisk pace, and Brosnan fell in beside him.

Brosnan said, "Why are you so careful? I could see a reason for the precautions you took when we were in North Africa, but why here?"

Piccard shrugged. "Habit, I guess. You'd want Annette to be safe, wouldn't you?"

"Certainly, and how is she?"

Piccard twirled his mustache and grinned. "Excellent. You'll see for yourself in a few minutes."

"Good."

"Not so good. I have to take her away from you in two or three days."

"Back to France?"

"Yes. You must know that we're getting ready for a big operation."

"And she has to help provide intelligence?"

"Yes. It's vital that we know of the size of the units and the movement of German forces in the area of her estate and the surrounding countryside."

"How long will she be there?"

Piccard shrugged. "Who knows? Maybe two months. By the way, your French is much improved, but you still have a Parisian accent. You will have to learn the accent of the people of the region around Lyon if you are to marry Annette some day and help her with her estate."

Brosnan laughed. "I'll have a good teacher."

Piccard stopped in front of a three-story flat and looked up and down the street. Brosnan recognized the building from a previous visit when he had come to London on leave from Portsmouth. Piccard inclined his head and in a low voice said, "Follow me."

Brosnan followed Piccard into a street-level entrance and into a stairwell. "You know the apartment," Piccard said.

Brosnan grinned. "Oh, yes."

"Good luck," Piccard said in English.

Brosnan said, "Your English is better, too. Thanks for everything." He bounded up the stairs to the third floor and knocked impatiently on the door of apartment 302.

"Who is it?" a familiar voice said in a delightful French accent.

"Beetle."

The door flew open and Annette gasped, her large brown eyes sparkling, and her slightly plain face beautiful in the dim light of the hall. "It *is* you!"

Brosnan took her in his arms and kissed her deeply. When he could get his breath, Brosnan said, "My God! We've got to do something about this!"

Annette laughed, her short brown hair jiggling slighty. "In a minute, Beetle, but first come in and tell me about you. How long do I have you?"

Brosnan sobered. "As long as you are here. Emile tells me you have to leave soon."

Annette shook her head slowly, her smile waning. "Yes, about two days, depending on flying weather." She forced a broad smile. "But we can have a good two days, yes?"

Brosnan picked her up and carried her lovingly to the bedroom.

Laying her on the low bed, filled with Moroccan cushions she had brought back from North Africa, he slowly unfastened the buttons of her long caftan that sensuously revealed the lines of her graceful body. She helped him remove his uniform.

"Mustn't mess this up," she said softly, "or I'll have to iron it in the morning."

Brosnan laughed. "That never stopped us before."

"No, it didn't, but I'm afraid I'm beginning to think like a housewife."

Brosnan's eyes saddened. "I've thought a lot about our relationship. You know I want to marry you, and I'm prepared to give up the Navy and move to your estate in France with you after the war. But what if something happens to one of us?"

Annette sighed. "I've thought about that, too—many nights when I was trying to avoid German patrols. But the war can't go on forever. We have to forget about it—about everything—for now."

Brosnan kissed her passionately and opened her caftan the rest of the way. "That's what I want, too," he said. He thought in that moment that she was even more lovely than she had been in North Africa, and he took her in his strong arms. She rose to embrace him and caressed the large pads of muscle across his shoulders. He kissed her again, and the two became lost in a separate peace, made even more sensuous by the months they had been apart.

*   *   *

The next two days they lived between joy and sadness. Each morning Annette called Piccard. Brosnan held his breath as she talked, and both days she turned to him with a big smile, saying "Not today, Beetle."

The rest of each day they walked hand-in-hand through the streets of London, trying not to see the bombed-out houses, and stopping in small restaurants and pubs for lunch, tea, and supper. They kept looking upward at the overcast and hoping it would last. In the early evenings, they returned to Annette's apartment for quiet hours of long conversation and the passionate embraces of a perfect love.

As they held each other on the second night, Brosnan asked, "What are the Germans doing to your estate?"

He could feel Annette's soft shoulder shrug. "Nothing bad. The estate produces a lot of wine, so the Germans protect the winery, the chateau, and the people of the village who work in the vineyards."

"And you use it as a base of operations?"

"Oh, yes. I'm safe while I'm there. The people protect me, and I can send out much intelligence. Now I have to go back because of the next big operation. I'll be needed there."

Brosnan said, "I know about it. We'll be in it, too."

*   *   *

The next morning Brosnan was apprehensive. Annette felt uneasy, too. The weather was unusually good. Great flying weather, Brosnan thought bitterly—just the kind a skilled pilot would need to fly a small craft low over France in the dark and find a small clearing on which to land. Annette rang Piccard's number and waited. She listened intently, and then Brosnan watched her head drop. When she turned toward him, he could see tears in her eyes. "Tomorrow morning," she said in a quavering voice.

They went out for one last walk, cursing the bright sunshine, but it was late afternoon before they had the appetite to eat anything. They had a late tea in a small, intimate cafe that Annette knew. They ate slowly, trying to stretch the time, holding hands across the table.

The night was all too short, and Brosnan made love to Annette as midnight rang out on Big Ben. A short time later, Piccard knocked softly. Annette, already dressed in dark clothing, wearing trousers and her short dark hair tucked up under a wool cap, let him in.

Piccard looked sadly at Brosnan. "Sorry, Brosnan, but she'll be back soon."

Brosnan's throat was so dry he could only nod, and he kissed Annette tenderly one last time. She turned quickly and followed Piccard out the door.

*   *   *

At dawn, Brosnan packed his meager belongings and took a cab to Paddington Station. The trip on the train to Portsmouth seemed to take forever. He tried to sleep, but he kept thinking about Annette. He imagined her climbing into a small reconnaissance plane—the frail aircraft flying through the bumpy air and coming down to a landing in far off France; Annette climbing out of a small door and running into the nearby vineyards to avoid German patrols.

He shuddered, the stark images startling him. The movement of the small aircraft he had dreamed about was actually the movement of the train car. Sleep was gone, and he knew the rest of the trip would be miserable.

CHAPTER EIGHT

An hour before dawn on the day the *Lawrence* was to leave Gravesend, Lieutenant Kelly arrived on the bridge. Chief Benson was busy putting a fresh chart on the chart desk, and the other quartermasters were moving about the pilothouse testing the ship's control equipment.

Kelly answered Chief Benson's cheerful, "Good morning, sir," and huddled over the chart desk. Benson asked with a straight face, "Ready to navigate, sir?"

Kelly shuddered, his usually strong face turning slightly pale. "Only if I have to."

Benson pursed his lips. "Sir, if you'd like a little advice, I think you ought to do as much navigating as you can on the trip south. The weather should be good enough to get in morning, noon, and afternoon sun sights and hopefully some evening and morning stars."

Kelly sighed. "I'll give it a try."

"Good, sir, I'll have the sextants ready."

Thirty minutes before dawn, Captain Fannon came on the bridge, stretching and yawning.

Kelly said, "Good morning, sir. The ship is ready for getting under way."

"All the men back?"

"Yes, sir."

Fannon looked at Chief Barley, who was standing nearby, his wiry frame supported by the bulwark. "Barley, you don't even look tired. You didn't find anything of interest over there in Gravesend?"

Barley shrugged. "Not much, Captain; not many broads. Lots of nice pubs. The beer ran out early, and what we could find was luke-warm."

Fannon nodded sympathetically. "Portsmouth will be better on all counts."

Fannon went over to the outboard wing of the bridge with Kelly following him and sniffed the breeze.

Kelly followed Fannon's motions, his nostrils quivering and his mustache twitching. "What do you smell, sir?" Kelly asked.

Fannon said, "Nothing."

"Is that good?"

"Certainly. See those ugly black mud flats across the estuary from us?"

"Yes, sir, they must stink."

"They should. They have collected the debris of thousands of years of the flow of the Thames River. But we can't smell them this morning. That means that the breeze, such as it is, is coming off the pier and blowing toward them."

Kelly nodded, digesting the information.

Fannon looked at him out of the corner of his eye. "And that means we won't have any trouble getting away from the pier. All we'll have to do is cast off all lines except ONE and the wind will push off the stern."

Kelly said, "Sounds reasonable, sir."

Fannon turned to hide a smile. "It is. Take her out."

Kelly blanched. "But sir!" Fannon was already walking away, trying to hide a smile.

Kelly looked around the bridge for help, but the bridge crew was studiously going about the business of getting the ship ready to get under way, finishing the testing of the ship's control equipment.

Finally Benson took pity on him. "Sir, we're ready to get under way."

Chief Brill walked over, trailing his long black telephone cord and looked at him expectantly. "Sir, shall we single up all lines?"

"Er, yes."

"And should I tell Main Engine Control to stand by to answer all bells?"

By now Kelly was recovering his poise. "Thank you. Yes, Main Engine Control stand by to answer all bells."

Kelly walked over to the side of the bridge next to the pier. Remembering what the Captain had said, he turned to Chief Brill, who had followed him. "Take in all lines except One."

Below the deck force scurried about on the forecastle and fantail bringing in the heavy mooring lines.

Soon Brill said, "All lines in except One."

Kelly looked apprehensively over the side, watching the sliver of black water between the ship's side and the adjacent pier. Miraculously the ship began to move away from the pier, but Line One over the bow and through the bullnose held the bow in while the stern began to point out into the broad estuary.

Nearby Fannon watched the situation closely, trying to appear relaxed.

Kelly waited until the stern pointed out about 20 degrees from the pier and then said in a strangely calm voice, "Take in One. All back one-third."

Brill repeated the order about Line One, and then said, "Ah, sir, I think you need to relay the order about the engines inside the pilothouse to the man on the annunciators. He can't hear you out here."

Kelly's mouth opened slightly, but he recovered rapidly and walked over to the pilothouse door. "All back one-third. Right full rudder."

Benson said, "Sir, permission to sound one long blast?"

Kelly's eyebrows twitched. "Ah, please do."

Fannon relaxed noticeably. The ship began to back into the muddy waters of the estuary, and soon was twisted enough to face downstream.

Benson poked his head out of the pilothouse door again. "Recommend course one two zero at ten knots, sir."

Kelly was now obviously more confident. "All ahead two-thirds. Steer course one two zero," he ordered.

Fannon heaved a sigh of relief and walked over to Kelly. "Nice job," he said. "You're learning fast. Turn the conn over to the officer of the deck and try a little piloting on our way out. Benson will help you."

Kelly was sweating heavily, but he managed a smile. "Thank you, Captain. I actually enjoyed that."

Fannon turned to walk away and then stopped. "You should like it. Being a line officer is more than knowing the design end of engineering. Spend more time up here. You don't need an invitation. Chief Marusak can run the engineering plant any time you leave it."

Fannon turned away, but stopped again and said, "By the way, about that mustache."

Kelly put his hand to his mouth. "Yes, sir?"

"It looks like a five–year–old toothbrush. Do something about it."

*   *   *

At 0730, Kelly left Benson in charge of the navigation and headed toward the wardroom for a quick breakfast before going to the well deck to take the reports at morning quarters. Shortly after quarters, Kelly came back to the bridge and returned to the chart desk.

"Here we are," Benson said, pointing to a neat three-point fix on the course line he had laid out on the chart. "And we just turned to course one two zero. We'll be on this course for a couple of hours."

Fannon was sitting in his bridge chair. The buzzer next to it sounded loudly and Fannon picked up the telephone. "Captain here."

He listened carefully for a minute. Then he said, "Right away, sir. We'll be on this course for two hours. We're out of the channel and there are no ships in sight, and I can leave the bridge safely."

Fannon turned to Kelly. "I'm going below to the Commodore's cabin for a conference. Take over up here. Increase speed by two knots and start zigzagging using a radical plan. Call me if you need me."

Kelly said, "Aye, aye, sir."

*   *   *

In his cabin, Phelps spread a chart of the British Isles, the English Channel, and France on his cabin table. Stevenson, the Commodore's steward, brought out a plate of cookies and plunked it down in the middle of the English Channel.

Phelps said, "Good shot, Stevenson. We'll need some coffee to go with this, too."

Soon Fannon and Kuberski came in, said good morning, and sat down. Without being invited, Kuberski reached out and took a handful of cookies. Phelps smiled and mumbled something about "growing boys."

Fannon took one cookie, asked Stevenson for cream and sugar for his coffee, and said, "Commodore, we missed you on the bridge this morning."

Phelps sighed heavily and rubbed his puffy eyes. "I know. Blame it on that damned Tweety Terwilliger. I had to get him pretty well soused before he'd tell me anything about the results of the interrogation of those German prisoners we turned over to the British."

Fannon put his coffee cup down and said eagerly, "What did you find out?"

"They were the crew of one of the latest U-Boats—hand-picked men, and well trained."

Kuberski stopped chewing and listened carefully.

The Commodore went on. "And if we hadn't captured them, they'd soon have been at sea on another new submarine raising bloody hell."

"I take it the British were pleased."

"Damned right. They wanted to give you an award."

Fannon laughed. "No thanks. It was routine, and I don't deserve anything special."

Kuberski raised his heavy eyebrows. "Maybe we could get something in the way of awards for the boat crews. They really took a beating."

Fannon nodded. "I'm already writing up citations for several of ours."

Phelps sat down abreast of the chart showing the coast of England. "I got you two down here to talk about the forthcoming operation, and I hope you'll pass this on to Brosnan, Captain."

Fannon nodded. "Yes, sir. I sent Brosnan on five days leave to London to conduct a little, er, liaison with the intelligence community."

Phelps laughed. "If you mean to see his fiancée, I think that's a fine idea."

Fannon grinned. "I thought you would."

Phelps continued. "When she leaves for France, we'll know the starting date is getting close. Right now we can guess the invasion will start in June because of weather factors and that it won't be at Pas-de-Calais."

Fannon shifted in his chair so that he could point at the coast of France. "About here, at Normandy?"

"Good guess. In preparation for an invasion somewhere in France, thousands of troops are training in western and southern England, and the ports from Gravesend to Penzance are filled with ships."

Kuberski said, "I'd hate to be the poor staff bastard who has to plot the routes from the loading areas to the landing beaches."

Phelps grinned. "Don't worry, Stanley, I won't volunteer your services for that thankless job. You'll be busy just getting our four ships there."

Fannon said, "I take it we'll get a lot of operation orders soon."

"About ten pounds worth. I think this is all we can do today. Stanley, take the rest of the cookies with you. The Captain and I have a little more to talk about."

Kuberski left, and Fannon settled back with another cup of coffee. Phelps said, "I thought we should do a litle personal planning for the next two weeks in Portsmouth. It may be the last slack time we'll have before the invasion preparations begin to crank up. I think we can both take a week's leave and go up to my, er, Claudia's estate. It's only a couple of hours by automobile from Portsmouth, and we can get back quickly if we have to."

Fannon nodded. "I don't see why not. Brosnan will have had his leave, and the captain of the *Hanly* can certainly cover for you."

Phelps was pensive. "I know Claudia's sister Cornelia will want to see you, and from the way you glow when I mention her name, I take it you two are very close."

Fannon grinned. "I've asked her to marry me after the war is over. She has agreed and wants to spend most of the time on my quarter horse ranch."

Phelps shook his head and frowned. "But you promised to help me breed speed and stamina into Claudia's racing stock."

Fannon sat up. "Don't worry. Cornelia and I will take care of that. We'll have you winning races in a few years."

Phelps sat back in his chair. "Good. Then we'll leave for Claudia's estate the day after we get in. Her Rolls will come down and collect us."

* * *

On the bridge at dawn the next morning, Chief Benson was searching the long shore of the entrance to Portsmouth Harbor for navigational landmarks. Lieutenant Kelly, binoculars glued to his deep-set eyes, was helping.

Fannon came to the bridge and headed for the wing. "Kelly, I think you'd better secure up here and head below for breakfast before we get into port. You'll have a lot to do as acting executive officer."

Kelly grinned. "Thank you, sir, I was beginning to think I wasn't going to get anything to eat."

Fannon shrugged. "I remember many mornings that I went without when I was executive officer. That's one of the hazards of being one. You work harder than the captain and you have fewer privileges."

Fannon watched Kelly disappear down the ladder and went to the pilothouse followed by Benson. Fannon looked at the chart and laughed. "I take it that's Lieutenant Kelly's morning fix." He pointed to a triangle as big as a shilling.

Chief Benson said, "Yes, sir, but he's improving. Last night's was as big as my hand. He's smart, though. Kept me entertained with a half hour's explanation of a new navigational system and the astronautical triangle."

"How was he with a sextant?"

"Almost dropped it once, but he got the knack of it quickly."

"My God! I hope you didn't let him use our best one."

"Oh, no, sir. Just our standby."

"Then you think he's getting somewhere?"

"Yes, sir, he's learning fast. Didn't you notice his mustache this morning?"

Fannon put his hand up to his own mustache. "Can't say that I did."

"Looks just like yours. Well trimmed. Maybe a little lighter color."

CHAPTER NINE

A week after returning to the *Lawrence,* Brosnan stood on the quarterdeck talking to Kuberski. The husky lieutenant was finishing a piece of a pastry he had foraged from the Commodore's steward. "I sure missed you when you were on leave. Kelly almost drove me nuts," Kuberski said, wiping the last crumb from his lips.

"Wasn't he a help to you as the acting Squadron Material Officer?"

"Hell, no. He kept giving the British yard boffins long-winded explanations of the theories behind the equipment they were supposed to be repairing. He sounded like a school teacher."

Brosnan stretched his arms and rubbed the muscles around his neck. "Knowing you, I'm sure you found a way to solve the problem."

"Well, I did have to make a few promises, but if the Commodore lets me down and doesn't bring back a good supply of Scotch, I might as well turn in my suit."

Brosnan laughed. "I'm sure he'll bring back a load just as he did the last time we were here."

"Yeah. The yard guys are still talking about the ten-year-old Scotch he gave them."

"I remember that it did the trick. We got a lot done."

"Yeah. I just hope Kelly hasn't killed off all the, er, good will we built up."

"Just remember that under Navy Regulations you have to keep any alcohol you bring on board under lock as cargo until we're in port."

"I know. I'll be careful."

Brosnan said, "Speaking of entertainment, did you manage to get ashore at all?"

Kuberski grinned. "Yeah. The skipper of the *Hanly* was acting as squadron commander and was very understanding. He gave me a weekend off."

"And you made the most of it."

Kuberski sighed. "Oh, yes. I met a nice girl when we were here about a year ago. She is here to take care of an art collection moved from London to escape the German bombings."

"And you got together with an artist?"

Kuberski bristled. "Well, what's wrong with that? I like art and so does she."

Brosnan looked at the short, bristling hair poking out beneath Kuberski's cap. "I guess I always thought you were a music-lover at heart. In fact, you let your hair grow and grew a mustache you'd look like Paderewski."

"Aw, cut it out. I'm not like that. I not only like art, I do a little myself."

"You did that stuff hanging in your room?"

"Yeah. Charcoal sketches and water colors. My girlfriend says she's going to teach me oil painting."

"And that was all you did. Just discuss art?"

Kuberski shook his head. "Of course not. She posed for me, too."

Brosnan laughed. "I knew it. Nude, of course."

Kuberski frowned. "You have no soul."

Brosnan changed the subject. "By the way, when are the Commodore and Captain due back?"

"Any minute now."

"I take it they went off to Lady Claudia's estate."

"Yeah. I hear it's quite a spread—lots of land, a forest or two, a herd of horses, a cellar of Scotch, and all that good stuff."

Kuberski sighed.

Brosnan asked. "What's the matter? No dancing girls?"

"No. Just Lady Claudia and her sister, Cornelia."

"The Commodore and Captain will have a hard time breaking away from that paradise."

How did Kelly do as acting executive officer for the trip south?"

"Okay, I guess. The old man was glad to see you waiting on the pier so you could take over for him while he went off with the Commodore."

"When did you say they were due back?"

"Any minute now."

*　　*　　*

Kuberski's "any minute now" grew to an hour as Brosnan paced up and down the quarterdeck. Finally, Chief Barley yelled down from the signal bridge. "Mister Brosnan, there's an old tired heap headed this way from the main gate."

Brosnan looked up the pier toward the street between the yard buildings. An ancient but highly polished Rolls Royce was pursuing a slow and dignified course toward the ship.

"That's it," Brosnan said, "and there's a big lorry following it."

Kuberski let out his breath. "Thank God! The overhaul is saved."

The Rolls made a wide turn and pulled up abreast of the brow. Commodore Phelps and Captain Fannon got out. Phelps stretched his legs and motioned to the lorry to come around astern of the Rolls.

"Quite a fleet he's got there," Kuberski said out of the corner of his mouth.

Phelps and Fannon walked across the brow and saluted the colors and the petty officer of the watch. "Report return aboard," they said in succession and stepped down onto the quarterdeck.

Brosnan and Kuberski saluted. Brosnan said, "We're glad to see you back, sir."

Phelps grinned broadly. "We hated to come back, but it's time to get to work." He turned to Kuberski. "Stanley, you know what to do with these boxes of, er, supplies."

"Yes, sir, and I assume I may leave a few boxes in your cabin for delivery to certain yard boffins?"

"Stanley, you learn fast. You're becoming an excellent chief staff officer."

Kuberski blanched. "But sir, I'm really a line officer at heart. You said this was temporary."

Phelps laughed. "I understand. Look at Brosnan there. He used to be my chief staff officer and now he's an executive officer well on his way to command soon."

Kuberski smiled. "Thank you, sir. If you'll excuse me, I'll get on with the, er, supply business."

Phelps said, "You'll find there are no cigars this time. Lady Claudia has grounded me."

Kuberski nodded. "Just as well, sir. I've stopped, too, and I know the signalmen will be happy."

Phelps shrugged. "I didn't know they were unhappy."

Kuberski tried to keep a straight face. "Sir, didn't you ever notice how alone you were on the bridge whenever you lighted off one of those things?"

Phelps ignored the question. "Stanley, I'll leave you in charge. While I still have the Rolls I'm going to go to Southwick, about seven miles north of here, to call on General Eisenhower."

* * *

Two hours later Phelps was back from his trip and asked Kuberski to assemble the four commanding officers and Brosnan for a conference. When the group had gathered in the Commodore's cabin, he began. "First, we're going to Belfast three days from now to join the Allied battleships, cruisers, and destroyers there now. We will be there until just before the cross-channel invasion."

Fannon pursed his lips. "Do we know what we'll be doing?"

"Not exactly. The planners are cranking out the paper-work now. We'll get the plan soon. Until then, get your ships in shape. You'll need to have all your personnel and equipment in tip-top condition. Once this begins, we won't have much time off."

Fannon nodded. "I take it you saw quite a bit of General Eisenhower at Prestwick."

"Yes. I spent more than an hour with him."

"What did you think of him?"

"Quite different for an Army officer."

"What do you mean?"

"Well, I'm sure he knew all about left-facing, heaving a rifle around, and all that Army stuff. But he's a great deal more. He has a firm command of the big picture, and he has a deft way of factoring the interests of all parties into an operation."

"I take it you're happy to be serving under him."

"Very happy. He'll do a good job, and as we Americans say, we'll get 'a fair shake.' "

CHAPTER TEN

On the morning before the division was scheduled to depart from Portsmouth, Brosnan made the rounds of the repairs completed by the British shipyard workers during the *Lawrence*'s stay in the shipyard. When he reached the forward engine room, he found Chief Basil Marusak and Machinist's Mate Bennaret bending over a feed pump, inspecting a weld on its surface. "How'd it go?" Brosnan asked.

Bennaret straightened up. "I didn't think that this could possibly be finished on time, but somehow the old geeks in the yard made it and even did a good job. They seemed to speed up the last two days."

Brosnan looked at the pump and smiled. "I think Mister Kuberski had something to do with it. He put a little of the Commodore's fuel in their boilers."

Bennaret laughed. "On the China Station we called that 'squeeze.'"

Brosnan nodded. "They have several words for it here. It gets the job done."

"It did the trick on this pump," Marusak added.

Brosnan stood up. "I take it you're ready down here now?"

Marusak smiled. "We're ready for anything. Bring on the big one."

* * *

As Brosnan walked up the deck, he heard a loud pounding of feet behind him; he stopped and turned. The new supply officer, Ensign Edward Parma, was hurrying toward him, breathing hard. Parma was a short, swarthy officer, of mixed origins, who had lived in North Africa for several years before his family had returned to the States. After College NROTC and his comissioning as an ensign in the Supply Corps, he attended Supply Officer School and upon graduation was ordered to the *Lawrence*. The officers of the wardroom nicknamed him Pasha almost immediately upon his arrival.

"Sir," Parma said, trying to control his breathing, "Can I see you for a few minutes?" Parma's young face was etched with worry.

Brosnan nodded. "Certainly, but what could be so bad?"

Parma took a deep breath and said in a confidential tone. "Sir, I heard the Commodore brought aboard several cases of booze in Portsmouth, and Lieutenant Kuberski locked it up in one of the forward storerooms. I can't get him to tell me a thing about it. He just laughs and tells me to see you."

"Well, you have. Don't worry about it. It's not a Supply Department item. I have the situation under lock, as regulations require, and only Lieutenant Kuberski and I have the keys. It is legally cargo, and will not be consumed aboard ship. It will be landed in port under very close supervision. Just tell anyone who asks you about it to see me, and I'll take care of it."

The worry lines in Ensign Parma's round face eased. "Thank you, sir."

"Did you get all the fresh food, dry provisions, and spare parts you ordered?"

"Oh, yes, sir. We're fully loaded."

"Then stop worrying and get your department ready for heavy weather."

* * *

An hour later Brosnan finished his inspection of the ship, consulted with Lieutenant Kelly regarding the Engineering Department, and informed the Captain that the ship was ready for getting under way. Brosnan then went to the quarterdeck to inspect it and found Lieutenant Aronson there with the day's duty. Severn Aronson was youthful in appearance, but his steady gray eyes showed a maturity beyond his years. As he walked up and down the quarterdeck with Brosnan, he was about a head shorter than the executive officer's five feet, ten. But unlike Brosnan's well-muscled neck and shoulders, Aronson's frame was slender and graceful.

"Commander, when I was over in the yard earlier to make sure we finished all of our paperwork, I ran into a new officer who is about to report for duty. He was just checking in and should be here soon."

"Who is he?"

"A former shipmate of mine on the *O'Leary* named Hans Gerlach, a nice guy. He was an all-American fullback at Ohio State. A helluva linebacker, too. Played both ways."

"How was he as a shipmate?"

Aronson laughed. "You'll have to meet him to see what he's like. He's six feet, four and about two hundred and twenty pounds—all muscle."

"That sounds okay."

"You don't understand. On the football field he was used to having people either get out of his way or get run over. As soon as you get used to him and give him the right of way, you'll get along with him fine. He may have been a great athlete, but he doesn't trade on it. He can't help the right-of way-thing."

And if you don't give him the right of way?"

"He'll pick you up afterwards and apologize. As I said, he's a nice guy."

Aronson looked up the pier. A rickety taxi was approaching the brow trailing a stream of smoke. "This must be Gerlach now." Aronson grinned. "The springs on the taxi are straining. He carries a lot of weight."

Brosnan watched as the taxi stopped at the bottom of the brow. The door popped open, and a large naval officer slowly backed out of the rear seat. The taxi driver watched him warily, collected his fare, and drove off quickly as soon as the officer had pulled a seabag and a large suitcase out of the rear seat, nearly taking the door off in the process.

Aronson nodded to Brosnan. "That's Gerlach, all right. Give him plenty of room." Aronson looked carefully at the large officer. "From the way his uniform coat bulges, I'd say he's put on another ten pounds."

Brosnan looked at Gerlach. "Must have been all that shore duty. He looks a little soft."

"Maybe, but he likes to stay in shape. He'll find a way to take it off."

"Diet?"

Aronson laughed. "I don't think so. He likes to eat too much. He'll probably lift weights."

"I take it he's of German descent."

"Yes, sir. His father is German and his mother is Dutch. He speaks both German and Dutch."

"Good. That'll take a little pressure off of you in the interpreter department."

Gerlach turned toward the ship, looked her over fore and aft, and then picked up his baggage as if it was two toys. He started for the brow, holding the seabag in front of him and the large suitcase in back of him.

On the quarterdeck at the top of the brow were two big brass shell casings, carefully polished and weighted, and used to mark the beginnings of the quarterdeck. The petty officer of the watch stood behind the forward shell casing, telescope tucked under his left arm, waiting to greet the new arrival. Aronson noted how close he was to the shell casing and started to warn him, but it was too late.

Gerlach stepped down off the lip of the brow and brought his baggage to his sides. The seabag knocked the after shell casing at least ten feet aft, where it rolled around noisily. The suitcase caught the forward shell casing a little lower and pushed it into the startled petty officer. Aronson moved forward and managed to catch him before he fell, but the telescope flew into the air. The alert messenger standing nearby caught it before it hit the deck.

"Jesus!" Brosnan muttered. "What an entrance!"

Gerlach, hardly noticing the confusion around him, put the baggage down on deck and saluted the colors. Then he saluted the petty officer of the watch, who had been righted by Aronson. "Lieutenant (junior grade) Hans Gerlach, reporting for duty," he said in a voice only a notch below Kuberski's. "Sorry about the shell casings."

The petty officer of the watch retrieved his telescope from the messenger and managed a shaky salute. Brosnan, trying to cover the petty officer's embarrassment, stepped forward and said, "I'm Lieutenant Commander Robert Brosnan, the executive officer. Welcome aboard. This is Lieutenant (junior grade) Severn Aronson, the gunnery officer."

Gerlach smiled. "Glad to be aboard, sir. Aronson and I were shipmates."

Aronson said, "It's nice to see you again, Hans. Come with me, and I'll show you your quarters. The messenger will bring your baggage."

The messenger was already struggling with the heavy suitcase and seabag Gerlach had carried so easily up the brow. Brosnan stood well back as Gerlach went by. He said, "When you're squared away in your quarters, come to see me and I'll take you to call on the Captain."

*   *   *

Just before lunch there was a very loud knock on Brosnan's door frame.

Brosnan answered, "Come in."

Gerlach pushed the curtain back, ripping it slightly, and entered the room. "All squared away," he said. "I'd like to call on you and the Captain."

Brosnan stood up carefully, keeping well clear of Gerlach. "We can forget the call on me. I'll take you right to the Captain. He's expecting you."

On the way up the three ladders to the bridge level, Brosnan decided he liked Gerlach. The problem was going to be to harness his power and use it to best advantage. Gerlach's broad face, perfect teeth, and strong jaw bordered on a handsome ruggedness, and the Lieutenant had an enthusiastic eagerness that seemed to communicate itself to others with whom he dealt with. Brosnan could hear Gerlach pounding up the ladders behind him, rattling the side rails, and he speeded up to keep Gerlach from stepping on his heels.

At the top of the second ladder, two men were waiting to go down the ladder. Brosnan noted that when they saw Gerlach they grinned and moved back several feet. Apparently Frenchy Bennaret had passed the word around to the crew about how to deal with Gerlach. Unfortunately, the word arrived too late to help the petty officer of the watch, and Brosnan grinned remembering the clanging shell casings and the flying telescope.

The Captain lived in his sea cabin on the bridge level because of the crowded conditions brought on by the Commodore and his staff. Brosnan knocked, and when Fannon said, "Come in," Brosnan entered, followed by Gerlach.

Brosnan said, "Sir, this is Lieutenant (junior grade) Hans Gerlach, who has just reported aboard."

Fannon stood up and offered his hand to Gerlach. "Glad to see you aboard."

Fannon rubbed the hand Gerlach had just grasped and pointed to a chair next to his small desk. "Please sit down. We're a little crowded in here. Beetle, you'll have to sit on the bunk over there."

Brosnan cringed as Gerlach passed the Captain en route to the chair, but Gerlach got there without casualty.

Fannon sat down at his desk and said, "I understand you served in the *O'Leary* with Aronson."

"Yes, sir. He left the ship some time ago. We were sunk recently, and since that time I've been on leave and at sonar school."

Fannon looked at Brosnan. "That's great. Aronson has been doubling as sonar officer. Now he can concentrate on being the gunnery officer."

Brosnan nodded, wondering how Gerlach would fit in the small sonar control corner of CIC. "That should work out fine, Captain. I'll make all the necessary arrangements."

Fannon chatted with Gerlach about his recent duty for a few minutes until Brosnan broke into the conversation. "Sir, I think we'd better leave to get ready for lunch."

Fannon looked at the clock. "Ah, yes, I'll see you both in a few minutes."

On the way down to the wardroom, Brosnan stopped suddenly. Gerlach said, "Did you forget somthing?"

Brosnan shook his head. "No, I just remembered something. You'll be sitting next to Lieutenant Stanley Kuberski, the biggest eater and the biggest man next to you we have. Now the poor junior officers at the end of the table will really starve."

*   *   *

Before lunch, Brosnan introduced Gerlach to the officers of the wardroom and showed him his seat next to Kuberski.

Kuberski said, "Aronson tells me you like to eat. Lucky for you I'm on a diet now. I'll leave a lot on the serving platters for you."

Gerlach grinned. "I'm on a diet, too. All that shore time put ten pounds on me."

Down at the far end of the table, Doctor Taylor, the Mess Treasurer, commented, "Best news I've had for some time. All of us down here can stand to put on some weight and it will help lower the mess bill."

About 1300, after a pleasant lunch, Brosnan looked at his watch. "Let's go, gentlemen, it's time to get the ship ready to leave. We get under way at 1400, and the girls in Belfast are waiting for you."

CHAPTER ELEVEN

Just before 1400 an ancient pilot creaked slowly up the ladder to the bridge. Brosnan had greeted him at the brow and escorted him carefully to the bridge. The pilot looked at Brosnan slyly. "Did you have a good time in Portsmouth, Sonny?"

Brosnan shrugged. "Can't say that I did, sir. I just saw it passing through on my way back from leave in London."

The pilot grinned, showing a three-tooth gap in his uppers. "You Yanks always like to go to the big cities where the best girls are."

Brosnan shook his head. "Not in this case. I went to see my fiancée."

"Good English girl?"

"No, French."

The pilot shrugged. "To each his own. Personally I used to like the Irish girls best of all."

Fannon was waiting patiently at the top of the ladder. "Good morning, Captain," He said to the puffing pilot. "We're all ready to go."

"Good day to you, Skipper. Nothing to worry about. I've handled this type of ship before, and the channel is simple. Just tell the other ships to follow us."

"Would you like some tea, sir?" Brosnan asked.

"Yank coffee if you have it. A lot of sugar. And if you don't mind I'll sit in the Skipper's chair for a few minutes. Them ladders got to my war wounds."

Fannon said, "Where did you catch it? In France? The Mediterranean?"

The pilot laughed. "No, sonny, World War I. On a battle cruiser at Jutland."

Brosnan noticed that Fannon colored lightly. Fannon said, "Sorry, you don't look that old."

"I don't feel it inside, but I'm an old gaffer and I know it. The Navy had to call a lot of us up so we could take the place of the younger ones who could then go to sea. If you're ready, please single up all lines, and I'll take her out. Thanks for the rest and the good coffee."

Getting away from the pier was easy for the veteran pilot, and in an hour he was escorted below by Brosnan and lowered slowly down the sea ladder and into the heaving pilot boat by Gerlach, who had to use all his strength to steady him. Brosnan waved a farewell, and the four ships of Destroyer Division 32 were off, steaming at 20 knots and zigzagging.

* * *

Inside the pilot house Phelps and Kuberski were watching Benson plot the track they would take from Portsmouth to Belfast. It led westward around Land's End on the southwest tip of England and then north through St. George's Channel to the Irish Sea.

Benson said, "About six hundred miles, sir, at 20 knots and zigzagging we'll average 18 knots. That's about 33 hours."

Phelps said, "We'll aim to get into Belfast Harbor at dawn on the third day. Tomorrow we'll practice some tactics, conduct some firing, and test the equipment we've just had repaired. That will slow us down just enough."

Fannon was listening. "Sounds good to me, Commodore. We're getting rusty, and the newer ships that just joined need some work-up with us."

Phelps nodded in agreement and turned to Kuberski. "Stanley, make up a message outlining an exercise plan." Then he turned to Fannon, "Skipper, how about a little bridge game tonight? We haven't played in some time."

Fannon shook his head. "Sir, I'd like to, but I don't like to leave the bridge in coastal waters. Brosnan and Kuberski can join you, and I hear young Aronson is pretty good."

Phelps smiled in anticipation. "Stanley, set it up when you've finished the message."

*   *   *

Phelps strolled out to the bridge wing where Brosnan was watching the crew move about the topside securing the ship for sea. Phelps said, "Good idea to batten down. We'll get some Atlantic rollers before we get to Land's End. Tomorrow we'll be in the Irish Sea, and the weather should be better."

Brosnan grinned. "My roommate, Doc Taylor, doesn't take to this seagoing."

Phelps said, "We'll just have to play late tonight."

"Fine. I wouldn't be able to sleep anyway."

Phelps rubbed his long, heavy jaw. "I guess I can tell you this. Lady Claudia and I took a brief trip to London. While we were there, we ran into Brigadier Tweety Terwilliger. He owes me one. He told me Annette would be coming back just after the invasion starts. They want some up-to-date intelligence about certain areas inland where she's been operating."

"Sounds important."

"It is. She has developed into a first-rate intelligence agent. The Free French, the British, and, in fact, all the Allies depend on her."

*   *   *

The bridge game that night started out fine. Aronson was a little nervous but soon steadied down. By midnight they were roughly even, and the increasing motion of the ship began to make it hard to keep the cards on the table.

The Commodore eventually called a halt to the game, and Brosnan left for the bridge. He looked at the navigational chart and noted Benson's last radar fixes. They indicated that the Division would round Land's End about 0200. Once in St. George's Channel, the ships would leave the large, rolling seas of the Atlantic behind. Brosnan decided he would wait to retire until the Division had made the turn. Trying to sleep in the same room with Braxton Taylor before then would be a waste of time anyway.

Brosnan began to pace on the open bridge. His foul-weather parka was adequate protection against the May weather, and he watched the low hills of the Cornwall Peninsula slide by in the moonlight. The Scilly Isles to the south were too far and too low to for him to see.

After Brosnan had taken a few turns, the pilothouse door opened, and the Commodore's tall figure appeared, buttoning up his British style parka and pulling on his gloves. "Ah, Beetle, a man after my own heart. Up here getting a little fresh British air, I see."

"Yes, sir. The air is good, but I keep thinking how empty the land is without Annette. But I know you and the Captain don't feel the same way. You have a wife and an estate nearby and the Captain has a fiancée who stays at home."

"Yes, I understand your feelings, and I hope Annette gets back soon."

"Thank you, sir, but coming back won't be easy. She says she may have to go to Portugal and come back by sea. Or she may have to be taken out by submarine. Most dangerous of all, she might have to be picked up by a light aircraft operating from a cleared area near her home."

Brosnan could see the Commodore shudder. Phelps said, "I hope that won't be the case. I don't like travelling by any aircraft; and those small, skinny things she'd be in scare me to death."

CHAPTER TWELVE

On the second morning en route to Belfast, Commodore Phelps was on the bridge at dawn, testing the wind, looking at the seas, and wondering how much ceiling the medium gray clouds would allow later. Kuberski was studying the exercise message lying on the chart desk he had composed the day before, muttering to himself and shaking his head.

Brosnan, watching him at the chart desk, said. "What's wrong, Stanley, did you leave something out?"

Kuberski sighed. "Hell, no, I just wonder if we can do all this stuff."

Brosnan nodded. "Maybe not, but it's easier to cancel an exercise than it is to add one. Anyway, the weather may interfere with the whole thing."

Kuberski straightend up. "Well, you make me feel better. Let's go below and shoot down some formations of hotcakes. We can get back up here by 0800."

*   *   *

At 0800 on the bridge, Kuberski wiped off some syrup drops left over from breakfast, consulted the exercise plan one last time, and asked the Commodore's permission to signal "commence scheduled exercises," by flag hoist to the ships in company with them. The Commodore eagerly gave his permission, and Kuberski's plan began to unfold. Exercise followed exercise. Ship tactics, flag hoist drill, and even a high-speed simulated torpedo attack on an unsuspecting coastal freighter.

When the ceiling improved in the afternoon, the ships fired at big, red helium-filled balloons simulating dive bombers. When Kuberski's repertoire had been exhausted, Phelps said, "Tell the ships to leave formation in order to conduct individual exercises and to test all equipment."

Kuberski sighed with relief. "Aye, aye, sir. This staff stuff wears me out."

Phelps laughed. "You did fine, Stanley. That's what it's supposed to do."

*　　*　　*

Early the next morning the hills surrounding Belfast appeared over the horizon. Phelps and Fannon stood on the open bridge watching the green shores of Ireland grow as they steamed west toward the harbor entrance. Benson was busy determining their position by radar.

Phelps searched the shore through his binoculars. "Ah," he said, "I see Belfast Castle on one of those hills. It's one of several castles in the area that have been destroyed and rebuilt many times throughout the centuries. Benson, you can use that castle for a visual fix."

Benson replied, "Thank you, sir. I have enough points now to shift to visual navigation. We're right on our planned track."

Phelps and Fannon walked over to the chart desk and looked over Benson's shoulder. Phelps said, "Looks good to me."

Fannon nodded in agreement and returned to the bridge wing to look at the castle through his binoculars. "I see it. I'd like to take a closer look when I go ashore."

"We'll have to wait and see. It may be off limits because of the war."

As the ships got closer, Phelps said, "Look at the buildings in the city. I see a lot of missing roofs and unrepaired ruins. The Germans made a heavy air raid on the town in 1941, and caused considerable damage."

Fannon lowered his binoculars. "Did they damage the city's shipbuilding capacity?"

"No, the shipyards have continued to build a large percentage of the Royal Navy."

* * *

By 0800 the division was moored in a nest next to a stone quay. Phelps went below and soon appeared on the quarterdeck. Fannon thought he might be leaving and was on the quarterdeck to see him off.

Phelps came out on to the quarterdeck adjusting his uniform and running a hand over his jaw to see if his shave had been satisfactory. He looked at Fannon. "I'm going over to the *Tuscaloosa* to call on Admiral Byrd, who will be in command of our fire support group for the exercises and probably for the actual invasion. I'll be back in an hour."

Phelps' estimate was a little off the mark. It was about noon when he returned. As he stepped on the quarterdeck, he said to Fannon, "If you'll invite me to lunch. I'll tell you what I found out."

Fannon grinned. "A good bargain. You're invited."

Phelps turned to Kuberski. "Stanley, you can pass the word to the other three commanding officers after lunch."

* * *

At 1200, the Commodore appeared in the wardroom, rubbing his hands and smiling. Fannon introduced the new officer, Gerlach, to him, and they took seats.

Even before the soup was served, Phelps began talking. "We're to be part of the fire support group of Task Force "O" that will assault an area in Normandy called Omaha Beach. We'll get an operation order that will detail all this in a few days. The order will be long and complicated. There'll also be a rehearsal at a place called Slapton Beach in a few days."

Fannon said, "You're more pumped up than this news would justify. Did something else happen?"

Phelps grinned. "Yes. General Eisenhower and Admiral Kirk will visit our ships here at Belfast on 19 May. Destroyer Division 32 is included in the inspection. The exact schedule will come out later, but they should be with us for an hour."

Fannon frowned. "We'll have to work like hell to get the ship ready."

Phelps shook his head. "No! No! General Eisenhower said he just wants to see our men and some of their equipment. It's an informal and personal visit."

Fannon was not satisfied. "I've heard of these informal visits before. Then all hell breaks loose if the ship isn't shining."

Phelps shook his head again. "I'll stake my reputation on General Eisenhower. If this is what he wants, this is what we'll give him."

Fannon remained skeptical. "We'll certainly comply with his wishes, but I hope this works out."

*　*　*

As planned , General Eisenhower and Admiral Kirk flew into the local airport on 19 May. Phelp's destroyer division was to be visited at 0900, and, accordingly, a jeep bearing General Eisenhower and Admiral Kirk drew up to the brow exactly on schedule.

Phelps had partially given in to Fannon's concerns and had the crews of the four ships at quarters, formed in two ranks, but wearing undress blues—a more informal uniform than would have normally been worn for a general's visit.

General Eisenhower jumped out of the jeep, almost before it had completely stopped, patted the breast pockets of his jacket, and looked over the ships as Admiral Kirk climbed out of the other side in a more stately fashion and joined him. Eisenhower said something to the Admiral, and Kirk nodded.

General Eisenhower bounded up the brow, saluted the colors and then the trembling petty officer of the watch, and asked for permission to come aboard.

The petty officer of the watch steadied under Phelp's suporting gaze and said in a firm voice, "Permission granted, sir."

General Eisenhower greeted Commodore Phelps and, with the famous grin on his face, said, "Commodore, I remember your call on me at Southwick, and I am honored to return it."

Phelps saluted. "General, I'm proud to receive you."

The smile on General Eisenhower's face faded as he looked around. "I think the word must have gotten twisted. I asked to see your men at their battle stations."

Phelps said. "I wanted to make sure they all got a look at you. They can be at their battle stations in one minute."

General Eisenhower grinned again. "Good. If you'll give the order for them to go to their battle stations, this young officer can escort me to your cabin, and we'll have a quick cup of coffee while they're getting ready."

General Eisenhower turned to Brosnan, standing nearby, "Son, please take me to your Commodore's cabin."

Brosnan saluted and turned to lead the senior officers up the deck.

* * *

In the cabin, Eisenhower said, "While you order the coffee I'll borrow the Commodore's latrine. That's the real reason I wanted to come up here. These inspections sometimes run long." He disappeared into the head, and Brosnan ordered coffee and stood chatting with Admiral Kirk. The General came out of the head just as Phelps and Fannon entered. Eisenhower looked at Brosnan. "Young man, now that you have your cap off, I'm sure I've seen you before."

Brosnan paled. "Ah, yes, General, we played bridge together in your club in London one night several months ago."

"Now I remember you. You and Admiral Cunningham clobbered us." Eisenhower turned to Phelps. "I believe I asked Cunningham to have this officer sent to my staff."

Phelps flushed. "Ah, General, I believe I'm responsible. Brosnan was the gunnery officer of this ship, and they were about to go into battle off Sicily. I substituted another bridge player from my staff, Lieutenant Commander Adrian Cooper. I hope he worked out."

Eisenhower snorted loudly. "Hell, he wasn't much as a bridge player."

Phelps swallowed and started to apologize, but Eisenhower imterrupted. "It was just as well. Planning for the damned invasion kept me so busy I didn't have time for more than a couple of nights of bridge."

"And Lieutenant Commander Cooper?"

"Oh, him. Funny thing. I put him in charge of my mess. Now we've got the best damned mess in Britain."

Phelps beamed. "Well, I'm glad. . . ."

General Eisenhower interrupted again. "He's also the best ass-kisser I've ever seen. Better than anyone in the Army. But, enough of this. Let's see the troops." He started out the door, stopped, and turned to the Commodore. "When this invasion has calmed down and you're back in Portsmouth, give my aide a call and we'll set up dinner and a bridge game. Bring young Brosnan with you, of course. We'll serve you some real steaks."

* * *

The inspection was inspiring to Fannon, who as commanding officer, closely followed General Eisenhower. The General stopped at each gun mount and at the areas leading down to the engine rooms and firerooms where the engineers were assembled. When he left each station, he had either spoken to, or looked at the face of, each man at the station.

Fannon found his own enthusiasm building, and when Eisenhower left to go to the *Hanly*, next outboard, he could hardly contain himself. As soon as Eisenhower was out of earshot, he turned to Phelps. "I'd take this ship into harm's way any where that man sent us."

Phelps was slow to reply. "You may be doing exactly that in early June."

"Do you know the date?"

"June 5th. But first, we'll stage a rehearsal next week."

*   *   *

By the side of 5-inch mount 52, where Bronski and his mount crew had been inspected by General Eisenhower, the gunner's mate watched the General and Admiral pass up and down the groups of men on the *Hanly*'s decks. Out of the corner of his mouth Bronski muttered to Swenson, "The old boy does a good job. He's got the guys over there ready to go to war."

Swenson, standing on his left, bristled. "Aren't you ready?"

"Sure, but I'm always ready to fight."

"You sure are. It's about time you took out some of your meanness on some Krauts instead of the poor Brits and Irish. They've suffered enough."

Bronski laughed. "Don't take all this stuff I do seriously. I just do it to stay in practice."

"Maybe so, but I'm getting a lot of bumps and bruises trying to keep you out of trouble."

General Eisenhower disappeared aft on the *Hanly*, and the crew of mount 52 was dismissed. As Swenson started aft, Bronski stopped him. "No you don't, Swenson. We've got some maintenance to do in the mount. All this inspection stuff has slowed us down."

CHAPTER THIRTEEN

The operation order for the cross-channel invasion arrived two days later. Phelps, sitting in the wardroom with Fannon and Kuberski, leafed through his copy. "This is bigger than the New York telephone book," he commented.

Fannon was struggling to unfold a large chart of the English Channel showing the movement of the various units from their loading ports to their assigned landing areas. He shook his head. "It would have to be that size just to list all the units whose movements are shown here."

Phelps handed his copy of the operation order to Kuberski and joined Fannon studying the chart. "Bloody hell—or, I mean damn!" he said. "We'll have to study this for a few days and then have the other skippers over for a conference."

*   *   *

Two days later, Phelps called over the commanding officers of the four ships of his division to the *Lawrence* wardroom for a conference. When they were assembled, he stood over the huge movement chart on the wardroom table. "Gather around, gentlemen, and let's go over this chart. I know you've all been studying this. Are there any questions about the movement chart or the operation order?"

Fannon cleared his throat. "Maybe we should put this aside for a few minutes and go over the rehearsal plan and movement. It's complicated enough by itself."

Phelps nodded. "I've thought of that, but we may be limited in time after the rehearsal, so I'd like to go over the operation order as best we can. If we know the operation, the rehearsal should be easy."

Fannon acquiesced. "You may have a point there. Fortunately for us in the fire support group, life will be relatively simple. We leave Belfast, pass through the Irish Sea, head south around Land's End, and then. . . ."

Phelps broke in. "All hell breaks loose. All those amphibians will be coming out of some eighty ports and anchorages stretched along the southern coast of England and trying to follow these tracks."

Fannon laughed. "All we really have to do is try to follow our own track and try to avoid them."

The commanding officer of the *Hanly* said, "Doesn't seem too difficult."

Fannon answered him, "Maybe not for you; all you have to do is follow the flagship in column."

Phelps turned to Fannon. "And all you have to do is fall in astern of the American battleships *Texas* and *Arkansas* and the cruisers. The *Tuscaloosa* will be in the rear of the column."

Kuberski laughed, "She's one of a kind. We ought to be able to keep her in sight."

Fannon was still not happy. "Yes, and there will be about fifteen destroyers of various countries behind us trying not to run over us."

Phelps said, "I see we've all been directed to show screened blue stern lights on our wakes."

Fannon nodded. "That should help."

Kuberski said, "I counted 168 LSTs in the operation. Also hundreds of APAs, AKAs, and miscellaneous landing craft from several nations.

Phelps said, "We won't see most of them, but our own task force will have enough amphibious lift to carry four Army regiments, and we'll be screened by five destroyers in addition to our own ships in the fire support group.

There'll be nine patrol craft, six steam gunboats, and a few miscellaneous craft. It will be a helluva show. I think you'd all better go back to your own ships now and do a lot of studying before we leave port."

*　　*　　*

A week later, after Phelps, his staff, and the officers of the division had digested the giant operation order for the forthcoming invasion, Admiral Hall, Commander of Task Force "O," led his large force south through the Irish Sea.

Their destination for the rehearsal was a beach known as Slapton Sands, on the southern coast of England, near Torquay. Commodore Phelps' division was part of the fire support group under Admiral Bryant. Their task during the run south around Land's End and then east to the beach was to screen the larger ships and then shift to screening the whole assault force against actual or simulated submarine or aircraft attack.

Admiral Hall's flagship was the amphibious command ship *Ancon* that he shared with Major General Heubner, who commanded the Army units making the landing. These troops were now loaded in four separate assault groups, each composed of a conglomeration of large American APAs, AKAs, LSTs, various Dutch and British transports, and a gaggle of LCIs, LCTs, and miscellaneous small amphibious landing craft.

Standing on the flagship bridge, Phelps swept over the groups of ships with his binoculars. "My God!" he said to Fannon. "There's one of every kind of ship ever built in this force, and they're manned by all of our allies."

Fannon laughed. "And a few that seem to have risen out of the deep instead of having been built."

Phelps nodded. "You're right. All of our ships and their personnel can really use this rehearsal. An amphibious landing is the most complicated kind of warfare ever invented."

Fannon laughed. "And isn't it always assigned to the rankest amateurs?"

*　　*　　*

The next day at dawn, the rehearsal began at Slapton Sands; soon, tanks, trucks, and hundreds of vehicles carrying thousands of troops thundered ashore and back into the interior, scaring farmers and their livestock already traumatized by many previous rehearsals by other forces.

At the end of the day, Admiral Hall and General Heubner declared themselves satisfied, and the tanks and trucks tore up the beach a second time as they re-embarked in their assigned ships and craft.

For Phelps, the operation was simple. His division manned radio circuits and simulated fire on targets ashore, as designated by shore fire control parties.

"Won't be this easy for those lads when the Jerries are shooting at them," Phelps observed.

Fannon, remembering the landings they had supported with their gunfire in Italy and Sicily, sighed. "It will be even worse if the weather's bad."

*　　*　　*

Two days later the fire support group ships were back in Belfast, and the transports had scattered to their several home ports along the southern coast of England. At their berth in Belfast Harbor at the stone quay, Phelps held a conference with his commanding officers to review the lessons learned from the rehearsal in order to prepare for the actual assault.

The final plan called for the Belfast-based ships to depart at dawn on 3 June in preparation for a D-day at Normandy of 5 June and an H-hour of 0630. Phelps was not sure the entire force was ready, but he knew his division, after their operations in the Mediterranean, was trained and ready. He was not worried whether his ships would perform. It was the large mass of untried and inexperienced ships the division would have to thread through that worried him.

CHAPTER FOURTEEN

Two days before the scheduled landing, Admiral Hall led the warships at Belfast out into the Irish Sea and south toward Land's End. The ships of the force formed up correctly and closed promptly, showing the results of the rehearsal.

Brosnan, standing on the bridge wing, watched the massive old battleships *Texas* and *Arkansas* leave their piers and steam out the harbor entrance to join the screen already formed off the harbor entrance. The destroyers had been patrolling off the mouth of the bay for more than an hour, while the ponderous battle wagons ploughed through the harbor's dark waters.

Phelps joined Brosnan on the bridge wing as the *Arkansas* poked her blunt nose out of the entrance and took position astern of the *Texas*. The Commodore examined her bristling upper works with his binoculars. "Looks familiar except for the added antiaircraft armament on the top side," he said. "I made a midshipman's cruise in her."

Brosnan grinned. "You slept in a hammock?"

"Damned right. Best sleeping there is. I wish I had one in my cabin here."

Brosnan groaned. "I wish I had one for Doctor Taylor. Nothing else seems to help his sea-sickness."

Barley looked up from his telescope. "The cruisers are coming out, and the *Texas* has hoisted the guide flag."

Phelps said, "Thank you. We'll be forming in a circular screen soon."

Fannon had been quiet, watching the other ships of the screen. Then he said, "Chief Barley, have someone keep a watch on the destroyer *Frankford*. Commodore Sanders will be sending some signals to the screen soon."

Barley turned to Fannon. "Acton has him, sir."

In a few minutes Acton shouted, "Hoists going up on the *Frankford*." Then he called off the rising and fluttering signal flags and two men bent on similar flags and hoisted the signal groups.

Lieutenant Farraday, who had the deck, grabbed the signal book, looked up the signals, and shouted, "Form screen AS1! Circle six! We're in station four!"

Fannon said, "Answer them and head for our station as soon as they're executed."

When the signals flying on the screen flagship fluttered down, Barley and Acton and the watch lowered the *Lawrence*'s hoists, and Farraday increased speed to 25 knots and headed for their station.

As they rounded into station and slowed, Fannon said, "Well done."

Brosnan watched the other destroyers take station. He looked back toward Belfast as the Allied cruisers sortied and formed a column astern of the battleships.

Belfast began to fade into the distance. Brosnan shook his head. "We may not see that place again for some time," he said softly.

Fannon heard him. "Right. Let's just hope we survive to see any city again."

*　　*　　*

Barley crossed to the other bridge wing to get a better view of the screen flagship. Acton followed him. Barley said, "Keep a close watch on the battleship *Texas*. Admiral Bryant is in tactical command, and that's where our course and speed signals will come from."

"Already done it, Chief. I got a man on him."

Barley laughed, "You're learning fast. Now see if you can get us some coffee. This won't be a long trip, but it'll be a tough one, even though they're getting better. These ships haven't operated much together."

Acton came back with two cups of coal-black coffee. Barley took one and drank deeply. He coughed and wiped the water from his eyes. When he got his voice back, he said, "Damned good stuff! You're learning how to make it. It'll sear your tonsils."

"Don't have any," Acton said.

"Well, give some to Mister Brosnan. He needs a little cauterizing."

*   *   *

With the ship at battle stations for the sortie, Bronski, the mount captain of 5-inch gun mount 51, had his head out of the top of the mount lazily watching the maneuvering ships. Below in the mount, the crew lounged near their respective stations. For them the period was boring. They had little to do and could not see out, because the side doors were closed for general quarters. Swenson came back from the pointer's station and poked Bronski on the knee. "Bronski, what's going on?"

Bronski looked down at Swenson. "Not a helluva lot. Just a lot of ships running around. Looks like some chickens that had seen a fox come near their yard. I guess someone out there knows what they're doing. Wanta come up and take a look?"

"Sure."

Bronski climbed down, and Swenson took his place on the narrow seat. After a few minutes he climbed down.

Bronski said, "How'd you like it?"

"The countryside back at Belfast was pretty. Too bad we didn't get ashore."

Bronski swore. "The damned brass kept us aboard for two weeks."

"Well, I can see why. They wanted to keep the day of the invasion secret. Some of the Army troops ashore were held behind barbed wire."

"Why the hell did they do that? We're hundreds of miles from Germany."

"Yeah, but only a few miles from the Irish Free State. Those bastards might do anything, including getting the word to the Germans."

Bronski sighed, "Can't trust anybody these days."

*   *   *

The fire support group steamed steadily south through the relatively calm Irish Sea until early morning on the 4th. At 0500, Farraday came up to the bridge, waving a decoded dispatch. Fannon read it quickly and swore. "D-day postponed 24 hours," He said to Brosnan. Then he turned to Farraday. "Get the word to the Commodore right away."

Before Farraday could leave, Phelps burst onto the bridge, trailing a wave of British aftershave. "Good morning, all," he said.

Fannon said, "Not such a good morning. This dispatch just came in."

Phelps read it and sighed. "I can see why you think the day isn't so good. I just looked at the latest weather map. Conditions really stink and are getting worse. We'll be lucky if the postponement is only one day."

Barley stuck his head inside the pilothouse door. "Signal in the air, 'Turn one eight.'

Phelps nodded. "Sure. We'll reverse course for 12 hours and then try again."

Fannon went over to the chart desk and studied the weather map laid out over the chart. After a few seconds he shook his head. "I'm glad I don't have to make these decisions. I don't see how the weather can moderate enough to let us land for at least three days."

Phelps shook his head. "That would be bad. I'm afraid General Eisenhower might have to postpone D-day for at least two weeks to wait for favorable tides."

Fannon rubbed the bristles now forming on his unshaven face. "I hate to think about that. We'd have to unload and reload the troops again. The longer we put this off the more likely it is that the Germans will find out about it."

Phelps shook his head "I think that's why General Eisenhower won't postpone the landing for more than one day."

Brosnan, who had been standing nearby during the conversation, added, "If he makes this call like he plays bridge, he'll gamble and go for it."

CHAPTER FIFTEEN

Early the morning of 5 June, with Belfast just a few miles away, the signal was made to reverse course and head south once again. Phelps, Fannon, and Brosnan stood on the wing watching the signalmen scurry around the signal bridge answering the flag hoists.

Phelps said, "Well, you were right, Beetle. I just looked at the latest weather report, and General Eisenhower is going to gamble."

Fannon nodded. "I hope he's right."

Phelps laughed. "This may be hard for General Eisenhower, but it's easy for us. All the destroyers in the circular screen just reverse course. Those big ships in the column must change course by following the flagship around in column so that she'll still be in the lead. They haven't had much practice doing that, and they all have different turning circles."

Fannon nodded. "The old girls look like circus elephants. That's a lot of steel to turn around."

Phelps took off his cap and scratched his head, "About 32,000 tons, as I remember."

"We're lucky we're well west of the weather in the English Channel. It must be pretty bad over there."

Phelps put his cap back on and pulled it down firmly against the increasing wind. "The weather map doesn't look too good for tomorrow, and I hope General Eisenhower has made a good decision. We'll have about 3,000 ships crossing the channel when he gives the final word."

Brosnan came out onto the bridge wing. "Sir," he said to Phelps, "we are just about to round Land's End, and the transports and landing craft for our force should have left their ports along the southern coast of England by now."

"Thank you, Beetle," Phelps said.

Fannon said, "We should pass them about midnight so we can get to the landing area first."

"Yes, sir. I make it about 0100, but we will still have to stay behind the minesweepers."

*   *   *

About midnight, Phelps, Fannon, and Brosnan stood on the port wing of the bridge, straining their eyes to look for the transports CIC had reported having contact with on surface search radar. CIC also reported it had trouble tracking the contacts. "Looks like an anthill someone has stepped on," CIC reported. "Must be two hundred ships over there."

Brosnan went into the pilothouse to look at the PPI. Kuberski and Farraday, the officer of the deck, were in the pilothouse studying the radar PPI and concentrating on the column of ships ahead. Now and then Farraday glanced out the pilothouse door at the loom of the ships to the north.

Brosnan asked, "How's the column ahead doing?"

Farraday looked at the PPI again and said, "They're in a pretty good formation."

Brosnan went back outside to the bridge wing and reported to Phelps and Fannon.

Phelps nodded in the gloom to acknowledge the report and looked over the side at the waves slapping against the side of the hull. "The waves must be at least four feet. I feel sorry for the smaller ships."

Brosnan said, "From the appearance of the formation on the PPI radar, they're keeping up."

Barley, looking forward through his large signalman's telescope, suddenly shouted, "I see them!"

Farraday heard him and poked his head out of the pilot-house. "Captain, CIC says we're just about to pass ahead of the leading amphibs."

Fannon turned around. "Thanks. Does CIC have any contact with the minesweepers?"

Farrady went back to the squawkboox and talked with the CIC watch for a few minutes. Then he reported, "CIC says the channels from the transition area south of the Island of Wight to the French coast have been swept and buoyed. There is another minesweeping flotilla just ahead of the battleships, and Admiral Hall is trying to speed them up so we can get to our area on time."

Phelps said, "From my memory of the plan, we should be arriving in our fire support area about 0200."

"Right," Fannon said, "the channels for us were swept yesterday and marked with lighted buoys."

Phelps cleared his throat. "I saw that dispatch, too. I also saw the one that reported a minesweeper had blown up. I don't want us to go so fast we rush those little guys. They have a tough job to do."

Farraday stuck his head out again. "The *Arkansas* has sighted the first lighted buoy and is entering the swept channel."

"We hope it's swept," Fannon continued. "We don't want to go down like the minesweeper you talked about."

Phelps shrugged. "It's a chance we'll have to take."

*   *   *

In half an hour, Barley reported sighting the first lighted buoy. The *Lawrence* steamed slowly by the bobbing little sentinel. Brosnan clenched his fists, half expecting the deck to heave up over a mine explosion. But nothing happened, and more buoys came in sight. Brosnan began to relax. Maybe they would make it, at least until the Germans began to fire at them.

Farraday reported, "CIC says the large ships are turning into their fire support areas. It's now 0220."

"Good," Fannon said. "Right on time. "Benson, let the Commodore and me know when it's time for us to turn into our fire support area."

Chief Benson was bent over the chart desk under a dimmed red light, plotting navigational fixes. In a few minutes he said, "Captain, time to turn to course one one zero."

Fannon looked at Phelps, standing next to him with his hands thrust deep in the pockets of his parka. Phelps said, "Go ahead. The other ships will follow without signal."

Farraday gave the order to the helmsman, and the *Lawrence* slowly swung to port. Now the men on the signal bridge turned toward the black loom of the low-lying hills beyond the beach, watching for a reaction from the Germans. But nothing happened, and the ship slowly glided to a stop in her assigned area.

Brosnan went into the pilothouse and looked at the face of the PPI. The beaches designated "Omaha" were clearly visible on the radar, because of the high bluffs behind them. Pointe du Hoe, a towering bluff to the right of the beach, was unmistakable. Moving his eyes left, the four small villages behind the beach were recognizable as small clutters of light, and the beach itself was framed to the east by the small village of Port-en-Bessin. The destroyers formed up in a line about 4,000 yards off Omaha. Behind them, and to the east of the boat lanes, the *Arkansas* and the French cruisers *Montcalm* and *Georges Legues* were now anchored. Across the boat lanes to the west, the bright dots identifying the *Texas* and the *Glasgow* were plainly visible on the glowing PPI.

Fannon came in and looked over Brosnan's shoulder. "Where are the transports?" he asked.

Brosnan pointed to a blank space about 12,000 yards from the beach. "Here's their assigned area. They're just coming on the screen now. I estimate they'll be on station by 0300."

"Will that give them enough time to get their boats in the water, load the troops, and still make H-hour?"

Brosnan shrugged. "It'll be tight. I don't think the weather has delayed the big ships, but the smaller ones will be late, and the landing craft, when they're launched, will have a rough time loading."

Fannon sighed with fatigue. "General Eisenhower had to make a tough decision. Let's just pray for the best."

Brosnan noticed how tired Fannon seemed to be, and he realized he was feeling tired himself. His feet were numb, and his muscles reacted slowly when he tried to relieve the tiredness in his feet and legs. "Captain, you ought to sit down during this lull. We're going to be busy at daylight and maybe for several days and nights."

Fannon shrugged. "Good idea." He walked slowly over to his chair and settled into it.

* * *

Out on the signal bridge, Chief Barley paced nervously, waiting for dawn. "Acton," he said, "ask CIC for bearings on the *Texas* and *Arkansas* and keep a lookout toward them. As soon as we can see them, I want a man on each of them continuously."

Acton sighed. "Jeez, Barley, take it easy. They aren't going to signal us with a light now."

"Okay, I guess you're right. Then get some fresh coffee ready."

Acton said, "That makes more sense. Coming right up."

* * *

Down on the main deck, Chief Marusak and Frenchy Bennaret appeared from the forward engineroom access hatch.

Marusak walked over to the starboard side and peered into the gloom over the French coast.

Bennaret, following him, said, "See anything?"

"No. Chief Brill, the bridge talker, said we were only a couple of miles off the beach; but it's dark as hell, and I can't see anything. The weather isn't helping, either."

Bennaret shrugged. "The dampness stinks. That's one good thing about being in the engineroom. The temperature is always the same."

"Yeah, hot as hell."

"Well, it's still better then being in the deck force."

Marusak pulled a rag from his back pocket and began to wipe his hands, "Except when we're going through a mine-field."

"Damn!" Bennaret said, "Did we just go through one?"

Marusak laughed. "Someone always fails to get the word."

Bennaret took a deep breath and shivered deeply in the cool night air. "Just as well I didn't know. I mighta crapped in my pants."

Marusak laughed. "Well. you've got some time to think about it. The bridge said we'd be lying to here until dawn."

Bennaret nodded. "Good, but we'd better get our butts back below. If the Chief Engineer finds we're not down there, he'll have a tizzy."

CHAPTER SIXTEEN

Lieutenant Commander Brosnan called Edward Parma, the ship's supply officer, to the bridge. The young ensign pounded up the ladder, slid to a stop in front of Brosnan, and gave him his best Supply Officer School salute. "Yes, sir," he said eagerly.

Brosnan sighed. "Pasha, ease up. We've got days to go on this operation."

Parma smiled. "I know, sir, and the Supply Department is ready."

Brosnan tried to keep a straight face. It was easy. His facial muscles were too tired to lift his cheeks. "We planned to feed the crew sandwiches and coffee at battle stations just before dawn. Are you ready?"

"Yes, sir, 300 fried egg sandwiches, 300 ham sandwiches, 300 apples, and 600 cups of coffee—hot to go."

Brosnan tried to smile again, and this time his cheek muscles managed a weak grin. "Go to it, Pasha, and have the same menu ready at 1200 for lunch."

Parma's liquid brown eyes clouded. "But, sir, for lunch I planned roast beef and ham sandwiches, oranges, and tea." His face split with a broad grin. "British fare, don't you know. We're in their channel."

Brosnan's eyes rolled. "Of course. I should have realized that. Carry on."

*   *   *

Fannon and Phelps were in the pilothouse just before first light watching the PPI. Phelps said, "Look at all those landing craft being unloaded from the transports. On the radar they look like fleas jumping off a dying dog."

Fannon said, "They're eleven miles off the beach. It's too rough out there to make much speed, and the run to shore will take forever."

Phelps laughed. "It will certainly seem like it to the poor soldiers in the boats."

Phelps looked at the luminous dial on the bridge clock. "It's about 0500."

Fannon said, "Right on time for departure from the transport area. The LCTs have already departed for the beach."

Phelps looked closely at the PPI. "They should make it at 0630 as planned."

At 0515 there was enough daylight to see the bluffs behind the beach, and Brosnan began to pace nervously. He had witnessed the beginning of big landing operations at Sicily and Italy, and he knew the Germans, like the Italians, would begin to fire at the ships as soon as they could see them. He wondered why the Allied ships were waiting to comence their bombardment; then he remembered that the scheduled bombardment wasn't supposed to start until 0550.

At 0530, fire erupted from the shore, and huge splashes began to rise around the *Arkansas*. Phelps said. "I'm glad they've chosen the biggest target around."

Fannon grinned. "And the ship with the most armor."

Just a few minutes later there were other flashes amid the murky shore. A medium-sized splash rose just short of the *Lawrence* and fell back in a circle of dirty foam. "Here it comes," Phelps said. "Let them have it."

Earlier, Fannon had been pacing nervously, his hands thrust deep in his trouser pockets. Brosnan knew the Captain got nervous before action, but he also knew that Fannon would be the coolest man on the bridge once action started.

Fannon grinned, the fatigue disappearing from his face. He looked at Chief Brill, manning the bridge telephone. "Tell Gun Control to commence counter-battery fire."

Almost immediately all four guns fired, their projectiles splitting the heavy atmosphere and the spent powder forming smoke rings. Debris from the unswept decks and residue from the burned powder flew into Brosnan's face, but he had prepared for it by shutting his eyes as soon as the guns fired.

Wiping the debris off his face, Brosnan opened his eyes, raised his binoculars, and trained them on the barrage ashore. Kuberski was standing next to him, counting aloud the seconds of flight of the salvo. "Now!" he shouted in Brosnan's ear.

Ashore there were four closely-bunched explosions. Geysers of smoke and brown dust began rising in multiple columns, spread rapidly, and were carried away downwind.

The *Lawrence*'s guns kept firing, and the fire from ashore stopped abruptly. After the fifth salvo, Fannon let his binoculars fall to his chest and reluctantly ordered, "Cease firing."

Kuberski said to Brosnan with pain in his voice, "Damned good shooting. I wish I were still up there in the gun director. This staff crap is killing me."

Brosnan started to say something, but he was interrupted by the heavy boom of the 14-inch guns of the *Texas* nearby. Six projectiles from her forward turrets flew alost directly overhead, bound for batteries ashore that were still firing at her. The big projectiles roaring overhead toward their targets sounded like a heavy freight train.

Brosnan ducked instinctively. "My God!" he said. "If they fire a round short we'll go down like a rock."

Kuberski laughed. "Don't worry. Those guys are real gunners. They've all been on the same jobs for years."

*   *   *

At 0500 the bombardment scheduled by the operation order began, supported by Spitfire spotting aircraft, which corrected the fall of shot for the big ships. All four turrets of the *Arkansas* fired salvos every thirty seconds, joined by the *Texas* with her 14-inch battery and the Allied cruisers with their 6-inch guns and secondary batteries. Against the bigger guns of the heavies, the destroyer's 5-inch guns sounded like pop-guns, but their five-second rate-of-fire enabled them to put a huge tonnage of ordnance on target.

As H-hour approached, the guns of all ships maintained fire, augmented at H-hour by smaller ships firing thousands of rockets close in to the landing beaches. The rockets, plainly visible from the smoke trailing from their propellants, lifted in steep arcs, nosed over, fell rapidly, and exploded in a continuous roar. A few late ones caused loud crumps.

Phelps turned to Kuberski standing at his shoulder and shouted in his ear over the din. "Stanley, what happened to the air bombardment that was scheduled to hit the beach at 0630?"

Kuberski shrugged. "Sir, they went over a few seconds ago and headed straight inland. Looks like they dropped their bombs about three miles back of the beaches. Maybe they couldn't see the beaches when they went over them. There's a hell of a lot of smoke and dust over them."

Brosnan heard the exchange. "Commodore, I saw them go over, too, and they dropped well inland."

Phelps shrugged. "That will stir up a lot of cow turds in the fields back there, but it won't help the landing force approaching the beaches much."

Kuberski tapped Commodore Phelp's arm and pointed at the boat lanes leading from the assembly areas to the designated beaches. Five columns of landing craft, Army DUKWs and LCTs, were appproaching the beach. They were wallowing heavily and taking on water and heavy spray, but they were still making slow progress.

Phelps looked at them worriedly and then at his watch. "Just a little late," he said, "In these seas they're lucky to be there at all."

Brosnan began to search with his binoculars through the gloom and dust for the specific assigned targets he knew were being attacked by the fire support group. The *Texas* was concentrating on Pointe du Hoc, a bluff almost 120 feet high and about three miles west of the western edge of the designated beaches. According to intelligence, a heavy German battery was supposed to be positioned there, and a high priority had been given to neutralizing it. So far no fire had come from it, but, nevertheless, the *Texas* was raining huge 12-inch salvos on the location. Monstrous clouds of dirt and rock rose with each salvo, and when the salvos hit near the edge of the cliff, large pieces of rock and dirt tumbled down the side and splashed into the water.

Across the boat lanes in the other fire support area, the *Arkansas* and the U.S. and French cruisers concentrated their fire on batteries thought by intelligence to be emplaced in impenetrable positions. The destroyers were closing in to the beach as far as possible without running aground to engage smaller batteries and machine gun nests that might fire on the approaching landing craft. The louder crumps of the big guns rose above the smaller guns.

Brosnan shook his head in amazement. The duration of the scheduled fire might not be enough to knock out the German batteries and emplacements, but while it lasted it was spectacular. In a few minutes the landing craft began to beach, and the tempo of firing on the areas back of the beach decreased rapidly so the troops would not be hit by friendly fire. Soon the Allies would find out how much opposition was left.

With the cessation of firing, it was once again possible to talk on the *Lawrence*'s bridge.

Brosnan heard an ominous crackling of machine gun fire coming from the area around Port-en-Bessin, at the eastern end of Omaha Beach. Phelps ran over to the starboard wing and joined him. Both searched the area anxiously. "Damn!" Phelps said, "There's one battery our fire support didn't get. Our landing craft are catching hell!"

Brosnan raised his binoculars again. He could see heavily burdened troops racing out of the landing craft and splashing waist deep in the water. Some made it across the wide beach to the shelter of a low, concrete seawall, but for every man who made it, three crumpled onto the sand, either dead or wounded. Brosnan was sickened by the sight and watched two destroyers steam dangerously close to the beach and open fire on the machine gun batteries. Troops in the following waves managed to drag the wounded up to the protection of the seawall under the destroyer's covering fire.

Fannon had been looking in the direction of Pointe du Hoc. "Commodore!" he shouted, "The boats with the Army Rangers assigned to take Pointe du Hoc are having trouble. I'd like to help them out."

Phelps responded, "Go to it, Captain."

Fannon ordered the *Lawrence* to steam west along the beach, outboard of the group of landing craft struggling against a strong cross-beach current to reach the beach underneath Pointe du Hoc. Watching the operation, Fannon tried to recall the Rangers' landing plan. They were supposed to land on a rocky beach below the Pointe and scale the forbidding cliffs. But the currents had driven their boats five miles too far to the east. The British destroyer *Tallybout* and the U.S. destroyer *Satterlee* had also decided to provide cover for the Rangers, and the three ships steamed along the beach, looking for machine gun nests. As the landing craft slowly approached their assigned beach, a torrent of machine gun and mortar fire poured in on the hapless boats. All three ships answered with heavy fire trained at the flashes ashore, and projectile explosions erupted near the suspected battery locations. The hits sent pieces of fortifications and even machine guns flying, and soon the firing from the German defenses subsided.

"Well done!" Phelps shouted. "But the Rangers are not out of the woods yet. The beaches are still full of machine gun nests." As if in reply, a larger gun battery began firing on the Rangers, and Fannon looked up at the top of the bluff. Turning to find Aronson, who had his head out of the director, Fannon pointed at the bluff. Aronson nodded, and the gun battery opened fire. Brosnan watched the explosions ashore and listened to the bridge gang cheer at every one. After the fifth salvo, Fannon ordered, "Cease firing."

The landing craft were still laboring badly in the strong current, but shortly after 0700 they were able to ground under the cliffs. Once ashore, the Rangers quickly unloaded long scaling ladders and special equipment designed to fire large grappling hooks onto the top of the bluff. The hooks were attached to long ropes that the Rangers would use to climb the vertical face. As the assault progressed, the three destroyers concentrated their fire on the Germans at the top of the bluff. A few hand grenades came sailing down the cliff face toward the struggling Rangers, but the explosions inflicted little damage. In 30 minutes, the Rangers had scaled the cliff and engaged the defenders in hand-to-hand fighting. In another 15 minutes the attack was over, and the Rangers stood on the Pointe waving to the ship crews. From the bridge of the *Lawrence*, Brosnan watched as an American flag was hoisted aloft on a makeshift pole.

* * *

As the *Lawrence* steamed back to her station, her crew tried to catch up with the progress of the troops ashore and the efforts of the Army Engineers and the Navy underwater demolition teams to clear the beach of mines and obstacles.

Boat waves had been beaching as best they could every ten minutes since 0700, in spite of an insufficient number of cleared lanes to the beach. Even by 0930, wrecked boats, tanks, and vehicles cluttered the entry to the point where beaching had to be stopped.

Farraday came running up to the bridge. Gerlach had taken over his officer-of-the-deck job during general quarters so Farraday could stay in the radio shack and listen to the radio circuits ashore. "We've lost contact with all the fire control parties ashore," Farraday said.

Fannon swore. "How the hell can we support the troops on the beach if we don't know where they are?"

Phelps took a deep breath. "We'll just have to use our best judgement."

Fannon was still agitated, "I'll pass the word to the gunnery officer. We'll have to help him."

Fannon trained his binoculars on the shore behind the beaches. Brosnan, also sweeping the beaches, groaned.

"Somebody is laying rounds on the boats at the beach. Just as soon as they beach, they get hit."

"I see a couple of flashes," Fannon said. "Brill, tell gun control to take a look at that tall, white building next to the church. I think some German bastard is controlling fire from there."

Aronson responded quickly and Brill reported, "The gunnery officer says he sees the building and he asks permission to open fire."

Fannon said through clenched teeth. "Permission granted—and if the church gets in the way, blow it to hell."

The guns boomed out, and Brosnan watched the fall of shot. The first salvo fell a little short, but the second blew the top story off the building.

"Bingo!" Fannon yelled. "Now we'll see if the firing stops."

With the German spotter probably killed, the firing did subside, and Fannon began to search for other targets. Twice during the remainder of the morning, the *Lawrence* silenced German gun positions.

By noon, firing ashore had slackened, and Brosnan sent word to the supply officer to feed the crew at battle stations. Within a short time a big cardboard box of sandwiches and a wooden crate full of oranges was brought to the bridge. Kuberski and Brosnan, after making sure the bridge crew was fed, tackled the few sandwiches left in the box. The oranges were gone.

"Not bad," Kuberski said in a muffled voice through a mouthful of roast beef.

With Brosnan's last bite, enemy fire started again, and for the rest of the afternoon, the destroyers ranged through the fire support area, answering calls from the fire control parties ashore that had restored their communication links with the ships.

With the improved communications, groups of tanks, vehicles, personnel, and supplies converged on the beach. All the while, Kuberski seemed alternately ecstatic and morose. Finally, Brosnan asked, "Stanley, what the hell's your trouble? Settle down."

Kuberski shook his head. "I can't. I'm proud of the guys up there I worked so hard to train, and I want to be up there with them."

Brosnan laughed. "Come on. Soon you'll like this staff stuff. Down here you always know what's going on."

Kuberski was not amused. "Just what the hell *is* going on over there?"

"We're beating the hell out of the Germans."

"Oh, yeah, tell that to all those guys lying on the beach and all the boat crews that went to the bottom with their boats."

Brosnan started to reply, but he couldn't think of anything to say and sighed deeply. Kuberski was right. That morning, in just a few hours, they had witnessed the death or wounding of hundreds of American soldiers and probably hundreds of Germans. Brosnan gripped the edge of the bridge bulwark in front of him and looked toward the beach. A huge pall-like cloud of black smoke and brown dust hung over the landing area, almost blotting out the carnage ashore. An overwhelming stench of smokeless powder, burned diesel fuel, and smoldering equipment burned his nasal passages, and he resigned himself to several more days of it. He knew the acrid smells would not go away, and the slow progress of fighting ashore meant many more deaths. The commander sighed again and shook his head. Yes, Kuberski was right.

*   *   *

As the evening light faded, Fannon joined Phelps on the signal bridge. Phelps looked out over the landing area. "I don't know what happened to the Army's tanks and artillery, but without the destroyer batteries, I think the landing would have failed."

"Farraday says that's just what General Heubner told Admiral Bryant. It seems many of the tanks were driven out of the LCTs when the water was too rough and promptly sank. Most of the Army's artillery was destroyed on the beach."

Phelps nodded. "That accounts for it. Maybe tomorrow will be better. I suggest you go to condition III to rest your crew and give them one full meal."

Fannon stretched his tired arms. "Beetle, you heard the Commodore. Get the word to the officer of the deck and to the supply officer so he can prepare."

Brosnan grinned and muttered. "He'll be ready for anything."

*   *   *

Down in mount 51, the loading crews were slumped against the steel sides of the mount. Bronski said wearily, "The word just came down to set condition III. Chow will be served in the mess hall in half-an-hour."

The projectileman looked at Bronski. "I've counted every damned round we've fired. One hundred and sixty-eight."

Swenson, coming back from his pointer's station, heard the comment. "I predict two hundred tomorrow," he said.

As the gun crew began storing their telephones, Bronski made an announcement, "Hold it," he said. "Now the bad news. We've got the first watch."

The projectileman groaned and slumped to the deck again. "Ain't there any good news?" he asked.

Bronski answered, "It's not all bad. We're to be relieved by mount 52 for chow in an hour."

"Okay," Swenson said. "I guess I can get by the rest of the night on that. The sandwiches didn't do much for me."

Bronski added, "Don't forget the apple and orange. That may be all you get tomorrow. General Quarters will be at 0500."

CHAPTER SEVENTEEN

That evening most of the officers gathered in the wardroom for a simple evening meal. Some were so tired they headed directly for their bunks.

"Where's Doc Taylor tonight? Seasick as usual?" Kuberski asked Brosnan.

Brosnan, who had just sat down, said, "No. He isn't eating anything, but he's been holding sick call and inspecting the galley to make sure the food is okay."

Kuberski grinned. "Good. Sorry I put my foot in it."

Brosnan rubbed his aching neck muscles. Don't worry. Doc Taylor will be there when he's needed."

"What do we do tomorrow?" Gerlach asked.

Brosnan put his fork down. "Same as this afternoon. We shoot whatever the shore fire control party wants us to, providing we can communicate with them."

"And at anything that shoots at us first?"

Aronson took the ring off of his napkin and spread the white linen on his lap. "Damned right," he joined in. "That's the best kind."

Kuberski shrugged and rubbed his stomach. "Enough of this shop talk. Pasha, what's for chow tonight?"

Parma, as the ship's supply officer, planned the menu for both the crew's mess and the wardroom, although Doctor Taylor, as Wardroom mess treasurer, kept the wardroom mess accounts. Parma's liquid brown eyes sparkled. "Beef Wellington, mashed potatoes and gravy, and spring peas." He looked at Kuberski. "This is Spring, you know."

Kuberski scowled. "What's for dessert?"

"Apple pie."

Kuberski grinned. "You've got my vote. Beetle, give this man some kudos."

Parma's eyebrows lifted. "Kudos?"

"It's a Greek word for praise," Brosnan said patiently.

Parma shrugged. "Well, if you can't eat the damned things, I'd just as soon go without."

Brosnan got up and headed for his room, pausing at the door. "Don't forget, gentlemen, breakfast at 0400. General quarters at 0500. Don't be late."

*   *   *

On the bridge, Fannon was finishing his dinner from a tray. Phelps, having eaten in his cabin, joined the Captain on the bridge for a cup of coffee. The Commodore brought it up in a thick mug and sat in his chair, which was similar to the one Fannon was sitting in on the opposite side of the bridge.

Phelps took a deep draft. "Ah," he said. "That Stevenson is a genius. Even makes good coffee."

Fannon nodded. "Glad you're enjoying it. I prefer the signal bridge sludge myself."

Benson, leaning over the chart desk, tried to suppress a laugh, but his shoulders shook.

Fannon noticed but let the moment pass.

"I think this will be a quiet night." Phelps offered with a yawn. "The Germans don't have much of a surface force left, and the British have laid on a strong force north of the invasion area to protect us from surface attack."

Fannon nodded in agreement. "We ought to get a good night's rest tonight. Tomorrow and the rest of the next day and night may be different. I think part of our success so far has come from the deception plan we were part of earlier.

Probably as many as 15 German divisions and all of the German surface force are still waiting for us to land at Pas-de-Calais."

Phelps finished his coffee and looked longingly at the dregs. "I hope the E-boats stay up there, too."

Fannon stretched his arms over his head and yawned. I think we can afford to get in our bunks soon."

Phelps got up, taking his mug with him. "Good night, Pete," he said. "That's where I'm headed."

*   *   *

At 0430 Phelps, Fannon, and Brosnan arrived on the bridge. Phelps asked Gerlach, who had the watch, "Still quiet?"

Gerlach turned around, inadvertently knocking the Commodore's coffee mug from his hand. The mug bounced loudly on the deck but didn't break.

Gerlach said, "Sorry, sir," and leaned over to pick up the mug. His shoulder caught the Captain, who was also leaning over to pick it up, in the gut.

Fannon grimaced and backed away.

Phelps laughed. "Bloody hell, son, just stand still, and we'll move around you."

Brosnan, trying to smooth over the confusion, said, "I stopped in CIC on the way up. There weren't any requests for fire from the shore fire control parties last night, but the Army has alerted us to expect some at dawn."

Fannon circled Gerlach warily and headed for the bridge wing. Phelps followed him, and Brosnan assumed rear guard. Gerlach, red with embarrassment, shrugged and walked to the opposite wing.

"That young officer you just got is a real pistol," Phelps said, leaning on the bridge rail.

Fannon laughed. "More like a field piece. He's got a formidable recoil."

"Just keep facing him," Brosnan said. "That way you can make the first move and get out of his way. Actually, he's a fine officer and a very good sonar officer."

Fannon nodded, "Good sonar officers are hard to find. I guess we can keep out of his way for a while."

*   *   *

About 0500, CIC reported that all fire support ships were receiving assignments. Brosnan went below to CIC to watch the *Lawrence*'s assignment being plotted on the bombardment chart. Ensign Dillon Lee, known as "Squid," was plotting the front-line positions and the coordinates of the first target. Lee was a young, lanky Carolinian with short blond hair, almost invisible blond eyebrows topping a long face, and long arms and legs seemed to flow from his short trunk. In spite of his somewhat frail appearance, his movements were fluid and graceful, hence the name Squid.

Lee finished plotting and turned to Brosnan, "Sir, here's the first target."

Brosnan memorized the location and said, "Thanks, I've got it." He headed for the bridge.

On the bridge, Brosnan approached the chart desk and plotted the target on the navigational chart. When he had finished, he called over the Commodore and Captain. "Here it is. We start firing on it on call."

Fannon asked, "Do we know the Army's proposed scheme of maneuver?"

Brosnan shrugged. "We know where the front lines are." He drew an approximation of the data he had seen in CIC in front of the target.

Phelps said, "I suppose they'll advance wherever they find a soft spot after we destroy the targets they know about and can assign to us."

Fannon looked at his watch under the dim red light over the chart desk. "Just enough time for a cup of coffee."

Gerlach, trying to make amends for his *faux pas* the day before, said, "I'll send for some."

Fannon sighed. "Ah, no thank you. I'll take care of it. I want you to be free to keep a sharp lookout toward the beach. We wouldn't want anybody firing at us."

Gerlach's voice was more confident, and he started for the starboard door. "Aye, aye, sir, I'll take care of it." The messenger and the Boatswain's Mate of the Watch scurried out of his way, but Acton, coming in the door blind, took a shoulder block. Chief Barley, behind him, saved Acton from hitting the deck.

"Pardon me," Gerlach said. "I've got to get out here in a hurry to look for the enemy."

*   *   *

Just at dawn, CIC reported that the Army wanted gunfire support to commence.

Fannon acknowledged the request and said to Brill, "Tell Gun Control to commence firing."

Brosnan raised his binoculars and searched the target area. Debris began rising with every salvo, and soon Brosnan could see Army troops moving out of their foxholes and running forward. In a few minutes they had advanced to the target area, and the Army shore fire control party asked that fire be ceased. "You did it well," came the report. "We'll want more soon."

Brosnan turned his attention to the beach during the lull. The Army Engineers were clearing the sands of obstacles, and geysers of brown water erupted frequently, indicating where the Navy underwater demolition teams had blown up underwater obstacles. Brosnan asked Benson, "What's the tidal range here?"

Benson said, "Twenty-two feet."

Brosnan whistled. "Jesus! If the boats don't unload in a hurry, they're stuck there until the next high tide."

Benson agreed. "A little more than twelve hours," he said.

The morning passed slowly, with firing assignments coming in half-hourly as the Army pushed inland.

Phelps walked into the pilothouse, leaving Fannon on the wing. "Beetle, the Captain would like to see Chief Benson out on the wing. Something about water depths."

Brosnan relayed the Captain's request to Benson, and Brosnan and Phelps bent over the chart desk.

Almost immediately there was an explosion near the starboard wing. "Jesus!" Brosnan said, "The Captain and Benson are out there."

Phelps and Brosnan dashed out to the wing. Two geysers of water and foam from two projectile explosions were descending, but obviously another projectile had exploded against the outboard side of the bridge wing and shrapnel had penetrated to the inside. Two dozen small holes gaped in the metal of the bridge bulwark.

Brosnan spotted Fannon and Benson lying face down on the deck. Brosnan turned Fannon over slowly, as Phelps rolled Benson onto his back. Both Fannon and Benson were breathing, but blood was beginning to well out of numerous small wounds each had suffered in the upper body.

Another salvo of projectiles landed close aboard. Brosnan realized that with the Captain down he was now in command and had to do something or the next salvo might land on board. He turned to Gerlach, who was looking out the pilothouse door. "Move the ship, or we're in trouble! Tell Aronson to take that damned battery under fire!"

Gerlach nodded, and Brosnan heard him order, "Right full rudder! All ahead flank!"

It was what he would have done, and he filed away a reminder to commend Gerlach later.

Forward, the *Lawrence*'s 5-inch mounts began to fire rapidly. Brosnan turned back to the two men sprawled on the deck.

Fannon stirred and tried to get up, "What happened?" he said faintly.

Brosnan eased Fannon back to the deck. "Sir, please stay down until Doctor Taylor gets here."

Gerlach had sent word for the Doctor and stretcher bearers, and in seconds Taylor ran up and leaned over Fannon. The pharmacist's mate with him examined Benson, who also began to move.

After a quick check, Taylor said, "I think the Captain is just stunned. He has numerous small wounds, none serious." Taylor then turned to the pharmacist's mate. "How's the Chief?"

"The same."

"Okay, let's get them below."

Fannon, slowly regaining full consciousness, said, "I'm not leaving. Just put me in my chair."

Phelps, leaning over him, said, "Sorry, Skipper, you're going below for a thorough examination. You're too valuable to me. I can't afford to lose you."

"But what about the ship?" Fannon asked.

"Brosnan is right here. He'll take over until you've recovered."

When Fannon and Benson were taken below, Brosnan realized he was without a navigator, and the *Lawrence* was still operating quite close to shallow water, although Gerlach had slowed the ship. He turned to the messenger, "Go find Lieutenant Kelly and tell him to come up here on the double."

Brosnan went to the chart desk and quickly checked Benson's last fix. Benson's assistant, a young quartermaster whose duty it was to take and record bearings in a bearing log book, was standing next to the chart desk almost in a state of shock. His eyes were wide in a pale face, and his hands were shaking slightly.

Brosnan said, "Son, get a hold of yourself. You've got work to do."

The assistant took a few deep breaths, and some of his color returned.

"Sir," he said, "is Chief Benson dead?"

Brosnan grinned. "Hell, no. He'll be back up here tomorrow. In the meantime Lieutenant Kelly will navigate."

"But, sir—."

"Don't say anything more. I know you worked with him before on the trip south to Portsmouth. He'll do fine with your help. Go out on the signal bridge and get a cup of black coffee. You'll need it."

*   *   *

In a few minutes Lieutenant Kelly ran up to Brosnan. "Yes, sir, you sent for me?" he asked breathlessly.

Brosnan looked at him carefully. "The Captain and Chief Benson were just hit by shrapnel from a shell explosion. I'm sure they'll be out of action for at least 24 hours. You're now the ship's navigator."

Kelly paled and stammered. "But, sir—."

Brosnan said curtly, "No argument. You can do it and you must. Your assistant will be back in a few minutes. I sent him out to get a cup of coffee. He was a little shaken, but he'll do okay if you show a little self-confidence."

Kelly was beginning to function. "Yes, I know he will. I worked with him on our trip to Portsmouth."

Brosnan said, "This won't be too difficult. You have good radar bearings and at least two prominent steeples ashore you can use for landmarks. Just keep a fix going every two minutes, and keep me informed. I'll be looking over your shoulder if you need me."

Kelly fingered his neat mustache and said confidently, "Very well, sir. I've got it. You can go back to worrying about the rest of the ship."

"Good," Brosnan said, "Just don't put the old bucket aground. We'd make much too good a target."

*   *   *

The rest of the day passed in a partial fog for Brosnan. After a few hours he stopped worrying about Kelly and concentrated on commanding the *Lawrence*. Now he had to worry not only about the internal workings of the ship—its meals, routine, and cleanliness—but more importantly, as commanding officer, he had to worry about the ship's safety. Navigating in shallow water, the threat of fire from ashore, and the ever-present danger of accidents on board from their own guns were all crowding his thoughts. Brosnan knew, for instance, that one serious mistake handling powder, and the whole ship could blow up.

At dark, Brosnan secured the crew from general quarters and set condition III. Staring out at the fading shoreline, he knew he was stuck on the bridge for the rest of the night.

Then he thought about the Captain's chair. By tradition,

only the Captain could use it. Brosnan thought momentarily about breaking tradition, but rejected the idea. Perhaps if the Captain wasn't back by tomorrow, he would have to find some alternative. His legs and feet could only stand so much fatigue.

Phelps, about to leave the bridge, seemed to realize Brosnan's quandary. "Beetle," he said, "I know you don't want to sit in the Captain's chair, but no tradition says you can't use mine. Sit down, and Stevenson will bring you some dinner."

Brosnan broke into a smile. "Thank you, sir," he said.

Phelps shrugged. "You don't need to thank me. This is my flagship, and I have a strong propietary interest in it. If you should lose it, I'd have to move to another ship, and I like this one just fine."

CHAPTER EIGHTEEN

Before dawn, Brosnan climbed out of the Commodore's chair and rotated his head a few times to stretch his cramped neck muscles. In spite of a few moments of rest between false warnings that German air and E-boat attacks were imminent, he was still deeply tired and straining to concentrate fully on commanding the ship. As daylight approached, the young commander began to feel a new respect for Fannon's stamina and skill.

Barley came by and looked at him carefully in the eerie glow of the dimmed red lights. "How about some signal bridge waker-upper?" he asked.

Brosnan cleared his throat and rubbed his eyes. "Sounds good, Chief. A little sugar."

Barley brought him a thick, steaming mug, and Brosnan gratefully drained the contents.

Stevenson entered the pilothouse door carrying a tray of fried eggs, toast, and coffee.

"What's this?" Brosnan asked.

"The Commodore sent you some breakfast."

Brosnan finished it just as Tubby Raymond, who had the deck, sounded morning general quarters.

Dawn gradually illuminated the wreckage on the beach, the morning sun piercing a few rising columns of smoke from several razed buildings.

Phelps burst onto the bridge with his usual eagerness. "How's it going, Beetle?"

"Fine, Commodore, and thanks for the use of your chair and the breakfast."

Phelps shrugged. "You needed it. An exec trying to do two jobs needs all the help he can get."

*   *   *

An hour later, requests for fire support missions began trickling in, as the troops ashore started their push inland. About 1100, as the rounds continued to soar over the beachhead, Brosnan began to feel restless. "Brill," he said, "ask Gun Control how many rounds of ammunition we have left."

Brill reported to Brosnan a few minutes later, "Mister Aronson says fifty rounds of common per gun and about fifty starshells total for all guns."

Brosnan stepped out to the open bridge with his binoculars. The area behind the beach was calm, except for unloading activities. He could see heavy fighting raging a few miles inland, and a few tanks maneuvering in huge clouds of dust.

Kuberski, standing beside him, said, "It looks like the Army is making progress over there."

Brosnan lowered his binoculars. "Yes, but I don't trust the Germans. They may be laying low."

Just as Brosnan finished talking, a salvo of projectiles fell around the forecastle. Two huge geysers rose and then saturated the forward gun mounts. The third projectile exploded on the face plate of gun mount 51.

Brosnan shouted, "Right full rudder! All ahead flank!" The ordered increase of speed seemed to Brosnan to take forever, but actually the ship began to move faster within seconds. No other salvos from the shore followed, and Brosnan slowed just as Kelly reminded him that the *Lawrence* was approaching mined waters.

Down on the forecastle, Brosnan could see the forward repair party running toward mount 51. One side door opened, and a man jumped out, followed by a cloud of smoke. Another handed him a brass powder can, and the man on deck headed to the side and heaved it over.

*   *   *

When the projectile hit in mount 51, Swenson had been idly searching the beach through his pointer's telescope. Suddenly, the view turned red, and he heard a violent explosion. There was a sound like a hundred angry bees flying at him, and he could feel some of their stings. He tried to make a report over his telephone, but his lips wouldn't work, and he felt himself slipping away. Then his whole world turned red and then black.

*   *   *

Up on his elevated mount captain's seat, Bronski heard the explosion forward. Smoke rose from the front of the mount and also billowed inside. The smoke from the outside mixed with the salt water cascading on the deck and swept onto his face, almost tearing off his helmet. Bronski pulled his head inside the mount and wiped the water out of his eyes. Looking down, he saw several of the loading crew were lying on the deck unconscious. Two were still on their feet, but obviously shaken and probably wounded. One of them was the powder casing loader, still clasping a powder casing. A few grains of powder were trickling to the deck from a small gash in the brass casing.

"Jesus!" Bronski yelled. "Get rid of that thing!"

The loader looked at him dazedly, and was too confused to move and carry out Bronski's orders.

Bronski climbed down to the mount deck, opened the side door, and jumped out. "Give it to me!" he yelled to the powder casing loader. When he had it firmly in his hands, he walked gingerly over to the side and heaved it in the water.

Returning to the mount, Bronski tended to the wounded men. No one seemed to have any serious injuries or arterial bleeding, and so he left them in the care of the repair party and pharmacist's mate, who were now climbing in the open door.

Bronski followed them and climbed forward alongside the gun to the pointer's station, looking for Swenson.

Swenson was slumped over the pointer's controls. Bronski could see several holes in the front of the gun mount shield, and hydraulic fluid was splattered all over the area and over Swenson, mixing with the blood from numerous wounds around his face and neck.

Bronski swore. "Stay with me, kid! I didn't know you were hurt. I'll get you out of here."

Bronski grabbed Swenson's shoulders and gently pulled his upper body backward over the metal seat. Now he could see several wounds on his neck and face, but there didn't seem to be any arterial bleeding. He continued to drag him backward and laid him safely on the deck. Swenson's eyes were closed, but apparently undamaged, and his breathing was shallow but regular. Bronski felt for his pulse. It was weak but steady.

Bronski straightened up and watched as the wounded were loaded and taken out in stretchers. He looked around the mount to see if it was safely secured and that there were no loaded powder casings around. Then he climbed out of the mount and followed Swenson's stretcher to the wardroom.

*　　*　　*

Brosnan watched the action on the forecastle as the stretchers were taken away. He knew he could do nothing for the wounded at the moment, and he was concerned that Aronson had not been able to spot the location of the battery that had fired on them. "Probably mobile artillery," Phelps speculated.

Suddenly Brosnan was aware that Fannon was standing next to him. "Captain," Brosnan said, "you're not supposed to be up here in your condition."

Fannon shook his head gingerly and felt the bandages on his face to make sure they were still in place. "Couldn't stay away," he said.

Brosnan said, "Did Doctor Taylor say you were fully ready for duty?"

"Hell, no. He was too busy with the wounded. I'm alright now, and I relieve you."

Brosnan sighed. "Aye, sir. I loved being in command, but I'll admit I'm pretty tired. It's good to have you back up here."

Fannon looked over at the chart desk where Lieutenant Kelly was busy plotting a fix. "Is he navigating?" he asked.

Brosnan nodded. "Yes, sir; and doing a good job of it. He's also helping me as acting executive officer. He'll be able to qualify soon."

Fannon said, "I'm ready to take over up here. I'd appreciate it if you'd go below see how the wounded are—and don't be in such a hurry to get back up here."

Brosnan dragged his heavy legs down the ladder, holding tight to the handrails to keep from falling. As he eased himself along, he thought how much he admired the Captain, and he remembered his feelings when he had seen him stretched out on the deck of the signal bridge. Much as Brosnan thought he could be a good destroyer captain, he knew that Fannon was better: Fannon could handle the ship better; he knew the needs of his crew better; and he seemed to have that sixth sense of what the enemy might do. Brosnan realized he would have to learn all he could from Fannon. There might be a time soon when he would be in command for a longer time, or even in command of his own ship. Brosnan breathed deeply. Just being a good executive officer was hard enough.

*   *   *

Brosnan pushed open the wardroom door and looked around. Four men were lying on the deck, covered with blankets, obviously waiting their turn to be treated on the wardroom table by Doctor Taylor.

Taylor was bending over Swenson, who was stretched out on the operating table. Brosnan walked over and looked over Taylor's shoulder. "How's he doing?" he asked.

Taylor, busy stitching up Swenson's wounds, said, "He's still unconscious. I'm trying to get these in before he wakes up so I won't have to use any anesthetic. Otherwise, I don't find anything much wrong with him. I don't think he has a concussion, but I'll know more when he wakes up."

How's the rest of the mount crew?"

Taylor gestured toward the men on the deck. "These are the rest of them. My pharmacist's mate has given them a quick examination and some morphine, and I'll take care of them in a minute. I've already sent Bronski back to his mount."

"Did you know the Captain was back on the bridge?"

Taylor laughed. "I didn't know about it, and I don't doubt it. I might have kept him away for one more day, but if he wants to go back to duty, I'll have to agree."

Taylor turned around and looked at Brosnan closely. "Besides, I think you need a little help."

*　　*　　*

Brosnan took a hot shower, changed clothes, grabbed a sandwich, and then headed back for the bridge.

Fannon was reading a stack of recently decoded dispatches. "Sounds like a busy night coming up," he said.

Brosnan's eyebrows shot up. "Bad news?"

Fannon handed the dispatches to Brosnan. "Looks like some air raids and an E-boat attack sometime after dark. Maybe a combination of both."

While Brosnan was reading the dispatches, Fannon patted the adhesive tape holding the bandages on his face. "Damned bandages," he muttered.

"What was that, sir?" Brosnan asked.

"Nothing important. What do you think will happen tonight?"

"After all our experience with the Germans, I'd say we'll get the full treatment. The only question is whether they come at us one at a time or all at once."

Fannon sighed. "They're good at coordination. We'll get them all at once."

Brosnan shrugged. "We'll take them any way we can."

* * *

Darkness came, and the concern among the ship's crew increased. Brosnan felt the tension, but was too tired to move around much and leaned on the bulwark, trying to stay awake.

About 2300, the CIC began receiving air contact reports from the screen commander in charge of the British destroyers protecting the British area.

Phelps said, "Sounds like a bunch of aircraft scouting targets for the E-boats."

"Maybe," Fannon said, but I think they'll attack at the same time."

Suddenly, gunfire erupted to the east of the British sector, and Brosnan could see the British ships directing fire at aircraft and also at surface craft. The TBS crackled. Fannon, listening intently to the clipped accents of the British radio operators, said, "They seem to be coming our way. Tell CIC to keep a sharp lookout on both radars."

Brosnan slapped his cheeks and stamped his feet to heighten his alertness. As he watched the action nearing, he could feel his fatigue fade as his adrenaline began pumping.

The squawk box blared. "Six surface contacts bearing zero seven zero! Range ten thousand yards! Course two two zero! Speed four zero!"

Phelps said, "They're headed right at us. Your target, Fannon. Fire when ready."

Fannon, watching the targets approach rapidly on the PPI, ordered, "Gun Control, fire when ready. I'm swinging to port so the after mounts will bear."

Chief Brill replied, "Gun Control acknowledges."

Within seconds, the first salvo screamed out over the water. The men on the bridge waited tensely. With mount 51 out of commission, only three mounts had fired.

Brosnan watched the soaring projectile tracers through his binoculars and saw them explode in the distance. Some produced a dull, red glow that flared briefly before disappearing. The other destroyers in the Omaha screen also had fired, and a hail of projectiles soon engulfed the oncoming E-boats. One E-boat exploded in a large fire and continued to burn brightly. Another direct hit sent a huge geyser of water and boat parts into the air, but the craft's hull did not burn. After another exploded in flame, a fourth turned away, trailing flame from its stern.

In a few seconds, the engagement was over, and the few remaining E-boats fled, zigzagging at high speed.

Brosnan let out his breath in relief and walked over to Fannon. "Captain, shall I set condition III?"

Fannon shook his head reluctantly. "No, Beetle, this is too busy a night. Besides, we haven't heard directly from the German aircraft yet."

Brosnan walked back to the bulwark and started to lean on it, but quickly straightened up. "If I lean on it, I'll go to sleep," he muttered. The exhaustion was descending on him like a blanket, and he began pacing up and down to fight off the weariness. Sleep and even rest were a long way off.

CHAPTER NINETEEN

By the morning of 9 June, Brosnan felt that the crew was so exhausted it was approaching the point where it could hardly function. The men plodded about the decks with leaden feet. Their eyes were blank and dull. They needed to get off of their feet and rest, even if only for a short time. Brosnan knew he, too, was tired, and he judged the officers and crew were just as tired. He talked briefly with Doctor Taylor about the situation, and the two went to the bridge to see the Captain.

Fannon, sitting in his bridge chair, saw them coming and grinned slightly. Only his lower face moved, and his eyes were glazed, although he still seemed alert. "You guys look like you're on your last legs. I can guess what you want, but this may be a busy day, and we have to be ready for anything at any time."

Brosnan decided to speak up anyway. "Captain, I think we've got to go to condition III. The crew isn't going to be much good to us in the shape it's in."

Fannon stretched his arms above his head. "How about those GIs ashore we're supporting? They've been going at it for three days, too."

"Yes, but at least they are lying in fox holes at night and getting off of their feet. Our men need a little rest."

Taylor nodded vigorously in approval. "They're in bad shape, Captain."

Phelps was standing nearby writing on a dispatch pad. He interrupted. "Fannon, I'm writing up a dispatch recommending that the *Lawrence* and *Hanly* be detached and head for Portsmouth for ammunition replenishment and urgent repairs. Both ships are very low on ammunition, and you have a gun mount out of commission. The *Hanly* has no surface radar."

Fannon said, "Yes, sir. We do need all of our mounts. Aronson says we can't fix the damage to the hydraulic system at sea, but that the yard could do it in a short period."

Brosnan grinned weakly, "I think we could all use a little overhaul time."

* * *

About 1100, Admiral Bryant, in answer to the Commodore's message, ordered the two ships to Portsmouth. When Farraday, who had the deck, announced their departure over the ship's loud speaker system, the crew was too tired to cheer.

Fannon asked Chief Benson, who had recovered enough from his wounds to resume his navigational duties, for a course to Portsmouth. When the *Hanly* was safely tucked in astern, the Captain ordered condition III set.

Brosnan stumbled down the bridge ladder and into his room. He tried to climb into his bunk, but he was too exhausted to make it. Instead, he threw a blanket and pillow on the deck, taking care not to get between Taylor's bunk and the wash basin. Falling onto his pillow, he was asleep before he could pull the blanket up over himself.

Taylor found him there, fully clothed, a few minutes later and pulled the blanket over him.

* * *

As the *Lawrence* steamed away from Omaha Beach, with the *Hanly* following, Phelps, Kuberski, and Fannon gathered on the bridge to watch the arriving convoys enter the swept channel leading to the transport unloading areas.

Phelps said, "Stanley, who's in these Liberty ships coming in?"

Kuberski thumbed through the thick operation order. "A replacement division of Army troops scheduled to relieve a division that made the initial landings."

Fannon said, "The Army is building up rapidly. Next we'll see prefabricated structures called Mulberries and other odd, large craft scheduled to be sunk in a ring around the beach to form an artificial harbor."

Phelps nodded. "I understand the British are building one, too."

"It was their idea in the first place." Fannon said. "We've got to use these artificial harbors until the Army can transport some harbors from the rear like Cherbourg, which have cranes to handle the major unloading."

Phelps said, "Those battles behind the beach will be going on for a long time. There'll be plenty for us to do when we come back."

*　　*　　*

The next day Brosnan had rested enough to return to the bridge. He watched Benson navigate the formation toward the entrance to Portsmouth Harbor.

Benson had a half-dozen bandages on his face and arms. Brosnan said, "You look like someone the first aid guys have been practicing on."

Benson grinned. "I feel like it, too. I've got a lot of bandages that don't show."

Brosnan looked over his shoulder at the web of fixes along their course line. "Small fixes," he said.

Benson nodded. "Thank you, sir. I understand Lieutenant Kelly did a good job navigating while I was out of it."

"Yes, he did. You were a good teacher."

"I didn't do much. He's a helluva smart guy. He just has to stick to mastering the simple stuff and stop trying to analyze everything."

Brosnan grinned. "I think he's got a good start in that direction."

*　　*　　*

Brosnan walked out on the bridge and looked astern toward France. He began to think about Annette, wondering how the invasion would affect her. Certainly the Germans would be moving units around the French countryside, and her observations would provide vital intelligence to the Alies. He hoped she would be able to do her job without being caught. If the Germans found her out, her life would be short. Spies caught in time of war knew what to expect. Swift execution, probably without trial, and the Germans would be ruthless.

He shuddered and turned toward the bow. Ahead he could see the pilot boat, and he started down to the sea ladder to meet the pilot. On an impulse, he stopped a passing man and ordered him to find Lieutenant Gerlach and ask him to meet him at the sea ladder. If they were to get the same ancient pilot, he would need Gerlach to help hoist the old gent up the ladder.

CHAPTER TWENTY

As expected, the same pilot who guided the *Lawrence* on her last visit to Portsmouth returned to the destroyer. Brosnan and Gerlach greeted him and easily hoisted him up the sea ladder, with Gerlach doing most of the work.

The pilot led the *Lawrence* to a familiar berth and soon had the ship moored, with the *Hanly* outboard.

Brosnan and Kelly stood on the quarterdeck watching the long brow being lowered into place by a travelling crane. A group of yard workmen stood on the pier, laughing and chattering, waiting to come aboard.

Lieutenant Kelly asked Brosnan anxiously, "Sir, can you help me with the Commodore? From the looks of those boffins over there, they're already thinking about drinking his booze, and I don't have any to give them."

Brosnan laughed. "Sure. Here comes Stanley Kuberski. He'll take care of it."

Kuberski strolled up to the pair, wiping his fingers on a handkerchief.

Brosnan asked, "Sweet roll?"

"Nah. A jelly doughnut. Pretty good."

Brosnan said, "Kelly, here, hopes you'll take the Brits standing over there to the Commodore and, ah, help persuade them to give us a good overhaul."

"Sure. I've got a key to the magic locker, and I know what he wants done." Kuberski looked at Kelly. "But you've got to simplify the paperwork."

Kelly nodded vigorously. "I've got it here. Only one page per job."

Kuberski grinned. "You're learning."

"I only make a mistake once. I didn't fall off a garbage scow," Kelly replied.

* * *

On the bridge, Chief Barley and Signalman Third Class Acton leaned over the signal flag bags watching the performance on the quarterdeck below. Barley said, "Those Brits on the pier can hardly wait to get aboard."

Acton nodded, "They always seem to do a great job. They'll have a lot of holes up here to weld shut. The bulkhead looks like an old colander my Grandmother used to use."

"Keep the coffee ready. We'll get the job done faster if you keep them well supplied with our signal bridge best."

Acton lifted a blond eyebrow. "I don't think that will do much. I think they'll be looking for something a little stronger once they get on board."

Barley laughed. "Chief Brill says they always come out of the Commodore's cabin laughing and scratching."

Acton added. "And carrying paper bags."

"Well, that may have something to do with it."

Acton looked over at the town behind the navy yard. "Are you going ashore here?"

"Damned right. I'm about to bust. Not having any liberty in Belfast was just about the last straw."

"Remember what Chief Benson said to you. You can't afford to get into any trouble now that you're a chief."

Barley rubbed his eyes and sighed patiently. "Kid, you worry too much and life is too short."

* * *

The British yard supervisers rushed up the brow as soon as it was secured, and Kuberski and Kelly met them and escorted them to the Commodore's cabin. Brosnan watched them go, trying to stay out of the traffic pattern.

An hour later the supervisers came back to the quarterdeck and left for their offices in the yard, carefully guarding their brown paper bags.

Kelly followed them and stood on the quarterdeck with Brosnan watching the Brits walk up the busy yard street. "Well," he said, "I think we'll have a good overhaul."

Brosnan grinned. "Yes, I'm sure we will."

Kelly shook his head and added, "You know, sir, they didn't teach us this stuff at MIT."

Brosnan heard a step behind them and turned. The Commodore was walking up the deck, followed by the Captain. They were deep in conversation. As the Commodore approached, he saluted the petty officer of the watch and stepped up on the brow. Apparently as an afterthought, he turned and said to Fannon, "I'll be back in an hour or two. I'll get transportation from the Captain of the Yard."

Fannon nodded and saluted. "We'll save lunch for you if you're late."

*   *   *

That afternoon Bronski and Swenson showed a party from the yard around the damaged mount 51. The head superviser explored with his fingers some of the bigger holes in the front of the shield and whistled. "Wouldn't wanna been behind these bloody holes when the projectile burst," he said.

Swenson grimaced and fingered his healing scars. "Wasn't much fun," he said.

Bronski looked at Swenson and then shouted, pointing to the fractured hydraulic piping and other damage around the pointer's station. "Look at that stuff. Looks like spaghetti. You were lucky, Swenson. Some of that mess protected you from more serious wounds. If it hadn't been there, your insides might have been hanging out just like that piping."

The yard superviser made some notes and did a few quick calculations on an old letter. Then he said, "Your Commodore says we should give this a high priority."

"You'll see to it right away?" Bronski asked.

"Damned right, mate, he can have anything he wants."

As the superviser walked away, Swenson said, "What's the Commodore's secret?"

Bronski took off his white hat and scratched his head. "Damned if I know, but it's all right with me."

*   *   *

Another yard superviser made a cursory examination of the holes in the bridge bulwark without recording a note.

As he started to leave the bridge, Chief Barley said, "Aren't you going to fix all this?"

The superviser grinned, revealing an uneven line of tobacco-stained teeth. "Oi! Or you betcha, as you Yanks would say. It ain't much. We'll weld all these tomorrow. You'll have to paint them, though."

Barley looked at Acton. "Can you handle that?"

"Sure, Chief, I suppose you're in a hurry to hit the beach."

"Yeah, although it ain't really a beach."

Acton nodded. "I could tell that from looking through the telescope as we passed it. Looks like a big gravel pit—and there isn't any surf."

"There will be when a channel storm works up. But it isn't the kind for surfing."

Acton shrugged. "I wouldn't even swim over there in a wet suit. Do the Brits really swim in these waters?"

Barley laughed. "I don't think so. All I ever see them do is sit on the gravel and drink beer—and that's good enough for me. I'll be back in 48 hours. Make sure we get a good paint job."

*   *   *

Just before lunch, Phelps drove up in a British staff car, got out, thanked the driver, and bounded up the brow.

Fannon met the Commodore. Phelps returned his salute and headed for his cabin. As he passed Fannon, he said, "Come with me." His invitation failed to include Brosnan and Kuberski. As the two senior officers disappeared into the interior of the ship, Brosnan looked at Kuberski and raised his eyebrows. "First time he's ever done that."

Kuberski shrugged. "Must be something top secret. But if he doesn't want to tell us, that gives us time to take a nap."

Brosnan said, "I'm with you."

*   *   *

In his cabin, Phelps invited Fannon to sit and then told Stevenson to close the door.

Fannon sat down and looked at the Commodore. "Something serious?"

"Not exactly. I didn't want Brosnan to hear this and raise his hopes that Annette might be coming back soon."

Fannon said, "You lost me before you started."

Phelps pursed his lips. Fannon idly thought that when he did that, he looked like one of his horses. Phelps pulled out a chair. "Let me start from the beginning. I called briefly on General Eisenhower, but he was too busy for anything but a brief conversation."

Fannon said, "I can understand that. Then what?"

"Eisenhower turned me over to my friend, Brigadier General Tweety Terwilliger."

"Then this must have had something to do with intelligence."

"Yes, Tweety owed me one because of our action with the German submarine crew a few weeks ago. They're still talking about that."

"You mean we're getting an assignment other than going back to Omaha Beach?"

"Yes. The *Lawrence* and *Hanly* are going to patrol a station in the channel for about five days. We'll have two British torpedo boats working for us."

"Sounds interesting, but what will we be doing?"

"Mostly acting as a rescue unit for Royal Air Force and Army Air Force bombers and fighters coming back from missions over France and Germany. There will be an increased offensive designed to paralyze the movement of German Army forces. That means a lot of crippled aircraft will be flying home."

"And we'll be a rescue point for those who can't quite make it all the way."

"Right, but there's more."

Fannon shrugged. "I guessed as much. What you've told me so far isn't anything Brosnan couldn't hear."

"You're right, and we'll tell him about this when we think it is the right time. The private part, and of course it's private rather than secret, is that sometime during that five-day period we might also be called to pick up one or more small aircraft being used by the British to evacuate intelligence agents from France. If they have to fly many evasive maneuvers, they probably wouldn't have enough fuel to make it back to England."

Fannon leaned forward in his chair. "You mean Brosnan's fiancée may be coming out?"

Phelps paused. "Terwilliger wasn't positive about that. That's why I don't want to get Brosnan's hopes up. He might expect too much."

Fannon nodded. "I agree. Let's let him be surprised if it happens. If it doesn't, he won't be disappointed."

Phelps changed the subject. "How are the prospects for our repairs? We only have three more days here."

Fannon grinned. "Thanks to you we'll make it. The *Hanly* is ready now. We should be ready tomorrow."

CHAPTER TWENTY-ONE

At dawn on the fourth day in Portsmouth, Chief Barley moved about the navigation and signal bridges, testing the fresh paint over the recently welded holes in the bridge bulwark. Occasionally he would stop by the signal bridge coffee pot to get some black coffee to help his hangover.

When he emptied the last cup out of the pot, he lifted the lid and inspected the inside. The coffee pot's insides were gleaming. "Acton," he said, "this pot looks great. Now get some more coffee in it."

Acton rolled his eyes and shook his head. "Don't worry, Chief, it'll be full when we station the special sea detail for getting under way."

Barley relented. "Good job on the painting. You can hardly see the holes."

Acton laughed. "I'll bet Chief Benson could find every one of them."

Benson was busy laying out the navigational charts for the trip out of the harbor, but he heard the exchange between Barley and Acton. "You're right, my friends—and I'll never forget how loud the explosions were, either. I thought I'd lost my hearing, permanently."

Barley looked closely at Benson. "Actually, I think I see a piece of your ear missing."

Benson felt his ear and frowned. "Yes, but not much. I can still hear you guys yattering."

Acton laughed, "It makes you look like a pirate."

Chief Barley tried to change the subject. "Acton, get the striker to do another sweep down."

"But, Chief—."

"Do it."

Chief Benson smiled as Acton walked away. "He's really a good kid."

Barley nodded. "Just needs a little prodding."

Benson put in the last thumbtack. "How was your liberty?"

Barley shook his head. "This is summer in England? I almost froze my butt off in my girlfriend's beach house. I had to double the strength of my drinks just to keep warm."

"You should have stayed in bed."

"I did that most of the time, but a guy's got to eat and drink now and then."

*   *   *

Just before the call came to station the special sea detail, Brosnan finished his customary inspection of the ship, checking its readiness for getting under way. The executive officer headed to the bridge to report to the Captain.

Fannon, drinking his third coffee of the morning, greeted him warmly. "Good morning, Beetle, are we ready for getting under way and ready for bad weather when we get to sea? I hear the English Channel has been in a helluva mess since we've been gone."

Brosnan raised his eyebrows and asked, "What's this about the English Channel?"

Fannon looked grim. "Terrible storm, or maybe it was just the usual English summer weather. Many of the parts of the arifical harbors were sunk or damaged, and unloading stopped for several days."

Brosnan shuddered. "I have great sympathy for how difficult those operations are, but mostly I think about the poor destroyer crews. Lots of rolling, lots of rain, and lots of cold water down their necks."

Fannon laughed. "That's about par for destroyers. But we've gotten off the subject. Are we ready for sea?"

"Yes, sir, all yard gear is off the ship. Everything topside secured for sea, and Kelly says the engineers will be ready on time. Mount 51 works fine, and we're full of amunition."

"Sounds okay. We won't be firing that much, though."

"At our briefing yesterday you said we were to man a rescue station in the English Channel. Won't we be firing there?"

"Oh, sure, at a few passing German aircraft, but not as much as on our last mission."

Brosnan looked closely at Fannon. "Captain, is there anything you aren't telling me?"

Fannon colored slightly, but appeared to concentrate on a passing tug boat. "Er, Beetle, not anything you really need to know. Let's get going. This could be an interesting mission."

*   *   *

The *Lawrence* and *Hanly* soon cleared Portsmouth Harbor, dropped off their friendly old pilot, and set course for the English Channel.

Fannon looked at the course line Benson had laid down. Benson commented, "These courses keep us in swept channels until just before we turn toward our station."

Fannon raised his eyebrows. "Our station is not swept?"

"Doesn't need to be, sir, it's too deep to plant mines in."

"Thanks. I feel better."

Fannon went out to the bridge wing to join the Commodore, who was watching the *Hanly* take station astern. Fannon said, "I take it the *Hanly*'s radar is okay."

Phelps nodded. "Good as ever. The Brits are good at radar repair. Also they stock some tubes we don't carry."

Fannon looked around to make sure Brosnan wasn't in hearing range. "Commodore, I take it you still feel that Brosnan shouldn't know about the outside possibility that Annette might be returning to England."

"Right. We don't really know how or when she'll be coming back. He'll know soon enough."

At dusk, the two ships turned south and out of the swept

channel. Just before dark, the *Lawrence*'s CIC reported two British PT boats, which soon darted out of the murk to join the destroyers. Phelps quickly contacted the boats on the TBS, and advised them where to take station. Once in the formation, the four ships began to patrol slowly in a large square.

As darkness drew on, apprehension grew among the bridge crew until it almost became palpable. The men did not know exactly what their mission was, although Fannon had passed as much information to them as he could without breaching security. Sensing the crew's anxiety, Fannon said to Brosnan in a voice he knew was loud enough to be heard by all the bridge watch, "This won't be too bad. There won't be any mines. We're too far from the German Navy bases for their surface forces to get at us, and it's too shallow for submarines to operate here regularly."

Brosnan, understanding the Captain's intentions, responded, "Should be pretty safe. All we have to do is keep a sharp lookout for any of our own aircraft heading this way."

Concerned that Brosnan's comments may have been perceived too optimistically, Fannon added, "But our own aircraft may be pursued by German fighters. We'll have to be careful to sort out the good guys from the bad guys."

Brosnan turned to the officer of the deck, Tubby Raymond, and started to give him instructions, but Raymond beat him to it. "I've got it, sir. I've already instructed my machine gun battery, and Aronson has done the same for the 5-inch battery and the lookouts."

"Thanks," Brosnan said, "You make my job easy."

Raymond laughed. "Well, I guess we're veterans by now. There isn't much we haven't done."

"Yes, but this mission may be a little different, and we don't want to shoot down a friendly."

*   *   *

As the night progressed, tensions eased, and the ships patrolled unnoticed and undisturbed.

Chief Barley prowled the signal bridge, checking on the

adjacent ships through his long glass. "Jesus!" he growled, "We might as well be back in Portsmouth."

Chief Benson, carefully keeping the track plotted, said, "This may be boring for you, but I'm going to be working all night to keep the ship's navigation going."

"All night?"

"Well, almost all night. Lieutenant Kelly is coming up to relieve me for a few hours."

Barley said, "I could take over for a few hours. There isn't much signalling going on."

Benson nodded. "I know you're qualified to do a quarter-master's duties, and I appreciate your offer, but Mister Brosnan wants Lieutenant Kelly to get in as much time navigating as possible."

Barley shrugged. "Fine with me, but we might be here for a long time."

Benson grinned. "Then I'll give you a call."

CHAPTER TWENTY-TWO

By dawn general quarters, the crew was relaxed—too relaxed, Brosnan thought after reading a dispatch from the Supreme Headquarters, Allied Expedition Force or "SHAEF." General Eisenhower's headquarters listed the bomber flights scheduled for daylight hours. As Brosnan ran his forefinger down the list, he let out a deep breath.

Fannon heard him. "You're reading the bomber listing?"

"Yes, sir. It is a hell of a big operation. This is just for the daylight hours of one day."

"And it will produce a lot of cripples and some business for us," Fannon interrupted.

Brosnan said, "I'd like to brief the crew over the telephone circuits about this."

"Please do. I think they need to be a little more focused. But before you do, let's get young Squid Lee up here to give us a more thorough briefing."

Brosnan called CIC on the squawkbox, and in a few minutes Lee appeared on the bridge carrying an armfull of charts, manuals, and operation orders.

Brosnan looked at him inquiringly, obviously concerned about the large amount of briefing material.

Lee laughed. "Don't be so concerned, sir. Whenever the Army does anything, it's very big with paper work. If I may drop all this on the Commodore's chair, I'll have the guts of it ready for your brief in about one minute."

Phelps said, "By all means. I won't need my chair. I'm going to be hanging over your shoulder like everyone else."

Lee put the material on the Commodore's chair and took a large folded chart off the top of the pile. Brosnan noted the smooth, liquid movements of Lee's long arms as he opened the chart and spread it on the chart desk, and he could see why the wardroom officers had nicknamed him squid.

The chart was so large that the ends drooped over the sides of the chart desk. Lee noted that Fannon was frowning and said quickly, "Captain, don't be concerned. We're only going to be using the center of this chart. The outer parts go clear to eastern Germany."

Fannon nodded. "Okay, we're ready when you are."

Lee began, "I think I can do all of the briefing with just this one chart. The other material is just for reference."

Phelps, Fannon, Brosnan, and Kuberski gathered around the edge of the desk. Lee cleared his voice. "First, the point of this mission is to disrupt the flow of German tanks, guns, and personnel toward the front for the next few days while the Allies conduct an offensive. The American and British Air Forces will try to destroy German vehicles and the roads they are traveling as well as trains and train tracks and German air fields and aircraft."

Fannon was skeptical. "They'll never do it. They never have in the past."

Phelps rubbed his jaw. "Well, I don't know. Depends somewhat on the forces we have available."

Lee stroked his pale eyebrows pensively while Fannon and Phelps were talking. Then he said, "Sirs, we'll be using all the aircraft we have in the theater. The American heavy bombers will be bombing in the darkness. British heavy bombers will take over in the daylight, and American and British fighter-bombers will work on rail and highway traffic during the days. It will be an all-out effort."

Fannon shook his head. "They'll have to convince me that the effort will make a difference. In the meantime, all those sorties are going to generate a lot of crippled and downed aircraft."

Lee said, "That's where we come in." Lee bent over the chart and began to point at specific features. "The main highways are in red. The rail lines are in green, and the large green spots are the marshalling yards. German airfields are in blue."

Kuberski, looking at the ocean part of the chart, asked, "What are those four yellow squares?"

Lee pointed to the southernmost of the squares. "This one will be us."

Kuberski said, "I see our square is between the southern airfields and the southern part of the battlefield."

Lee nodded. "Yes, and the others are more or less in direct lines between groups of bomber bases and the areas of the battlefield assigned to these groups."

Fannon looked relieved. "Then we don't have to do it all."

Phelps interrupted. "Only about a fourth. I assume all the aircraft crews will be briefed on our locations."

Lee pointed to a printed box on the chart. "Here are our assigned frequencies and call signs. Each rescue group will be transmitting continuously on a different frequency. Any bomber can shift to any frequency and home on it."

Fannon tightened his stare. "So can the Germans."

Lee was quick to answer. "Yes, sir, but probably only German fighters will be sent over the channel. SHAEF figures we can take care of most of them with our guns. If, not, there will be flights of Spitfires at coastal bases on strip alert ready to fly out and help us."

Fannon's eyebrows shot up. "How long will they take to get out to us?"

"About ten minutes."

Lee's answer calmed Fannon. "I guess that will be all right."

Kuberski frowned. "That's a long time to hold off a bunch of fast ME109s."

Fannon relaxed. "You don't have to worry about that anymore. Aronson will do the worrying."

Kuberski smiled bleakly. "You're right. Now if they strafe us, I can just duck behind the pilothouse."

*   *   *

About 1100, the first bomber flights began returning to England. Gerlach had been assigned to monitor the special air-sea rescue circuits set up in the CIC. The big air plot board was expanded to include not only the ship's radar contacts but also the whole English Channel. Gerlach sent a running summary of the aerial activity to the bridge over the squawkbox.

Over the next hour, the crew observed trails of condensate high in the atmosphere, as Allied fighters tried to intercept German fighter formations seeking the vulnerable bombers. Then, just before noon, Gerlach's voice became excited. "British bomber headed our way. Two ME109s in pursuit."

Fannon called the ship to general quarters and warned Aronson and Raymond to have their men and the lookouts keep a sharp watch.

The squawkbox came to life again, as Squid Lee reported. "We have contacts on radar. Bearing zero seven zero. Ten miles. Three aircraft."

Brosnan swept the horizon to the east with his binoculars, and was the first to spot the oncoming aircraft. "I see a bomber and two fighters. The bomber is beginning to trail smoke."

Aronson reported on the telephone, "We have them. Request permission to fire a salvo to one side of the bomber to try to scare off the fighters."

Fannon was hesitant, but he said, "Permission granted."

Lee, below in CIC, heard the order on the telephone. "We have the bomber on the radio. I'll warn him the salvo is coming."

Fannon said, "Tell him to fly right over us, and we'll debug him."

Moments later, Lee reported, "The bomber acknowledges our order, and he sees us."

As Brosnan watched the approaching bomber, he could see the German fighters making firing runs on it, alternately pulling above and swooping down toward its tail. The attackers were handicapped by the bomber's low altitude and the answering fire from her machine gun turrets, but the Germans still managed to pour out streams of bullets on each pass. As he watched the winking guns, Brosnan held his breath and cursed. The bomber would have to be lucky to survive.

As the bomber closed the ships, Raymond's 40-millimeter battery joined the 5-inchers, sending a steady stream of fire at the dodging fighters. The fire struck one ME109, which burst into flames and quickly disintegrated. Brosnan shouted, "Got the bastard!" The crew cheered.

The second fighter veered off in the middle of a run and headed for safety.

Gerlach could hardly contain his emotion over the squawkbox. "The bomber says thanks. Her engine fire is out, and she's headed for home on three engines."

Brosnan said to Fannon, "Captain, can we go to condition III so I can feed the crew?"

"I don't think so, Beetle. This stuff develops too fast. Let's feed them on station."

Brosnan sent word down to Pasha Parma, and in a half hour, the supply officer saw that a large tub of sandwiches was delivered to the bridge. Brosnan looked over the flag bags and could see similar tubs being carried aft by straining mess cooks. Parma, a clip board in his hand, was directing traffic.

*   *   *

At 1300, another British Lancaster bomber, trailing smoke, appeared from the east. Gerlach said, "He's going to ditch."

Phelps picked up the TBS and ordered the PT boats to stand by to rescue the bomber's crew and then to transfer it to the *Hanly*. In seconds, the huge, lumbering aircraft decreased altitude and slowed. The pilot brought his nose up as far as it would go without stalling, until the plane's tail cut gouges in the tops of the waves. With the propellers flailing at the water, the fuselage plopped awkwardly onto the surface, and the nose dropped into the rough seas. Then, in an instant, the whole aircraft nosed over on its back and settled upside down in the green water.

Brosnan watched the PTs speed toward the wallowing fuselage, with high tails of white water following the small craft. Men began to struggle out of the doors and hatches of the bomber fuselage. All were wearing yellow life jackets and brown suits and helmets. Plopping into the water, they began swimming toward the approaching PTs.

Just as the bomber began to sink, Gerlach reported, "The PTs say they have the whole crew aboard and are heading for the *Hanly*."

Phelps rubbed his hands together. "Bloody good show. Tell the PTs well done."

*   *   *

In midafternoon. Gerlach reported another Lancaster, escorted by a British Spitfire fighter, approaching at medium altitude.

"Is he in trouble?" Fannon asked.

Gerlach said, "He has wounded aboard and can't fire his machine guns. Says he'll be all right as long as the Spitfire is with him. He just wants us to cover him as long as we can."

In a few minutes the Lancaster appeared in the east, flying at about five thousand feet. Brosnan watched a Spitfire circling him.

Gerlach reported, "Two more contacts approaching at high speed."

Aronson yelled, "We see them. Two ME109s. Request permission to open fire."

"Permission granted," Fannon replied.

In an instant, 5-inch salvos began to blossom in the distance, walking slowly toward the Lancaster. Aronson stopped firing just as the ME109s merged with the British group. The three fighters swirled around the Lancaster, the Spitfire trying its best to protect the slower bomber. Suddenly, a burst of bright flame exploded from the engine of one of the German aircraft, and it began to spiral down. Brosnan watched it closely. "There's a parachute. Mark our position, Benson."

Brosnan looked at Fannon and started to say something, but the Captain interrupted, "Commodore, do we have to rescue that bastard?"

Phelps shook his head, "Later. He has to get in line behind our own troops."

The two remaining fighters swirled around the Lancaster, the ME109 trying frantically to get in a burst at the
bomber.

Fannon fidgeted, obviously hoping to get in a few rounds,
but the fighters were too close to each other and to the
bomber.

Phelps noticed his agitation. "Sorry, Skipper, but we can't
take a chance."

Fannon replied, "I agree, sir. But if they get close enough,
I'll release the 40s."

The bomber drew closer, and just before the group of aircraft came within range of the 40-millimeters, the Spitfire
began trailing smoke and headed for one of the PTs.

"He's out of it, Fannon said, "Now we can try for the
German."

Phelps added fiercely. "Give it to him." Fannon had never
seen him like that before.

Fannon passed the orders to commence firing to Aronson
and Raymond, and the machine guns spoke in their peculiar, staccato rhythm. As the Lancaster circled the destroyers, the *Lawrence* and *Hanly* poured up a cone of destruction,
and the ME109, trying to evade the fire, lost a section of its
tail. In a slow, few seconds the pilot lost control, and the aircraft nosed over and plunged into the sea, raising a huge
column of green water.

The Lancaster waggled its wings and continued to head
for home. Gerlach reported, "The Brit says thank you."

Both of the PTs were busy fishing the Spitfire pilot out
of the water, pointedly ignoring the floundering German.

Fannon looked over at the enemy parachute, filling with
water, "I'll try for the German. I see his chute."

Phelps shouted into the wind. "Go to it."

*   *   *

On the forecastle, the crew of mount 51, led by Bronski, spilled
out on deck and ran up to the cargo net secured to the out-

board side of the lifelines. Bronski couldn't see the parachute and asked Swenson, "What are we suposed to do?"

Swenson said, "Chief Brill, the bridge talker, said we're on our way to pick up a Kraut pilot. He's up ahead somewhere."

Swenson shielded his eyes and looked ahead, "There he is. I see a parachute in the water, and there's a head next to it."

The *Lawrence* steamed ahead at high speed while the men on the forecastle broke out small grapnels, heaving lines with monkey fists, and other equipment, and readied for a recovery.

Bronski, waiting expectantly, said, "It will be good to see face-to-face one of these bastards we've been shooting at."

Swenson shrugged. "He might be a nice guy."

"Swenson, you're always looking on the bright side. He'll be a bastard. All them Jerry officers are."

Lieutenant Gerlach trotted up to the forecastle. Bronski saw him coming. "Gangway!" he yelled. The men scattered quickly, and Gerlach panted to a stop.

Tubby Raymond, on the forecastle as First Lieutenant, said, "Up here to see the sights?"

"Nah. I speak German, and Aronson says I speak it better than he does, so the Exec sent me up here to talk to the pilot."

The *Lawrence* shuddered to a stop with the floating pilot almost abeam of the cargo net. The pilot swam over to it trailing the parachute. Bronski said to two men standing nearby, "Go down the net and cut away the parachute."

With the wet silk clear, the pilot climbed up the cargo net, and bounded over the lifelines. He seemed to be looking around for an offcier, spotted Gerlach, and walked over to him. He stopped with his face only inches from Gerlach's, and spewed forth a torrent of German. Gerlach listened patiently and then tried to reply.

*　　*　　*

Those on the bridge and up in the director watched in fascination. The exchange was so loud Aronson, leaning out of the director, could hear it, and he began to laugh.

Fannon looked up at him. "What's so funny?"

"The Kraut is complaining because the British pilot was picked up first. He says he was the first to be shot down and should have been picked up first."

Fannon colored and started to swear. "What did Gerlach say?"

"Not much. The German wouldn't listen to him."

Fannon turned back toward the forecastle. The German pilot was shouting at Gerlach, his face even closer. Then he grabbed the front of Gerlach's shirt in his wet hand.

Gerlach's reaction was so fast Fannon wasn't sure just what happened. As near as he could make out, Gerlach put both of his hands on the German's chest and pushed. The astounded pilot flew backward across the deck and slid into the base of mount 51. There was a loud thud as his head hit the steel ring of the heavy base, and he lay motionless, his arms and legs sprawled in all directions. Gerlach didn't move and stood staring down at the wet front of his shirt.

Fannon was speechless as he watched Bronski trot over and examine the prostrate pilot. When the Captain found his voice, he leaned over the bridge bulwark, cupping his hands. "Mister Gerlach, come up here."

Gerlach looked up, paused for a moment, and started running aft toward the bridge ladder. He was still looking up at the Captain's stern face, and failed to see Bronski's stern sheets sticking up as he leaned over the German. Gerlach's hip glanced off Bronski, and Bronski fell forward on top of the German, who was begining to stir. Both heads bumped into the steel ring, and now both men lay motionless.

Gerlach glanced at the two bodies as he ran down the deck and yelled over his shoulder. "Sorry, Bronski, but I've got to see the Captain."

Swenson hurried over to Bronski and helped him up. Bronski was groggy, and a welt was beginning to swell on his forehead. Swenson said, "You're supposed to keep your helmet on at all times. This wouldn't have happened if you'd had it on."

Bronski swore. "Swenson, you're an idiot."

* * *

On the bridge, Fannon watched Gerlach appear at the top of the ladder. All the signalmen scattered, leaving a clear path for the Lieutenant.

Phelps was standing nearby, unable to control his laughter, and tears streamed down his face. "Damnedest thing I've ever seen," he croaked between gasps of laughter.

Fannon, not as amused, looked sternly at Gerlach, standing before him. "Just what the hell was going on down there?"

Gerlach came to attention, sensing that the Captain was not very happy. "Sir, the pilot was complaining because we didn't pick him up first."

"What did you say to him?"

"I told him he was lucky we bothered to pick him up at all."

"Then he complained some more?"

"Yes, sir, he said he was going to inform Field Marshall Goering."

Now even Fannon began to laugh. "Tell him it will be a long time before he'll be able to do that."

Gerlach nodded. "I started to tell him that. Then he grabbed my shirt in his wet hands."

"Then you, er, bunted him?"

"No, sir, that's baseball talk. I just gave him a football double-hand shiver."

Phelps was laughing uncontrollably now. "He must have made you plenty mad."

Gerlach looked down at his wet, twisted shirt front. "Yes, sir. This is my last clean shirt. Now I'll have to wear it to dinner."

Phelps regained his composure. "No, you won't, Lieutenant—I'll have Stevenson give you one of mine."

Gerlach smiled. "Thank you, sir. Sorry to cause all this trouble."

"Trouble! You just made my day."

Fannon joined in. "Mine, too. But God only knows what the night will bring."

CHAPTER TWENTY-THREE

As dusk approached, Brosnan reviewed the dispatch summary from SHAEF. It listed only a relatively few scheduled night bomber missions, which suggested the *Lawrence* probably would not see much rescue business during the evening. Nonetheless, Brosnan felt a growing uneasiness.

Hours earlier, as the day bomber missions had been completed, Fannon had relaxed enough to let Brosnan set condition III and feed the crew a full meal. Brosnan tried to walk off his full stomach, and chuckled as he remembered Gerlach's recounting during the wardroom meal of the arrival of the German pilot. The pilot was now confined securely in one of the ship's storerooms, partially filled with some bales of cleaning rags and soap powder. Gerlach had visited him and reported that he was complaining that the quarters were not fit for a German officer.

"What was wrong with them?" Brosnan had asked.

"He said there was not enough room, and he didn't like his roommates."

"Roommates?"

"The bales of rags."

Kuberski laughed. "I've seen the storeroom, and it has more space than my stateroom."

Raymond, Kuberski's roommate, added, "Yeah, and the bales of rags are probably an improvement over your dirty laundry."

Kuberski threw a piece of bread at Raymond. Raymond caught it. "Thanks. I was just about to ask someone to pass the bread. It seemed to be stuck in front of you."

Brosnan returned to the prisoner. "We could always put him in a large empty fuel tank. He could walk up and down clear across the ship."

Doctor Taylor, ever serious, replied, "I don't think that meets the requirements of the Geneva convention for the treatment of prisoners."

Brosnan chuckled to himself, and continued pacing up and down, peering over the rolling waves. There was nothing out there but thickening darkness and a few tendrils of forming fog hanging above the surface of the sea. The only living things in sight were a pair of black and white seagulls skimming above the three-foot seas. Now and then, the pair paused and turned gracefully to investigate some small piece of debris on the surface and then resumed their patrol.

*   *   *

About midnight, CIC reported that the air search radar had detected a small, low-flying contact that was maneuvering so low it sometimes also appeared on the surface search radar. In moments, Squid Lee's voice grew more urgent. "There's a larger contact that appears to be following it."

Sitting up in his bridge chair, Fannon ordered, "Sound general quarters."

Brosnan, who had retired to the signal bridge for coffee with Barley, came trotting around the corner of the bridge structure and asked Fannon, "What's up, sir?"

Fannon began wondering if Brosnan's fiancée might be on board the fleeing plane and looked long at his executive officer before answering. "A small contact is closing us, and it's being followed by a bigger one."

When Aronson reported the gunnery department manned and ready, Fannon did not hesitate. "Fire at the larger target if you can do so without endangering the smaller one. It's probably friendly."

Brosnan searched the area ahead with his binoculars, but the darkness was impenetrable. A low overcast in the channel prevented any moon or starlight from illuminating the surface of the sea.

Suddenly a burst of machine gun fire appeared in the distance, the projectile tracers shooting through the black like fireflies.

"Damn!" Brosnan shouted, "The little guy is getting it." Silently, he hoped that his Annette wasn't coming out of France this way.

Aronson kept firing at the larger contact, using radar control. Suddenly, a blinding flash enveloped the *Lawrence* as the contact exploded, spraying burning aviation fuel over a wide area.

Brosnan cheered. "Got the bastard!"

*　*　*

The small contact was now approaching the formation. Commodore Phelps grabbed the TBS transmitter and ordered, "Contact is friendly. Don't shoot."

The contact passed close aboard the *Lawrence*, its engine coughing and sputtering. "He'll have to ditch!" Phelps yelled. "Turn on your running lights!"

As the aircraft passed, Brosnan observed a tiny four-passenger observation plane, similar to the one Annette had described to him, and he hoped she wasn't on board. Before it could make another turn, the engine quit, and the aircraft dropped abruptly into the water, turning end over end. The nearest PT boat put on a burst of speed and headed for the floundering craft.

Brosnan entered the pilothouse and hovered over the TBS speaker, waiting for the PT boat skipper to report. After only a few minutes, which seemed to Brosnan like hours, a British voice said, "We have all your chaps aboard. All unconscious. Can't see any major bleeding. Might be a few minor bone breaks. Can't do much for them on our small deck."

Phelps grabbed the TBS transmitter. "Come alongside the flagship and make transfer. We will lower stretchers."

Fannon heard him and turned toward Brosnan. "Have

Doctor Taylor and his pharmacist's mates and stretcher bearers ready by the sea ladder.

Brosnan left on the run. Flying down the ladder, he could hear the word being passed on the loud speaker to stand by to receive patients from the PT at the sea ladder. He was the first to reach the area, and he waited impatiently as Taylor and his men and the personnel of the repair parties congregated at the station, checking their equipment and peering through the dark night.

As the PT loomed out of the darkness, Brosnan directed the chief boatswain's mate to illuminate the port side of the ship with red flashlights.

The PT skipper, with the side in sight, skillfully brought his small craft alongside in spite of the channel chop. Fannon had turned the ship to put the port side in a lee, but there was still a small chop, splashing salt water as high as the PT boat decks. The patrol boat's powerful engines roared temporarily, as the PT backed down, and then the motors subsided to a loud rumble as the boat slid neatly alongside.

After mooring lines were secured, the chief boatswain's mate directed the process of lowering stretchers to the quietly bobbing PT. In the dim light of the flashlights, the British sailors quickly placed the survivors in steel mesh stretchers, and the men on the *Lawrence*'s deck carefully hoisted them on board.

Brosnan noted that the four figures were dressed in loose fitting black jackets and black trousers. Black wool hats covered their hair, and black camouflage paint disguised their faces. Brosnan approached, trying to find out if any one of them might be Annette or might know about her, but Doctor Taylor pushed him aside. "We've got to get them to the wardroom, where I can see what I'm doing," he said.

Brosnan shrugged. "All right, go ahead," he said, "They all look like men to me."

The stretcher bearers pushed Brosnan aside and carried the wounded up the deck.

Brosnan felt he was losing control of the situation and himself, and he trudged slowly back toward the bridge. The weariness he had pushed aside in the hope of seeing Annette flooded over him again.

CHAPTER TWENTY-FOUR

Brosnan trudged wearily back to the bridge as the last of the stretchers disappeared through the door leading to the wardroom. Behind him he could hear the PT's engines roar to life as the small craft veered away from the slowly steaming ship and returned to its lonely station.

As Brosnan climbed the ladder, he thought of Annette and hoped she was on her way to Portugal for a safe but slow return to England on board a neutral merchant ship.

Once on the bridge, he joined Phelps and Fannon, who were watching the PT disappear into the gloom. The boat's roiled white wake was clearly visible among the velvet waves long after the hull had been swallowed up in the darkness.

Fannon sighed. "Just like a quarterhorse," he said to Phelps. "They get up and go in a hurry."

Phelps was unusually quiet. "I hope you can infuse some of that quick get-up-and-go into Claudia's racing stock some day."

Fannon shrugged. "Should be easy. Those Texas-bred horses are always looking for a chance to excel, and I'm sure Claudia's mares will be very attractive to them, even if they are a bit slow."

Brosnan was listening to the conversation, waiting for a chance to interrupt. When Fannon said Lady Claudia's horses were slow, Brosnan expected the Commodore to make a cutting reply, but Phelps shrugged resignedly and said, "I'm afraid they are slow, but Claudia refuses to see it. She thinks they are great racehorses."

Fannon laughed. "But they can't win anything."

"She really doesn't care as long as they are sleek and well fed."

"We'll take care of that. I think we can keep them looking great and still develop some early speed."

Brosnan grew impatient and cleared his throat pointedly. Fannon turned to him. "Spit it out, Beetle."

Brosnan reported to Fannon that the survivors were all on board. Fannon listened carefully. Then he said, "I gather no sign of Annette?"

Brosnan replied with disappointment in his voice, "I couldn't get real close, but they all looked like men to me."

The TBS crackled, and the three moved closer to the speaker to hear the incoming message. It was the PT boat that had picked up the Spitfire pilot. "I say, my fighter jockey has a broken leg. My medic has splinted it, but he says it should be set as soon as possible. Can you take on the job?"

Phelps picked up the TBS transmitter and said, "Roger. Wait." He turned to Fannon. "Can Doctor Taylor do anything for him?"

In the red glow of the chart desks lights, Brosnan could see Fannon shake his head.

Brosnan interrupted. "Sir, we don't have an X-ray machine, and I've heard Doctor Taylor say he can't do much to set bones properly without one."

Phelps frowned and turned to Chief Benson. "Chief, how far to the nearest port?"

Benson was ready. "Folkstone, sir, fifty miles."

Phelps looked over the side. "The waves are definitely decreasing in height. Not too much chop. He should be able to make it in an hour and a half without shaking the patient up too much." He picked up the TBS transmitter and ordered the PT to proceed to Folkstone, unload the patient, fuel, and return to the patrol area.

"Cheerio," the PT skipper said, "we'll have an ale while we fuel."

The bridge crew grinned. Fannon noticed. "Don't worry, men, we'll be in Portsmouth soon."

Phelps said, "That reminds me. If we get another five days in Portsmouth, you and I should go to my, er, Claudia's estate for a few days."

Fannon grinned expansively. "Yes, sir, sounds like a fine idea. I ought to take another close look at her horses."

"Ha! You mean at Claudia's sister."

In the glow of the red lights, Brosnan could see that Fannon colored slightly. "Well, that would be nice, too."

*   *   *

In a few minutes, Farraday came up with a decoded dispatch and handed it to Phelps. Phelps read it under the red lights and said, "Two destroyers will be here at daylight to relieve us. Our ship and the *Hanly* are to proceed to Portsmouth at best speed."

Fannon scratched his chin pensively. "I wonder what that's all about."

Phelps said, "I know. I sent a dispatch a short time ago telling SHAEF we had picked up the French intelligence agents. I think they want to talk to them as soon as possible. This is Tweety Terwilliger's doing, I imagine."

Fannon turned to Brosnan. "Beetle, I want to make sure they are in as good a shape as possible before we arrive in port. Please, go down below and see how Doctor Taylor is getting along."

*   *   *

Chief Barley watched Brosnan go by on his way below and said to Acton, "Did you hear that? We'll be back in Heaven tomorrow."

Acton laughed. "I thought you didn't like England."

Barley grinned in the darkness. "I guess that depends on who you know who lives there."

CHAPTER TWENTY-FIVE

Brosnan blinked as he came into the wardroom. The large operating room light over the wardroom table was on, and in its circular glare, lying stretched out on the table, was the black-clad figure of a patient. Brosnan said, "Doc, how are you doing? The old man wants to know if you have any serious cases that will require a high-speed run back to port. We're planning to leave for Portsmouth at dawn."

Taylor turned and looked at Brosnan and then pointed at the three figures lying on the deck in one corner of the wardroom. "Those three are all right. They're banged up but conscious. They'll need a little work, but nothing serious. I can fix them later. I haven't examined this one on the table, yet."

Brosnan looked at the patient. A wool cap was still pulled well down on the head, and a peasant's jacket and trousers hung loosely on the body. "Is this one conscious?" Brosnan asked.

The chief pharmacist's mate interrupted, picking up a large pair of scissors. "Doctor, shall I start cutting off the clothing?"

Taylor hesitated. "I don't see any bad bleeding, and there don't seem to be any fractures of the legs or arms. Try loosening the belt and pulling off the trousers. I'll start on this end and get the jacket and shirt off."

160/

Taylor opened the jacket and then began undoing the shirt buttons. As he was about to open the edges of the patient's shirt, the Chief pulled off the trousers. "Jesus!," he said. "Look what I've got!"

Taylor pulled back the edges of the shirt. "Wow! Me too. This is a woman."

"And a helluva fine one, too," the Chief added.

Brosnan came closer and looked down at the figure clad now only in underwear and with the outer clothing pulled back. There was something familiar about the slim, slight body. He pulled off the black woollen cap. Short, dark hair tumbled around the face, darkened with camouflage paint and stained with blood. Brosnan grabbed some sterile bandages and wiped away the blood and paint.

"Do you know her?" Taylor asked.

"My God! It's Annette!"

"Who's Annette?"

"My fiancée. Is she all right?"

Taylor nodded. "Seems to be. There's a small bruise and cut on the side of the face. There're also some other minor cuts and abrasions, but no arterial bleeding." The Doctor paused and looked up at Brosnan. "Actually, I'd say she's more than all right. She's a knockout. You're a very lucky man."

Brosnan ignored the doctor's comment and spoke with a tone of urgency in his voice, "Let's get her cleaned up and covered. The officers will be coming through here soon when the watch changes."

"Good idea. They couldn't take too much of such a beautiful sight."

Taylor rang the pantry bell, and Jason, the steward, came in. Taylor said, "Jason, get a sheet and a clean towel and wet half the towel."

Brosnan said, I'll take care of cleaning her up."

The Chief offered, "I'm ready to help."

Brosnan shook his head, "Thanks, but I can do it."

Cleaning her up will be only a start," Taylor said. "Now I've got to make sure there aren't any broken bones and then sew up the cuts." He leaned over the table and began to examine her legs, arms, and ribs.

Brosnan watched anxiously.

Taylor said, "Beetle, when Jason gets back with that towel and sheet, you can cover her and begin the cleanup. The salt water has cleared some of her skin, but you can get the blood and the rest of that black grease off her face."

In a few minutes, Taylor straightened up. "No broken bones, and her spine seems okay. She doesn't have any major bumps on her head, and I don't think she has a concussion."

Brosnan said, "How can you be sure of that?"

"I can't until she regains consciousness, but I'm ninety percent positive."

Brosnan sighed. "That's a relief."

Taylor turned to the chief pharmacist's mate "Chief, get the sutures ready. We'll try to get most of them in before she wakes up."

Brosnan took the sheet from Jason and covered Annette. Then he took the towel and finished washing the blood and camouflage paint off of her face. Either the wet towel or the sting of the sutures brought Annette back to the edge of consciousness, and she moved her head and moaned. Brosnan bent over her and said softly, "Annette, Annette. Can you hear me?"

Her eyes opened slowly, but they were not focused, and she closed them against the glare of the overhead light. Brosnan brushed away her hair and, again, asked softly, "Annette, Annette. It's Beetle. I'm right here. Can you hear me?"

Her eyes opened again, and she struggled to focus them on the shadowy figure over her. Brosnan shielded her eyes from the glare. He was sure she recognized him. She said faintly, "Oh, Beetle, is that really you?"

"Yes, Annette, and you're going to be all right. Try not to move while the Doctor is working on you."

"Annette asked, 'How are the others?'

"They are slightly injured, but they should be all right."

Annette moaned. "I didn't think any of us would make it. That German fighter was all over us."

Brosnan stroked her cheek. "It's all over, Darling. We shot him down just before you crashed."

"One more pass and he would have had us. It was close."

"Don't worry about it any more. You're safe and in good hands."

Taylor turned to Brosnan, "I've closed the last cut, and she's all right. I don't think the blow to her head was severe. As I said, there's only one small bruise on her face. We'll try a cup of black coffee with some brandy in it as soon as she can sit up. I don't think there's any danger of a concussion."

Brosnan went to his nearby room and returned with his bathrobe. Soon Annette had recovered enough strength to embrace her worried fiancé. Taylor looked at the pair fondly. "Hey, enough of this romantic stuff, Beetle. Get her up, put her in your bathrobe, and we'll start the stimulant. We need to get all of these patients out of here so the stewards can get the wardroom ready for breakfast. Now that the seas have gone down, I'm actually hungry for the first time in days."

Brosnan said, "I'll put her in your bunk."

Taylor grinned, "I thought you would. I guess I'll sleep out here on the transom."

CHAPTER TWENTY-SIX

Brosnan took Annette to his room and carefully put her in his bunk. She protested. "Oh, Beetle. I'm so dirty and my hair is full of grease. Can't I take a shower?"

Brosnan shook his head. The Doctor gave me some pain killers and sleeping pills for you. You're supposed to get a good night's sleep. We'll take care of the other stuff early tomorrow morning."

He gave her the pills with a glass of water. After she had swallowed them, he leaned over and kissed her gently. "There's a lot I want to ask you, but not now. I'm going up to the bridge for a few minutes to tell the Captain about you, and then I'll come down again and be in the upper bunk. I'll be here for you if you want anything. Just call out."

Annette sighed. "I'm so tired, Beetle. I'll be asleep before you get out the door. I'm so glad to see you. I thought I was a goner, as you Americans say, when the machine gun started firing at us, and our aircraft started going down."

Brosnan put a hand on her lips. "It's all over, now. Go to sleep."

*   *   *

Brosnan left her, closed the door carefully, and went up to the bridge. As he approached Phelps and Fannon, the

Commodore said, "Well, Beetle, how are they? Ready to face General Tweety Terwilliger?"

Brosnan grinned in the darkness. "They're fine. Especially Annette."

Fannon was the first to react. "What! I thought the four were men."

Brosnan nodded, "So did I, but I didn't get close enough to see until I went to the wardroom. One of them was Annette, dressed like a man."

Phelps asked anxiously, "Is she all right?"

"A little shaken up, but Doctor Taylor says she should be back to normal after a full night's sleep. The others we took aboard are all right, too."

"Who's taking care of her?"

"Ah, I'd like to, sir, if you don't need me up here. I can get back up here in a hurry, should you need me."

Fannon grinned. "Go ahead below. It's calm now, and we leave for Portsmouth in a few hours. I'll call you if I need you. Otherwise, I'll see you about 1600, when we're scheduled to get into port."

*   *   *

Brosnan eased the door open carefully, but it was a useless precaution. Annette was soundly asleep, a hand thrown back over her head. Brosnan looked at her and then crawled into the upper bunk. He sighed deeply and began to think about how lucky they both had been. He was so exhausted he fell asleep before he could get very far in his thoughts. The last thing he remembered was Annette in a caftan.

Several hours later, Brosnan was awakened by the unusual motion of the ship. He put his hand on the rail of his bunk and held it there. Slowly he gathered his faculties and realized the ship was at full speed. He estimated they were making twenty knots from the vibration of the bunk rail. But the ship was very steady, and he was happy for Doc Taylor that he probably would not be seasick in the wardroom.

Brosnan looked over the side of his bunk at Annette. She was asleep but beginning to stir. He climbed quietly out of his bunk, took off his clothes, put on his bathrobe, and headed for the shower and a shave. After dressing in clean khakis, Brosnan pulled a chair over to the side of the lower bunk and sat down. The slight scraping sound of the chair awakened Annette, and she opened her eyes slowly. Then she opened them wide and reached for Brosnan. He held her tightly for several minutes, and then she said, "You promised me a shower this morning."

Brosnan released her. "So I did, but Doc Taylor will have to approve." He got up, opened the door, and went aft to the wardroom. Doctor Taylor was sitting alone at the table drinking coffee. In front of him were the remains of two sandwiches.

Brosnan said, "What's the matter? Can't sleep?"

Taylor wrinkled his nose and pointed at the leather transom. "Nobody could sleep long on that."

Brosnan laughed. "It's designed to be uncomfortable so young officers won't be tempted to doze off on it. Can you come look at one of your patients?"

Taylor grinned. "I could look at her all day."

Brosnan said, "Now, now. Let's be professional."

Taylor followed Brosnan to the room they normally shared. The Doctor knocked and the two entered. Annette was still lying patiently in the lower bunk. Brosnan said, "You may not remember Doctor Taylor. He's the one who patched you up."

Annette grinned. "Oh, yes, I remember him. He's the one who graciously loaned me this bunk. I am most grateful for everything."

Taylor beamed. "You look fine to me. Do you have any particular pains?"

Annette shrugged. "A lot of small ones here and there. Nothing big."

Brosnan said, "You should have a lot of small ones. That little plane spun like a kite."

Taylor nodded in agreement. "Not a pretty sight. I think

you can get up, get dressed, and have breakfast. It will be ready shortly. I'll have Jason save you whatever you want. We have a couple of big eaters in the mess."

"Would a soft-boiled egg be too much?"

Taylor laughed. "Easy. Our big eaters don't bother with such delicate fare. Hot cakes or waffles might take a reservation, if you change your mind."

Annette laughed. "The egg will do nicely, thank you."

When Taylor had left, Brosnan helped Annette up and put her in his bathrobe. He looked out in the corridor. It was clear, and he motioned Annette to follow him. "The shower will be unused this early," he said.

In a few minutes they were back in Brosnan's room. Annette tried to dry her hair while Brosnan rummaged through his clothing locker for a set of khakis that Annette could wear. Finally they decided on a shirt with the sleeves rolled up and a pair of trousers also rolled up and held snugly with a belt. She sat down, and Brosnan put his slippers on her feet over a pair of wool socks. "There," he said. "You look like you're ready for breakfast."

Annette pulled Brosnan down on the bunk beside her. "In a few minutes," she said. "I'd just like to have you hold me for a while."

Brosnan was apprehensive. "This isn't like you. You sound like you know you're going to be leaving for France again soon."

Annette sighed. "Yes. In a few days after I have been debriefed. After they squeeze all the intelligence they can out of me, they'll want me to go back to France and get in position for the next offensive."

"Next offensive? We haven't even finished this one."

"Oh, Beetle, in this business we have to live in the future. Maybe you haven't heard."

"Heard what?"

"The Allies will be landing in Southern France in a few weeks. This time there will be Free-French Army forces in the initial landing, and I'll be working directly with them. I'm very proud."

Brosnan shrugged. "I'm sure you are, but I hope General De Gaulle and his officers aren't as stubborn as they have been in North Africa—or you'll be in trouble."

Annette sighed. "Yes, I understand what happened there, but this is my country, and someday it may be yours, too, I hope. I have to do my duty."

Brosnan shook his head. "Well, let's make you as strong as we can. You need some breakfast."

*   *   *

Annette's entrance into the wardroom created a sensation. Most of the officers had not heard that she was aboard, and her slightly pale but still beautiful face, along with rolled up khakis and bed room slippers, was the last thing they expected to see.

Kuberski, attacking a pile of hot cakes, looked up for more syrup, and saw her first. In accordance with the etiquette he had been learning from Tubby Raymond, he stumbled to his feet and stood at attention.

Brosnan grinned. "Take it easy, Stanley."

By now the other officers had noticed her arrival, and all of them tried to stand up. Squid Lee backed into Jason who was passing behind him with a pitcher of cold water. Jason narrowly avoided spilling it down Gerlach's neck.

Brosnan said, "Gentlemen, please be seated. This is my fiancée, Annette Duchamp. She arrived unexpectedly last night, courtesy of British Intelligence airlines. Not the most comfortable way to travel."

Annette nodded politely and said, "Gentlemen, I am honored to meet the friends of my fiancé."

Brosnan started the introductions around the table. When he had finished, Kuberski gave up his seat next to Brosnan's and moved to the foot of the table.

Jason brought in a single soft-boiled egg and some trimmed toast. Kuberski stared at the meager breakfast and looked at Doctor Taylor, the mess treasurer. "My God, Doc! Is that all we can spare?"

Taylor grinned. "That's what she ordered. She wanted to leave all the hot cakes for you."

Kuberski put down his fork and turned to Annette. "Ah, may I ask what you were doing in France?"

Brosnan quickly interrupted. "Sorry, Stanley, that's classified."

Kuberski colored slightly and picked up his fork. "Of course. I should have known better." Then he raised his heavy eyebrows innocently. "But I'd like to visit your vineyards some day."

Annette grinned. "You like wine?"

Kuberski's eyebrows went up again. "Not really. I'm a beer man; but I'd still like to visit you."

CHAPTER TWENTY-SEVEN

After breakfast, Brosnan took Annette to his room. For hours they talked, and Brosnan listened intently as Annette described her life in France as a spy. Her emotions rose as she told him about the time the Germans had narrowly missed discovering her activities. While she had been away, gathering intelligence, German soldiers had tracked down a radio transmitter hidden in a tool shed on her estate. The man she had placed in charge of communications had been captured and was executed without trial.

Annette began to shake, and Brosnan took her in his arms and patted her back. "That's enough," he said. "We'll have years later to talk about this."

"Oh, Beetle, I hope so, but our luck can't hold out forever."

"Just one more big operation, and we can leave the rest to the armies."

"You are right, Beetle. In Mid-August, Free French units will be part of the assault forces landing in Southern France."

"And you'll be working for them."

"Yes. After I finish my debriefing at SHAEF with General Terwilliger, I'm to be transferred to the intelligence forces of the Free French."

"I suppose you'll like that."

Annette shuddered. "I've seen all of the war I want to see, but it will be thrilling to serve my country directly at least once."

A knock on the door interrupted their talk. Brosnan said, "Come in."

Jason opened the door. "Sir, lunch is ready."

*　　*　　*

After lunch, Brosnan took Annette to the bridge to meet the Commodore and Captain and to watch the ship enter port. As he reached the top of the ladder leading to the signal bridge, Barley was waiting for him. "Good morning, Mister Brosnan, were we sleeping in today?"

Brosnan looked at him, grinned, and stepped aside to help Annette, who had been following him, over the last step.

Barley's jaw dropped as he realized Annette, though dressed in officer khakis, was a woman. "Ah, er," he mumbled.

Brosnan grinned at him. "You said something, Barley?'

Barley finally found his voice. "Ah, sir, I said, 'we'll be sweeping down today.' "

Brosnan laughed. "That's what I thought you said." He turned to Annette. "Annette, this is Chief Signalman Barley. The best signalman in the business. Barley, this is my fiancée, Annette Duchamp."

Annette looked at him shyly. "Hello, Mister Barley. I've heard a lot about you."

Barley, never at a loss for words where the ladies are concerned, grinned widely and said, "Pleased to meet you, Ma'am. I hope some of it was good."

Before Annette could reply, Brosnan took her elbow and escorted her to the starboard wing of the bridge where the Commodore and Captain were talking quietly. Brosnan cleared his throat. The two stopped talking and turned around. Phelps and Fannon beamed. "Ah, Beetle," the Commodore said, walking toward Annette. "I've been looking forward to this moment. Please introduce us."

"Annette, may I present Commodore Horace Phelps and Captain Peter Fannon. Gentlemen, this is my fiancée, Mademoiselle Annette Duchamp."

Phelps and Fannon saluted, and Fannon said, "Welcome aboard, Miss Duchamp. I'm sorry I couldn't welcome you properly last night."

Annette laughed. "I wouldn't have remembered your greeting anyway. I believe I was unconscious. In fact, I hardly recognized Beetle—I mean Lieutenant Commander Brosnan."

Phelps frowned, obviously concerned. "Has the doctor seen you this morning?"

"Oh, yes, I'm in good health, except for a few stitches and bruises."

Fannon pointed over his shoulder to the rapidly nearing shores of Portsmouth. "We'll be entering port soon. Beetle, I'm sending for Lieutenant Kelly to take us into port. You will be free to explain to our guest what it's like to bring a ship into a harbor."

Brosnan started to protest, but thought better of it. "Thank you, sir, I appreciate the opportunity. If you'll excuse us, we'll go up above where we can see better."

*   *   *

The same old British pilot boarded the *Lawrence* and brought the ship into harbor. Fannon asked him to let Lieutenant Kelly conn the ship alongside the pier, and the pilot, bribed by a cup of steaming coffee, stood aside and chatted with the Commodore while Kelly nervously executed a slightly wide landing.

"Not bad, sonny," the pilot said.

Fannon looked slightly pained, but said, "Good job, Kelly. You're learning fast."

*   *   *

Brosnan took Annette below and waited while she changed into her own clothes, which had been cleaned and dried in the ship's laundry. While she was changing, the Commodore sent for Brosnan.

When Brosnan arrived at Phelps' cabin, the Commodore said, "Beetle, I've talked this over with the Captain, and we both agree that Miss Duchamp should be properly escorted to SHAEF and turned over to Brigadier Terwilliger. Obviously you are the man to do it."

Brosnan smiled. "Sir, I couldn't think of anyone better qualified."

Phelps pulled at his long jaw to hide a smile. "Well, I thought about Lieutenant Kuberski, since he's a member of my staff, but ah. . . ."

Brosnan paled, "But, sir. . . ."

Phelps relented. "But of course I'll need him, so I've decided that you're the man for the job. But I want you to make sure General Eisenhower doesn't see you. He might still get after me to have you transferred to his staff."

Brosnan forced back a grin. "Oh, no, sir. I'll be careful."

Phelps also kept a straight face. "Of course you should stay there at least two nights to look out for Miss Duchamp. I don't trust those over-sexed young Brits at SHAEF. I'll give you a note to take to Brigadier Terwilliger in which I'll ask him to put you up somewhere in the village. Of course, where Miss Duchamp stays is up to her."

Brosnan grinned broadly. "Sir, I think I can take care of that."

"Off you go, then." Phelps said. "Don't lose a minute."

CHAPTER TWENTY-EIGHT

As soon as the *Lawrence* was secured at the mole, Brosnan departed with Annette. Crew members, busy adjusting the mooring lines and preparing the ship for yard work, still managed to look up as Annette passed and to admire her with a few low whistles. Even the floppy clothes and the snug woollen cap could not hide her beautiful face and graceful walk. Brosnan's admonitory scowls could not completely control the crew's conduct after such a long period at sea, and he resigned himself to their demeanor, because he knew it was a tribute of sorts to Annette.

Two hours later the Commodore and Captain came to the quarterdeck, followed by Jason carrying two bags. Lieutenants Kuberski and Kelly were standing nearby to see them off. Phelps stopped and addressed Kuberski, "Stanley, I gave you the location and telephone number of Mrs. Phelps' estate. Don't hesitate to call me if anything important develops or we suddenly get orders." He turned to Lieutenant Kelly. "Kelly, I understand you will be acting as commanding officer until Lieutenant Commander Brosnan returns. Lieutenant Kuberski and the commanding officer of the *Hanly* will be available to you for advice. The same goes for you about calling Captain Fannon. We'll be together at the estate, and if all goes well, we'll stay about a week."

Kuberski and Kelly both nodded. Kuberski saluted, "Aye, aye, sir. I think we've got it. Enjoy yourself, sir. We'll try not to bother you."

Phelps and Fannon took their departure and boarded a Rolls Royce waiting for them on the pier. Kelly scratched his head and said to Kuberski. "How did the Commodore's chauffeur know to be here?"

Kuberski rolled his eyes. "He didn't until I went over to the yard office and called him for the Commodore. The estate is only about two hours away."

Kelly watched the Rolls motor away. "Nice piece of machinery."

Kuberski shrugged. "Rather have a Cadillac."

*   *   *

Liberty call on board the *Lawrence* was sounded at 1200. Bronski and Swenson were among the first to arrive on the quarterdeck and to leave the ship. "Where are we going?" Swenson asked.

"Just fall in alongside me and stop when I say stop," Bronski answered.

The thirsty pair left the main gate and headed along a street lined with small stores and pubs. Bronski examined the pub signs carefully as they swung down the street, uniforms carefully pressed, white hats pushed slightly back and well-tied neckerchiefs flapping in the breeze.

Suddenly Bronski halted, staring at a sign just ahead. Swenson, taken by surprise, surged ahead and then stumbled to a halt. "You didn't say stop," he complained.

Bronski looked at Swenson and shook his head, "Do I have to tell you everything?"

"No, but what are you looking at?"

"That sign. It's just what we want. A Polack pub."

Swenson read the sign. "It says 'The Swinging Pole'. That doesn't mean it's for Polacks."

Bronski grinned. "Close enough. Let's go in."

*   *   *

Two days later, Brosnan returned to the ship in a jeep driven by a British soldier. Kuberski met him as he came on board. "I see from your transportation and your smile that you had a good time."

Brosnan nodded and grinned, obviously very happy. "Yes, but we have a problem. Come on down to the wardroom, and I'll tell you about it."

After Jason had provided a series of large sandwiches for Kuberski and a cup of black coffee for Brosnan, the executive officer spoke. "First, I had a great time with Annette. She finished all of her debriefing by the end of the first day, and then we had the second day all to ourselves."

"What did you do the first day?"

"As soon as I got to SHAEF, I learned that General Eisenhower was in France visiting the front for a few days, and so I was able to move around the headquarters without worrying about running into him."

"But you saw Brigadier Terwilliger?"

"Oh, yes, and he told me some news we need to act on immediately."

"Is it bad?"

"Yes, and no. This is all top secret."

Kuberski nodded, "I'll keep my trap shut."

"A big Allied landing is being planned for the South of France about August 15th, code named ANVIL," Brosnan explained. "Some of the forces involved will come directly from the States; some are already in the Mediterranean, but most of the troops and ships will come from the forces that took part in the landings at Normandy and are now regrouping."

"Including us?"

"Yes. That's the bad part. We'll soon be receiving a dispatch from headquarters, ordering us to leave two days from now. That means we have to get word to the Commodore and Captain to get back here by tomorrow at the latest."

Kuberski put down the last sandwich and looked up at the overhead. "I could phone him."

"I don't think so. Security on this is too tight, and if General Terwilliger found out we made an unsecured call he'd have me sent to Murmansk. You'll have to make the trip in person."

"Couldn't I call and ask him to send the Rolls down?"

"You won't have to. General Terwilliger said he would arrange a car or a jeep for you. Just give him a call. Finish your sandwich first. You're making me hungry."

"What'll I tell them about what we'll be doing?"

"Tell them we'll get dispatch orders tomorrow to leave in two days. The *Lawrence* will escort a troop convoy through the Straits of Gibraltar to Oran in Algeria, arriving about 28 July. Then we go to Naples, Italy, to prepare for the landings, but don't mention that. We'll get a copy of the operation order when we arrive."

* * *

After several hours in the dark, warm confines of the Swinging Pole, Bronski and Swenson had just finished another round of ale when the heavy front door swung open and Chiefs Brill and Marusak and Frenchy Bennaret entered on a crest of loud conversation. Chief Marusak looked around in the stale gloom and grinned when he saw Bronski. "Can we join you?" he asked.

Bronski pushed back some chairs and gestured at the barmaid. "Sure. Room for all. Chief Brill, can I ask the bar maid to bring a cushion for you?"

Chief Brill scowled, but sat down next to Bronski. "Bronski, I'm tall enough to see over the table without any damned cushion—and in my office, I'm tall enough to reach up to the top shelf where all the liberty cards are kept, including yours. Do I make myself clear?"

Bronski reddened slightly. "Sorry, Chief, but I'm always getting the prod about how tall I am."

Brill looked at him more calmly. "I see you've acquired some other dashing features, too. Where did you get those cuts and bruises along the edge of your scalp?"

Swenson piped up. "Some he got when a shell hit our mount. The rest he got from bumping his head in the mount because he's so tall."

Brill grinned. "I guess we all have our problems."

By the time the next round of ale arrived, Swenson, buoyed by the earlier rounds, was feeling full of himself, despite the presence of several senior petty officers. He looked at Chief Marusak. "So how did you guys choose this place? Did you think it was a Polack bar?"

Marusak and Brill looked at each other. Brill said, "I'm Irish and Chief Marusak is a Czech. Not a Polack in the crowd except Bronski."

Bennaret said, "And I'm a Frog."

Swenson grinned, adding, "And I'm a Swede."

Bronski picked up his stein and made a toast. "What diference does it make what country our ancestors came from? We all wear the same uniform, and our blood is all the same color."

Swenson looked at Bronski's head scars. "Yeah, it is—and lately I've seen a lot of yours."

*   *   *

Early the next morning, Kuberski departed from the *Lawrence* in a jeep sent by General Terwilliger and arrived at the estate about 1000. The entry driveway ran for a half-mile between twin rows of Lombardy poplars. "Blimey", the British Army driver said. "Looks like a bloody park."

Kuberski studied the main building as they approached. The residence was a substantial country house two stories tall, with a third story of dormers. The walls were made of light colored sandstone, and the roof was black slate. Outbuildings were connected to the left side, and a series of separate buildings could be seen in the distance to the right. Kuberski took them to be stables and equipment and feed sheds. A riding track, at least a full half-mile in circumference, lay just beyond the main house.

Kuberski exited the jeep and thanked the driver.

"Matey, can you get back all right?" the driver asked.

Kuberski laughed. "I think so, but not if they make me ride back on a horse."

After the jeep had departed, Kuberski stood for a few minutes admiring the house and the landscaping. Then he walked to the front door and pulled on an old-fashioned bell rope. In a few minutes the door was opened by a pleasant-faced man, obviously the butler. "Yes, sir?"

Kuberski said, "I'm Lieutenant Stanley Kuberski of Commodore Phelps' staff. I've come to see him."

The butler shook his head, "Sorry, sir, but he's out riding

with his guest, Captain Fannon, and his step-daughter, Miss Cornelia. They won't be back until lunch time. Lady Claudia is here. May I take you to see her?"

"Please do."

The butler said, "My name is James. Please follow me. Since you sent away your transport, I presume you'll be staying on with us, sir?"

"I'm afraid not. I'll have to return today and so will Commodore Phelps and Captain Fannon."

James shook his head sadly. "Too bad. We were just settling in. Madam will be very unhappy."

James led Kuberski to a tiled terrace behind the house. From it, Kuberski could see a series of white fenced fields and densely wooded areas, which followed streams stretching into the distance. A small village broke the horizon a few miles away.

Lady Claudia was sitting under a large tan umbrella. James led Kuberski to the umbrella and cleared his throat. "Madam, may I present Lieutenant Stanley Kuberski. He is a member of the Commodore's staff."

Lady Claudia turned to Kuberski, looked at him with interest, and smiled graciously. "Ah, Lieutenant, welcome, and please come and sit down. I feel that I know you well. My husband talks about you frequently."

Kuberski walked forward and bent over Lady Claudia's hand, as Tubby Raymond had once instructed, and then sat down next to her. Moving a porcelain cup and saucer toward him, she asked, "Would you care to join me in a cup of tea or perhaps sherry would be more appropriate?"

Kuberski cleared his throat nervously. "Well, Ma'am, it was a long trip. A sherry might help to allay the fatigue."

Lady Claudia giggled, her plain face breaking into a beautiful smile. "Allay the fatigue! That's one I'll remember. I like you, Lieutenant, may I call you Stanley?"

"Please do, Ma'am. I feel very honored that you'd call me by my first name."

As they drank their tea and sherry and chatted, Kuberski became increasingly charmed with Lady Claudia. He thought she seemed a bit too thin and somewhat angular, but the charm of her open manner and gentle face conveyed a unique inner beauty and grace. He decided that the Commodore was a very fortunate man to be married to such a lovely woman.

In the middle of Kuberski's second sherry, Lady Claudia shaded her eyes and looked toward the nearest clump of woods. "There they come now, just in time for lunch. Stanley, I assume you will be here for lunch."

"Oh, yes, Ma'am, but not much longer. We'll all have to leave soon in order to get back to the ship before dark."

Lady Claudia frowned. "I was afraid of that. Then we'll all have an early tea."

*   *   *

A half-hour later, the Commodore, the Captain, and a young lady whom Kuberski assumed was Lady Claudia's younger sister, Cornelia, trotted to the house. Grooms met the riders immediately and secured the horses' reins while the trio dismounted.

"Ah, Stanley," the Commodore said. "I was afraid that I'd be seeing you."

Kuberski smiled apologetically and said, "Sorry to be the bearer of bad tidings, sir."

Phelps shrugged. "We were lucky to have this much time." He turned to Cornelia. "This is Lieutenant Stanley Kuberski, of my staff."

Kuberski bowed. Cornelia smiled and then suddenly curtsied. "You Americans never cease to surprise me," she said.

Phelps kissed Lady Claudia. "Darling, we'll all go up to bathe before lunch. Would you mind showing Stanley Lord Stagger's art collection while you wait for us?"

Cornelia laughed. "Oh, please, Mother, don't bore him with that."

Kuberski, now openly admiring the curves that seemed to substitute for the angles of her older sister and the more conventional and beautiful face, said, "I would very much like to see it."

As Lady Claudia led Kuberski away and the others

headed for their rooms, she said softly, "You don't really have to see it, Stanley; you could have a sample of Lord Stagger's Scotch whiskey instead."

Kuberski grinned. "I've already had a small sample of it on board ship. I keep the keys to the Commodore's shipboard locker, and a bottle was broken when it was brought on board. But I would like another on the rocks, and could I see the collection, too?"

Lady Claudia laughed. "Of course you can, and I'll be glad to show it to you. Anyone who could persuade my husband to give up those awful cigars can have anything he wants." She paused. "Anything except Cornelia, of course. She's already engaged to your Captain Fannon."

Kuberski colored. "I know that, Ma'am. I'm afraid my admiration might have been a little too unguarded, but I haven't seen many pretty girls during the last year."

They entered the library, and Lady Claudia poured Kuberski a generous tumbler of Scotch while he stopped in front of the first group of paintings.

As she handed him the drink, he commented, "You have *three* Degas paintings?"

Lady Claudia's eyebrows went up. "Why Stanley, you do know something about art."

"Yes, Ma'am. That and how to shoot guns."

*   *   *

Later, over another Scotch, Kuberski briefed the Commodore and Captain about the forthcoming operation. After an excellent lunch, orchestrated deftly by James and tainted with a somber atmosphere, Phelps suggested that the party retire for siestas before a heavy tea and departure.

Kuberski protested. "But, sir, I don't need any rest."

Fannon cleared his throat and raised his eyebrows.

Kuberski colored. "But then it will be a long trip and I could certainly use it."

"You might rather look over the estate," Phelps offered.

Cornelia smiled wickedly. "Maybe you'd like to ride out on a horse."

Kuberski paled. "Ah, no horses, Ma'am. I'll walk."

"What's the matter, Stanley?" Fannon inquired. "You don't like horses?"

"Can't stand them, sir."

Cornelia giggled. "Why?"

Kuberski's face reddened, and he unconsciously put his hands near his tail bone. "Got kicked once."

* * *

The trip back in the well-polished Rolls was slow and comfortable, but sad. Kuberski tried to lighten the mood by entertaining his seniors with anecdotes about his past trouble with horses. But Fannon finally sighed heavily and said, "Don't bother, Stanley, we'll just sleep."

Two hours later, the car rolled up to the mole and back to the war. As Kuberski climbed out of the comfortable leather seat and looked at the gray steel sides of the *Lawrence*, his thoughts returned for an instant to the beautiful serenity of Lady Claudia's estate. Then he sighed and headed on board. As he went over the brow, he looked back at the Rolls and said under his breath, "To hell with the Cadillac. I'll take a Rolls every time."

* * *

Barley and Acton had the day's duty, and Barley was prowling the signal bridge trying to work off his frustration over having to stay on board while Bronski and the others had enjoyed one last night ashore. Barley had been standing on deck listening to the loud conversation and the occasional bursts of song as the "Flying Poles" made their way through the yard to the ship just before midnight. "Disgusting!" he said to Acton. "They're drunk."

Acton bristled. "What's wrong with that? They're back on time."

Barley grinned. "Who said there was anything wrong with it? I'm just mad because I wasn't with them."

CHAPTER TWENTY-NINE

The next morning, Fannon announced at quarters that the division would be leaving that afternoon to escort a convoy to Oran. The crew received the news with mixed feelings. Barley was unhappy, because he would be leaving a girlfriend who lived in a comfortable apartment on a nearby beach—even though it was a rocky one—with an endless supply of whiskey. Barley's girl worked as a barmaid and regularly smuggled home in her ample brassiere at least two pints of whiskey, more than enough to satisfy Barley. Bennaret, on the other hand, was happy to be going back to a more tropical climate and the varied, but dubious, pleasures of Mediterranean ports. Acton shrugged indifferently to the news. "All the same to me," he commented. "No good surf anywhere around here." Swenson was happy to go, because Bronski told him to be happy. And Jason only grinned when Brosnan asked him how he felt. "Same old job in the wardroom, and I don't get much liberty wherever we are."

*   *   *

The division got under way in the early afternoon and before dark had formed an antisubmarine screen around a dozen transports coming out of ports just to the east of Portsmouth. Barley swept the transports' decks with his telescope. "A hell of a lot of Limey soldiers," he said. "I'm glad I'm not going to be fighting ashore with them."

"Why not?" Acton asked.

"Don't like wine, and that's all they'll find in France."

Brosnan, standing nearby, heard him. "Don't be too sure, Barley. The French make Cognac and a helluva strong apple brandy. I think it would be strong enough for you."

Barley shrugged. "Weil, in that case, I'll volunteer if any signalmen are needed ashore."

Brosnan walked over to the shore side of the bridge, leaving Barley and Acton to argue about how many troops were embarked in the transports. He leaned on the bulwark and watched the British shore recede as the formation turned and steamed south. Annette would still be there, he thought, but not for long. She had expected to return to France within the week, and was very optimistic about her mission. At first he thought she was trying to counter his pessimism with her exuberance, but she explained to him that she believed the Germans in Southern France would not fight well.

"Why not?" he had asked.

"All they'll want to do is get out of France before the Allies cut them off from Germany by action in Central France. They won't be really much concerned about trying to uncover our intelligence apparatus," she suggested. But Brosnan remained concerned about her safety. "Don't worry, Beetle," she had assured him. "We're both going to make it, as you Americans say. I can feel it."

Brosnan sighed, remembering the conversation, and he hoped she would be right. Both of them faced difficult tasks. Walking to the other bridge wing, he found Barley and Acton still arguing, but their debate suddenly held little interest for him. Lost in his private thoughts, Brosnan headed below to his bunk. Perhaps he could get in a short nap before dinner, but more likely he would toss in his rack for the next hour. Either way, a few minutes of rest would be better than listening to Barley and Acton.

Brosnan's apprehension was justified. Even the gentle motion of the ship failed to put him to sleep, so he spent the time thinking about the great moments he and Annette had shared in London and in North Africa. He imagined how wonderful life would be in France, if they could both just survive the war. But before too long, a loud knock on the door interrupted his reverie. It was Jason. "Mister Brosnan, five minutes to evening meal," he said.

*   *   *

On the third day of the operation, Gibraltar lay ahead in the morning mists. Brosnan had come to the bridge to see landfall made, eager over the prospect of seeing the looming bulk of the big rock. Barley arrived before him and presented him with the usual white mug of steaming coffee.

Chief Benson, navigating the *Lawrence*, walked out on the bridge wing, putting his binocular strap around his neck. Brosnan said, "Looking for the rock?"

Benson said, "Yes, sir. We have it on radar, but the bearings are fuzzy. Too much overcast for morning sights, but last night's star fix was good. I'd still like to take a few visual bearings before we turn into the entrance to the straits."

Barley stepped forward with his telescope and steadied it on the bulwark rail. After a few minutes he said, "I've got the high point."

Benson sighted his binoculars down the axis of Barley's telescope and focused the lenses carefully. "Thanks, I see it, right where I thought it would be." Soon Benson was able to get a visual bearing on it and then disappeared into the pilot house to add the fix to his navigational plot.

*   *   *

As the convoy turned east and headed for the channel abreast of Gibraltar, Phelps and Fannon talked. Phelps said, "I'm always nervous when we go through this channel. It would be easy for German submarines to lie in wait, masked by the shallow areas and the heavy currents."

Fannon called down to sonar on the squawkbox. "Sonar, this is the Captain. Be alert during the next two hours as we go through the straits."

Aronson's confident voice came back. "The gear is carefully tuned, sir, and we'll be careful. I know you don't want to lose any of those Limey troops."

*   *   *

The passage was surprisingly easy, and the green water of the Atlantic gave way to the seemingly blue seas of the Mediterranean. Two days later, the skyline of Oran appeared on the horizon. Brosnan watched the shoreline carefully, as the formation approached the harbor entrance.

Through his binoculars, he thought he could see the restaurant terrace where he had first met Annette. Then, his attention was diverted by a question from the Captain, and when he looked over again, a mosque obstructed his view. Brosnan thought about the pleasant hours and days he had spent with Annette at the beginning of their relationship and of their decision to get married when the war ended. He sighed and rubbed his eyes, trying to focus his thoughts on the present. He knew he had responsibilities to carry out, and he hurried down to the main deck to make sure the ship was ready for entering port. The *Lawrence*'s visit would be short, and he decided to stay on board and let Lieutenant Kelly go ashore. Oran held nothing for him anymore. It was only a quick stop before heading to Naples and then to France, where an end to the war would begin.

CHAPTER THIRTY

As the *Lawrence* and her sister ships glided toward the mole, Barley and Acton swung their telescopes back and forth, eagerly searching the buildings, wide boulevards, and terraces behind Oran's waterfront. Barley was excited. "I can hardly wait to get ashore," he said.

Acton rolled his eyes in disgust. "Didn't you get enough of it the last time you were here?"

"I was only ashore for one day."

"Sure, and you got the clap and were restricted the rest of the time we were here."

"That's what I mean. I never got a chance to shop."

"What the hell would you buy?"

"Some perfume and silk skivvies for Sadie."

"Sadie?"

"Yeah, you know, my girl in Portsmouth."

"Oh, that one. I heard she was pretty nice, but you never let me meet her."

"Didn't want to get you involved. She said she liked young blond men, and it was too big a chance to take."

"Won't we have trouble buying things in the shops if we don't speak French?"

Barley rubbed his angular chin. "I thought of that, and I've asked Frenchy Bennaret to go with us."

"And he said yes?"

"Sure. He owes me one. I got him out of trouble with a big Mick in Belfast."

* * *

Tubby Raymond, as first lieutenant, was at his station on the forecastle supervising his crew as the *Lawrence* moored. Aronson's station was normally on the after deck house, but Brosnan had put the chief gunner's mate in charge there and had directed Aronson to go forward to learn about the forecastle and the anchor, the windlass, and the assorted other equipment.

Raymond explained the windlass system, which dropped and hoisted the heavy anchor, and handling procedures for the mooring lines. When Aronson was satisfied, the pair turned and watched the mole as the Captain brought the ship in parallel to it. Four sleepy-looking Arabs working on the pier hiked up their long gowns and trotted to the heaving lines, as the weighted monkey-fists on their ends landed on the mole. Then the linehandlers pulled them toward the nearest heavy iron bollards on the pier.

Raymond watched as the forecastle crew payed out the heavy mooring lines attached to the heaving lines. Now and then he applied a little body English but he gave no orders. When he was satisfied that the lines were properly secured, he turned to Aronson. "You don't have to do anything as long as all goes well. The chief boatswain's mate does all the work."

"And if all doesn't go well?"

"The old man will shout down instructions, and you still won't have to do anything."

Aronson laughed. "Sounds like a great job."

Raymond sighed. "You're better off aft where the old man can't see what's going on."

Aronson said, "Why does the old man, who is so good otherwise, feel he has to run the forecastle?"

Raymond shrugged. "Damned if I know. I guess all skippers are like that. Sometimes he seems a little nervous, but he always seems to know what he's doing. A little close scrutiny is a small price to pay for such a good skipper. I'd trust him completely with my life."

Soon the ship was secured snugly alongside the rough stones of the ancient mole. Raymond leaned over the side to make sure the *Lawrence*'s steel sides were protected from the rough surfaces of the huge stones by cane and rope fenders. Then he stood back as the crew doubled up the mooring lines and joined Aronson, who was examining the scenery. "How'd you like to go ashore this afternoon?"

"Sure. I can be ready right after lunch."

*　　*　　*

At 1300, when liberty call was sounded, Barley made tracks to be the first man off the ship. Once on the dock, he waited impatiently for Bennaret and Acton, who had to wait their turn to leave with the lower-rated men, to join him. "Let's go," he said, "I want to get to the Casbah before they're all gone."

Acton frowned, "You mean girls?"

"Naw, not them. There are so many here they'll never run out. I mean good souvenirs."

"Okay," Acton said suspiciously. "But I'll be watching you the entire time."

Barley grinned. "I suppose you're hoping I'll get myself on the VD list again, so you can move in on my girlfriend."

Acton shrugged. "I wouldn't mind."

Bennaret shook his head. "Knock off the small talk and let's get going. I've got some things to do after we finish shopping that won't wait."

*　　*　　*

After the quarterdeck was clear of the liberty party, Tubby Raymond and Aronson went over the brow and strolled up the roadside toward the city.

Aronson said, "I really need the exercise. Let's walk as far as we can."

Raymond patted his ample gut. "Me, too. I figure I can do five miles before I have to eat something to renew my strength."

Aronson raised his eyebrows. "You look strong enough as you are to me."

Three hours later, Raymond and Aronson sat in front of two beers at a small table on a restaurant terrace. Raymond said, "Beetle Brosnan told me this is a great place to find girls. It's where he met his fiancée, Annette."

Aronson looked up and down the sidewalk. "A hell of a lot of women, all right, but all of them are wearing chaidors and veils."

Raymond nodded. "Yeah. I think most of the French women have left for England and are waiting there to get back to France."

Aronson sighed. "My legs are shot, and I think we've struck out. Let's have another beer and some dinner and then take a taxi back to the ship."

"Suits me. I couldn't walk it."

* * *

The Casbah in Oran was like most others in Mediterranean ports. Narrow, winding streets led to a collection of small shops and smaller apartments. The crowded stores bulged with goods, pawed over by eager customers with big expectations and appetites but small wallets. Since the start of the war, the loss of American and European tourists had made the proprietors eager to sell to almost any customer. Most prospective buyers were other Arab men, but today there was a sprinkling of U.S. Navy uniforms in the marketplace.

Suddenly, a commotion erupted in one of the exit streets, and three white-clad figures came running out of the Casbah. An Arab, screaming in high-pitched Arabic, followed them, carrying a large package.

The first man out was Barley, who carried several small packages. Bennaret and Acton followed in close pursuit, and only slightly ahead of the angry Arab. As the group came out of the Casbah, a French policeman blew his whistle and held up his hand. Barley skidded to a stop in front of him, and Bennaret, runing all out, crashed into Barley from behind. Acton, stopping behind the group, turned to head off the onrushing Arab. The policeman blew his whistle once again, shouted a command, and the Arab halted, blowing heavily and still spouting in Arabic.

The policeman approached Barley and said something to him in French. Barley looked at the officer blankly and turned to Bennaret. "Frenchy. What did he say?"

Bennaret shrugged. "Search me. I don't speak French."

"What the hell, aren't you a Frenchman?"

"Sure, but I was born in Milwaukee of French parents and put in an American orphanage when I was two."

Acton moaned. "Now we're in a hell of a fix. I can feel the heat from this damned Arab three feet away."

Barley shrugged and looked helplessly at the policeman.

Then a voice said, "Can I help you guys?" It was Chief Benson.

Barley felt better momentarily, but slumped whan he saw who it was. "I don't think so, Benson, unless you speak French."

Benson said, "I'll try. I took it for three years in high school." He turned to the policeman and began to question him in halting French. They talked for a few minutes, and then Benson returned to Barley. "The Arab says you agreed to buy the water pipe he is carrying, and then you changed your mind. He wants you to pay him."

Barley raised his eyebrows. "When I first saw it, I thought it was a nice souvenir. But then after he wrapped it up, he told me it could be used to smoke dope as well as tobacco. I figured I couldn't bring it back to the ship, so I tried to tell him I didn't want it anymore, but he wouldn't listen."

Benson laughed. "I'll try that on the policeman." Benson talked with the officer again. After a few minutes of conversation, the policeman pointed to the Arab and said a few words. The Arab shrugged, muttered a few more words, picked up the package, and trudged back into the Casbah.

Barley asked, "What was that all about?"

Benson said, "Something about doing something to his mother if he didn't let you alone. Also he put you guys in my custody and said I'd have to take you back to the ship."

Barley shrugged. "Suits me."

Bennaret frowned. "I didn't get *my* shopping done."

"Too bad," Acton said, "You'll have to wait until we get to Naples."

Bennaret sighed. "But I might explode."

The group ignored Bennaret and headed toward the mole. Approaching the dock, Acton accidentally bumped into Benson's package, which gave off a metallic clang. Acton said, "Sorry, Chief, I hope I didn't damage whatever was in your package."

Benson laughed. "I don't think so."

Barley grinned and punched Acton in the ribs.

Acton flinched. "What?" he asked Barley.

Barley said out of the corner of his mouth, "Ask him what's in the package."

Acton shrugged, turned to Benson, and pointed to Benson's package. "What is that?" he asked.

Benson reddened. "Ah, it's a water pipe."

*   *   *

The next day, the division left Oran, bound for Naples, and escorting the same convoy of ships it had brought into the harbor.

Barley watched the shoreline recede behind the formation. He sighed and turned to Brosnan. "Don't care if I never see Oran again. Bunch of crooks. It's Portsmouth for me."

Brosnan shook his head. "You won't see Portsmouth for some time. Maybe not until the end of the war."

Barley's face fell. "No other way?"

"Well," he offered, "We could get damaged in the next operation and have to go back to England for repairs."

Barley thought for a moment. "How about just a quick end to the war?"

CHAPTER THIRTY-ONE

Three days later, as the *Lawrence* approached the west coast of Italy, the lookouts sighted the top of Mount Vesuvius towering over the coastal overcast.

Naples Harbor, below Vesuvius, was crowded with Allied shipping. Smaller landing craft and escorts were nested together, either at piers or in the harbor at anchorages or buoys, and large combatants and transports lay haughtily alone among crowded anchorages. Fannon brought the flagship through the anchorages with the aid of an excitable Italian pilot, who had been picked up at the entrance to the harbor. The Captain declined the pilot's offer to bring the ship all the way in and moored her at an assigned pier without incident. Soon the other ships of the division were secured alongside.

Fannon took off his cap and wiped his brow.

Phelps noted his action and grinned. "Tough job, but you did it well."

Fannon replaced his cap. "Thanks, but it wasn't so difficult. Most of this perspiration comes from the summer heat."

Phelps nodded. "Today is the first of August—right in the middle of the hot season."

Fannon blew a bead of perspiration off of the end of his nose. "I wish we could go to some of the nearby beaches and cool off a little."

Phelps shook his head. "Not much chance. We won't have much time. And besides, the beachheads will be pretty well chewed up by the tanks and wheeled vehicles that the Army is using for rehearsals and training."

Before Phelps could leave the bridge, the signal light on an American cruiser moored at a nearby pier began to blink. Barley turned on his own signal searchlight, called for Acton to record the message, and began receiving. Phelps and Fannon strolled over to the signal bridge wing and began to read over Acton's shoulder. Acton was recording the incoming message in deliberate block letters on a rough message blank, held on a large clipboard.

Fannon watched the first few sentences form on the message blank and then said to Acton, "I take it that cruiser is the *Augusta*."

Acton nodded, trying to be careful not to miss a word. Barley, relaxed and confident in what he was doing, kept calling out the words and still conducting a conversation. Barley said, "Yes, sir, the *Augusta*. She's Admiral Davidson's flagship. A beautiful sight."

Phelps limited his reply, trying not to distract Barley. "Oh, yes, she's a beauty."

Fannon, paying more attention to the text of the message than the appearance of the *Augusta*, remarked, "It says 'You and your commanding officers are to come aboard for a conference right away.' I'll send an officer to the nearest headquarters to borrow a car."

Phelps shook his head. Don't bother. We can walk, and we all need the exercise. Please send the full message down to me when it's in, and make sure the other skippers are notified. I'm going below to change."

*   *   *

Fifteen minutes later, Phelps led the four commanding officers over the brow and down the broad esplanade toward the flagship, about a half-mile away. The sun was hot, and almost overhead, and in the 15 minutes it took to walk to the *Augusta*, all the officers were soaked.

Phelps wiped his brow and shook his head. "Maybe this walking wasn't such a good idea after all."

Fannon pulled out his handkerchief, "We won't look so good when we get there."

Phelps laughed. "There's a war on, and Admiral Davidson won't care how we look as long as we're ready to fight."

The Commodore led the group up the *Augusta*'s brow to her quarterdeck. All five saluted the colors aft, and Phelps asked the officer of the deck for permission to come aboard.

The officer of the deck saluted smartly and said, "Permission granted, sir." He turned to a lieutenant standing nearby and wearing on his shoulder the twin-stranded golden aiguilettes indicating he was an aide to a rear admiral. "Lieutenant Radford will escort you to the conference in the Admiral's cabin. Please follow him."

As they walked across the larger quarterdeck, Fannon's eyes swept the spotless area. "Jesus!" he said to Phelps out of the corner of his mouth. "This ship has more men cleaning the quarterdeck than I have cleaning my whole ship."

Phelps laughed. "And look at all the brass plaques and decorations they've got to shine. They must be left over from the *Augusta*'s tour as flagship of the Asiatic Fleet, when she was carrying the President around."

As they entered the flag cabin, Admiral Davidson rose, smiled, and moved forward to shake hands with the Commodore. "Good to see you, Horse. It's been a long time since I was a struggling four-striper in the Navy Department and you were a hard-working aide to our boss."

Phelps grinned broadly as he shook hands. "Yes, sir, those were busy times, but not as busy as we are here now. He turned to the four redundant officers waiting expectantly nearby. "Sir, I'd like to present my four commanding officers to you. I made them all walk here for the exercise, and I'm afraid we're all a little hot and sticky."

Davidson shook hands with the four captains and said, "They look fine to me, and as if they're ready for the action they're about to get."

He turned to his aide. "Radford, please seat our guests, and we'll begin the conference."

At the table were the commanding officer of the *Augusta*, Colonel Walker of the U.S. Army's First Special Service Force, and Lieutenant Colonel Bouvet of the French Romeo Force. The destroyer officers shook hands and assumed their chairs in the second row. Phelps seated himself in the front row.

Admiral Davidson picked up a pointer and moved in front of a large chart of the southern coast of France.

"Gentlemen," he began, "this is the first of a series of briefings for the members of my force, called 'SITKA FORCE,' or Task Force 86. The landing force, commanded by Colonels Walker and Bouvet, will be carried in the ships of the transport force, commanded by Rear Admiral Chandler. The troops are already embarked and are being trained now. The force will also include a naval gunfire support group that I will command. Commodore Phelps's division will operate with this naval gunfire support group.

Initially, and during the trip to the objective area, the division will serve as part of the screen of the naval gunfire support group. Commodore, I have picked your division, especially, for this mission because of your outstanding reputation for rendering naval gunfire and for your ability to protect our ships against radio-controlled bombs."

Phelps, trying to contain his pride for his ships, looked carefully at Colonel Walker. "Yes, sir, a home-grown capability. We think we're as good as the professional Army teams."

Colonel Walker clenched his teeth a bit and looked at the overhead, but remained quiet.

Lieutenant Colonel Bouvet raised his eyebrows and said in a heavy French accent. "What is this thing you talk about? A radio-controlled bomb?"

Phelps said, "The Germans have the ability to control large rocket-powered bombs, carried to an area by big bombers and launched and guided to their targets by radio signals transmitted by the mother aircraft. The bombs can be controlled at long range. The Army trained several teams to intercept the radio signals and to jam and interrupt the German's control of the bombs."

"And what happens to the bomb?"

Phelps grinned and made a diving motion with his hand, "Kerplunk!"

"What is this 'kerplunk?' " Bouvet asked.

Fannon explained, "Once the control signal is interrupted, the bombs dive into the water and are destroyed. Not enough Army teams were available to put aboard all ships off the Anzio beachhead, so the *Lawrence* improvised our own control system."

"And you can kerplunk this damned Nazi threat?"

"Damned right!" Fannon said. "We haven't missed yet."

Bouvet turned to Admiral Davidson and grinned. "Ah, I think I feel a little safer now."

Davidson extended his pointer again. "We're getting off the main subject. When you gentlemen leave here today, you will be given copies of an operation order for the operation, which has been named ANVIL. D-Day will be 15 August. On that day, a large force of American, Canadian, and French troops will land and assault a 50-mile stretch of coast from here to here." Admiral Davidson's pointer swept west to east along the southern coast of France, from Toulon to the Antibes. "The invasion will proceed under cover of American, French, and British ships, joined by the naval vessels of several other allied countries." Davidson put his pointer on the middle of the area. "This line divides the French area on the west from the American and Canadian areas to the east. Our group will operate next to the line, landing both French and American Special Forces. All of the details regarding the individual tasks to be carried out are in your copies of the operation order, issued by Vice Admiral Hewitt, who will serve as the overall comander of the operation. The Army commanders will be Lieutenant General Alexander Patch, Major General Lucian Truscott for the American Army, and General of the Army de Lattre de Tassigny for the Free French forces.

"Gentlemen, that is all for now. Lieutenant Radford will

distribute copies of the Operation Order as you leave. Good luck to you all."

*　　*　　*

As the group left the quarterdeck of the *Augusta*, Fannon took one last look around and muttered, "Sure could use some of these men."

Phelps heard him. "The Navy has plenty of men now and we need to have at least one large flagship that will out-do the British in spit and polish."

Fannon chuckled. "Then we've got it."

Fifteen minutes later, the group returned to the *Lawrence*. Phelps handed his copy of the operation order to Kuberski, and Fannon gave his to Brosnan. Phelps turned to the other comanding officers. "Gentlemen, we'll meet in my cabin at 0900 tomorrow. That will give us time enough to digest all of the operation order."

*　　*　　*

At 0900 the next morning, Kuberski met the three commanding officers and escorted them to the Commodore's cabin to join Phelps and Fannon. Stevenson, the Commodore's personal steward, circulated among the officers with coffee, and after all arrived and were served, Phelps spread a chart of the Western Mediterranean on the table. "Gentlemen, let's get on with it; we'll get under way soon for rehearsals. Yesterday, we received general information in the briefing from Admiral Davidson. According to the operation order, we have a few days before we get under way for a rehearsal by landing on Ponza and Zannone islands. Then we return to Naples the following day, and the whole force gets under way on the 13th."

Phelps leaned over the chart and pointed to Sardinia and Corsica. "We pass between these islands through the Bonifacio Strait the night of the 14th and arrive off our objective before dawn. Our forces will land at night to ensure the element of surprise, but for the first time in the invasion of Europe the main forces will land during daylight after air and naval preparatory bombardment."

Fannon laughed. "I'll bet Admiral Hewitt had a hard time persuading the Army to land in daylight."

Kuberski said, "The Army and Marines have been doing it in the Pacific for some time."

Fannon nodded. "This way, our naval gunfire support and air support will be able to knock out many of the coastal defenses using direct fire and spotting to correct it.

Kuberski said, "And we'll even be able to target some fortifications and mines in the water."

Phelps added, "The Germans, according to the Intelligence Annex, are well-entrenched, but they've been suffering losses from several days of aerial bombardment. Then on D-day our carrier-based air wings will take over the assault. This landing won't be as hard a job as the one we had in Normandy. Also, the weather will be better and the tides amount to only about eight inches."

Phelps reached for his coffee cup and continued. "As Admiral Davidson said, our task is to escort the naval gunfire support group composed of the *Augusta, Dido, Lorrain, Omaha,* and *Cincinnati* to the objective area, and then to join them and four other destroyers covering the special force as it lands under cover of darkness. The ships have three missions: First, to land French commandos on Cap Nègre; second, to knock out enemy batteries; and third, to capture the two easternmost of the Isles d' Hyères."

Fannon said, "Then we won't be firing in advance of the landings?"

Phelps smiled and shook his head. "No, but we'll be busy after daylight."

*   *   *

The rehearsal on the 6th proceeded as planned, and then the ships sat in port until the 13th. On the *Lawrence*'s main deck Frenchy Bennaret came topside with Chief Marusak and looked toward the Naples waterfront. Bennaret had been supervising a crew cleaning the sooty firesides of a boiler, and his face, below a dirty rag tied around his head, was covered with sweat and black carbon. Marusak had poked his head in the fire box from time to time and was relatively clean.

Bennaret said, "Chief, this heat is awful. Even up here in the fresh air it's bad."

Marusak laughed. "Just study harder and make chief and you won't have to dive in those boilers any more."

Bennaret took the rag off his head and wiped his face. "I wouldn't mind if I could get ashore. Why aren't we getting any liberty?"

"Something about security. The big brass is afraid the Italians will find out about the next operation and tell the Germans."

Bennaret sighed. "And I didn't get my ashes hauled in Oran, either. I tell you, I think I'm gonna explode."

Marusak laughed. "Try more hard work and a cold shower."

Benaret was not amused. "In this weather, even the cold water in the showers is hot."

Marusak shrugged. "Then all that's left is hard work. Let's go below."

CHAPTER THIRTY-TWO

At long last the 13th arrived, and the enormous armada got under way from Malta, Naples, Salerno, and a host of smaller ports along Italy's east coast. Fortunately, Commodore Phelps's destroyers got under way first and took screening positions around the transports of the SITKA Force. Since the SITKA Force was ordered to be in position off its landing beaches at 2200 on the 14th—well before the other groups were due to arrive at the various positions for their landings—the destroyers were directed to get under way first and to lead the other groups through the Strait of Bonifacio between Sardinia to the south and Corsica to the north.

Fannon looked back at the milling throng of ships getting under way from Naples. "Glad we're not in there now," he said to Phelps.

Phelps, watching the process through his binoculars, agreed. "Indeed. The *Augusta* almost got rammed by a British cruiser. That wild pilot you had coming in the first day here must have been aboard."

Fannon laughed. "He was a real Neapolitan pistol."

Phelps nodded. "I'm glad you didn't let him conn your ship to the final landing. You might have ended up a block or so inland."

In spite of the crowded conditions, all the group's ships were under way by 0900 and beginning to join up in a rectangular cruising formation.

* * *

The large ships of the naval gunfire support group for the SITKA Force, other than the *Augusta*, were in Malta and were scheduled to join the formation at about noon. Barley and the signal gang on board the *Lawrence* kept a close watch for the ships to the south, with each signalman vying for the honor of being the first to sight them. Soon after CIC reported multiple contacts on radar, Barley sighted the cruisers, escorted by two British destroyers, steaming over the horizon. The heavy ships maintained their own formation about five miles ahead of the ungainly transports. Barley, watching their maneuvers, commented, "They don't seem to want to join us *peons*."

Acton snickered. "We ain't *peons*, Barley, that's Spanish. We're in Italian waters, so we're *paisanos*."

"Whatever we are, those troops will be the main performers soon."

Acton shuddered. "I'm glad I'm not going ashore with them in the middle of the night."

* * *

All that day, the SITKA Force steamed toward the Strait of Bonifacio. Phelps paced the bridge, contemplating his responsibility for protecting the transport group from air or submarine attack.

Kuberski, watching him, tried to ease the strain. "Commodore, don't worry so much. We're too far away for the German Air Force to get at us, and there haven't been any submarines reported in this area for some time."

Phelps stopped pacing. "I agree about the air threat, but if the Germans have any submarines left, they'll come after us. Certainly they know we're about to land somewhere on the coast of France. Italian spies must have gotten the word to them of our concentration around Naples and the rehearsals and training of our ships and troops."

Kuberski scratched some breakfast egg from his shirt front. "I agree, sir, and our Army Air Force has been bombarding the southern coast of France heavily for two weeks. That should send them a signal."

Phelps sighed and said patiently, "Then you agree that I have something to worry about?"

Kuberski looked at the formation of heavy combatant ships steaming steadily ahead. "Yes, sir, but maybe those clowns up there will run over any submarine out here first. Then we can go elsewhere."

*   *   *

In spite of Phelps' apprehension, the SITKA Force continued to steam peacefully across the translucent blue seas. The swells were moderate and the only signs of life were small clouds of flying fish, which occasionally lifted from the calm surface, glided for a ship's length, and then plopped back into the water, acting as if there were no other life within hundreds of miles.

As darkness fell, CIC reported Sardinia and Corsica on radar, and Phelps bent over the PPI watching the ships ahead approach the Strait of Bonifacio. The navigator of the *Augusta* was setting the course for the whole formation, and Chief Benson's job was simple. All he had to do was maintain a navigational plot in case the *Lawrence* was suddenly detached. Phelps asked him, "How are we doing, Benson?"

"Looks good to me, sir. We should begin to transit the strait about 2000. I've laid out the tracks that all the groups have been directed to follow."

Phelps approached the chart and bent over it, adjusting the dim red light above. "I see that after the group is clear of the coast of Corsica, the ships all head north toward Genoa until dark tomorrow."

Benson said, "Yes, sir, a deception intended to make the Germans think we are all going to land further east on the coast, near Genoa. At dark, the ships all change course to the west. Then they head directly for their objective areas, taking whatever speed is required to arrive early the 15th."

Phelps said, "I see we also head directly west for our area."

"Yes, sir. We have to do that because we have to be on station by 2200 the 14th."

* * *

The coasts of Sardinia and Corsica slid by the attacking force as the ships, darkened and silent, glided along the calm seas. Brosnan leaned on the bridge bulwark and watched the rugged coasts in the pale blue moonlight. There were a few lights visible, and Brosnan thought how the war already had ended for thousands of Italians on the islands. Now they could get back to leading normal lives, and he wondered how long it would be before he could do the same. Soon he might leave his own country behind and become a European.

When the shores began to recede astern, Brosnan yawned, stretched, and headed below for the last full night of sleep he knew he would have for some time.

* * *

The next day was much like the one before, except that occasional flights of American aircraft droned overhead, coming from airbases in Northern Italy and headed for the coast of France to drop their bombs.

Brosnan inspected the ship thoroughly to make sure all was ready for action. He looked in all the first aid boxes, checked the inventory of tools and equipment in the repair lockers, and verified that every piece of loose gear was secured to ensure that nothing would fly around in the event of a projectile explosion. Earlier, at morning general quarters, Brosnan had carefully inspected the ship's crew to make sure the men's helmets were properly fitted and that life jacket ties were in good repair.

By the time for evening meal, the executive officer was satisfied that the ship and her crew were ready for battle, and he reported the facts to the Captain.

Fannon said, "Thank you, Beetle, I'm ready, too. It's been some time since we've been in battle, but I don't think our men will forget what to do during routine action or to improvise if they must. They've been superb in the past."

Brosnan nodded. "Most of them won't forget, but we have fifteen new men. I think they'll be ready, too. The more experienced men have been hard at work instructing them."

Fannon yawned. "Let's have early dinner and taps at dark. We'll have to serve a simple meal at 2100 and go to general quarters about 2130."

Brosnan nodded. "I've got the schedule all set. Pasha Parma says he's ready to out-do himself at dinner and at the 2100 meal. We'll also be ready to serve breakfast on station at dawn, and the meals after that will be ready quickly and whenever I call for them."

Fannon laughed. "What's he got for breakfast?"

"Spam sandwiches, hard-boiled eggs, and bananas."

"Pretty good. Portable and easily eaten. The only trouble will be what to do with all those damned banana skins."

Brosnan laughed. "I think the flying fish will get most of them."

*   *   *

Brosnan went below to take a shower and to put on clean clothes in preparation for the battle that he expected in a few hours. When he was getting dressed, Jason knocked on his door and announced dinner.

As Brosnan approached the wardroom, he could hear laughter and loud conversation. It meant the young officers were relaxed and ready, and even eager, for what might happen. He remembered how tense they had been a year ago before their first action off Sicily and Italy. A year had made a big difference.

Kuberski looked at Brosnan as he came in the door and grinned. "Thought you weren't coming to dinner. I was about to start without you."

"Hungry?"

"Damned right. Always am before a ruckus. Let's get at it. Pasha has laid on a helluva feast."

Brosnan took his seat at the head of the table. The Captain was eating a solitary meal on the bridge as he usually did at sea. Kuberski sat at Brosnan's right and Kelly at his left. The other officers, still chatting, took their places in order of rank, except for Doctor Taylor, who as mess treasurer, sat at the end of the table.

Kuberski said, "Doc, I see you've put pressure on Pasha to give us one last good meal."

Taylor looked at Parma. "No, he did it all himself. All I have to do as treasurer is figure out how to pay for it. A lot depends on how much you and Gerlach eat."

Gerlach, waiting impatiently to be served, turned to Brosnan. "Sir, can you tell us a little about what will be going on ashore? Some of us haven't had much time to review the operation order."

Brosnan had finished serving himself from the platters brought around by Jason and his assistant. He looked at the huge steak on his plate with anticipation, but decided to answer Gerlach before attacking it. "Well, as you probably know, the French Army Landing Force will land to the left of us."

"Yes, sir, I got that far before the Captain sent for the operation order."

Aronson said, "Yes, he wanted to go over it for possible targets with me and Squid Lee."

Lee uncoiled his long arms and put down his fork. "They're laid out on the bombardment chart in CIC if you want to see them after dinner."

Brosnan managed to take two bites during the exchange, but Gerlach turned to him expectantly again, and he put down his fork. "Well, our first mission is to cut the road east of Toulon to prevent the Germans from moving toward our main landing forces. The Romeo Force will land at the Rade de Bones to do this. The Force has British, Canadian, American, and French troops."

Kuberski stoped eating, but spoke with his mouth full. "My God! I forgot about that. How will they comunicate?"

Brosnan said patiently, "The French have volunteered to take interpreters with them."

At the other end of the table, Squid Lee laughed. "How about the British? I can't understand most of them."

Brosnan ignored him and continued. "The first group will land in the dark using rubber boats, and their scouts will use surfboards."

There was laughter around the table. "Surfboards!" Parma said, "They aren't on the Navy stock list. The only person I know who knows how to use one is Acton, and we need him."

Brosnan looked patiently at the ship's supply officer. "Follow-on waves of LCMs will land vehicles for the troops to use in moving inland to block the highway."

Kuberski, now well into his second steak, said, "Tell them about the two islands. They'll be thorns in our sides if we can't neutralize them."

Brosnan looked longingly at his uneaten steak and at Kuberski's emptying plate and said, "Aronson, you and Lee tell us about it. You both know the targets."

Aronson said, "Certainly, sir. The two islands we're worried about are Port Gros Isle and Levant Isle. Intelligence reports indicate that there are big German guns there, and they'll have to be destroyed or neutralized to prevent their interfering with the Romeo operation or the later daylight landings."

Kuberski snorted. "Interfere! They'll make rubber bands out of the rubber boats."

Lee took over. "I don't think that will happen. Colonel Walker has 2300 Commandos—half American and half Canadian, all individually trained—and I think they'll do the job. Besides, we'll be riding herd on them, ready to fire on anybody who tries to interfere with their landings."

Parma asked, "In the dark? Do we know where they are?"

Aronson answered him, "Tubby Raymond and I will be ready to fire at the flashes as soon as we see them. The division's other three destroyers will be nearby."

Kuberski beamed expansively. "I trained you guys, and I have faith in you."

Brosnan said, "You won't be able to see much of the troop loading and movement ashore, so I won't go into it. It's unbelievable anyway."

Taylor said, "More surfboards?"

Brosnan laughed. "Yes, and these are motorized. Also kayaks and rubber boats. Their Commandos carry so many so-called razor-sharp knives, they probably won't be able to float if they fall off their surfboards."

Taylor said, "That's enough for me. I think you guys are conning me. I'm going to turn in."

CHAPTER THIRTY-THREE

Brosnan was on the bridge long before general quarters was sounded at 2130. He leaned on the bridge bulwark as Fannon brought the *Lawrence* to her assigned station and stopped her engines. Brosnan could tell that being motionless made the Captain nervous, and he felt the same way. "I don't like this. I feel like a sitting duck."

Brosnan could see Fannon shrug in the faint illumination coming from the pelorus. "We don't have any choice."

"I know, sir, but it never seems right to deprive a destroyer of her main defense, speed."

"You're right, and if we perceive any threat, I'll bend on speed in a hurry, although I don't know where I'd go. This swept area is mighty small."

Brosnan laughed. "I'd be happy if we could just circle."

The exec stopped worrying and looked around the area. Brosnan could not see much, but through the darkness, he could see the shapes of the other ships of the division floating ghostlike nearby.

He looked toward the shore beyond the nearby islands of Port Gros and Levant. Small lights belonging to fishermen and merchants blinked along the coast. Brosnan felt a pang of guilt as he realized some of them might soon be dead. Now they were going about their small tasks, blissfully ignorant of the fury about to be unleashed on them. Now they were faceless, unknown persons. If all went well and he and Annette married some day, they would be his countrymen and no longer impersonal. He sighed. Life was very peculiar and certainly unpredictable.

*   *   *

Brosnan stepped inside the bridge structure and walked over to the PPI, where Fannon was watching the increasing number of individual contacts on it. Fannon said, "Looks like bunches of ants coming out of anthills."

Brosnan pointed to some of the larger contacts. "I take it these are the anthills."

"Yes. Admiral Chandler is in one of the Canadian APDs configured as a flagship. The other larger contacts are 'Prince' Class Canadian and British APDs. Low-profile British LCA landing craft are towing ruber boats toward the landing area, and ahead of them are electric powered surfboards carrying scouts."

Brosnan laughed. "I told the wardroom officers about them, and I don't think they believed me."

Fannon nodded, the glow of the PPI glancing off his tense face. "I don't blame them."

Brosnan said, "I've told Farraday to put a receiver on the landing force radio circuit so we'll know what's happening."

"Yes, I know. He's over on the other wing now. Let's call him over."

In a few minutes Farraday came through the pilot house dragging a long cord behind him. "You wanted me, Captain?"

"Yes. What's going on?"

"So far nothing. I think they're still in radio silence. According to the schedule, their first troops have been cast loose and are paddling to shore now in their rubber boats. In a few minutes we should hear something."

Brosnan and Fannon searched the darkness between them and the islands. Fannon said to Chief Brill, standing near him with his telephone cord carefully coiled, "Brill, tell Gun Control to be alert. We may be needed any minute."

Brill delivered the message and then reported. "Gun Control reports ready, sir."

About 0130, Farraday began to listen carefully. Then he said, "All troops ashore. Complete surprise. No casualties. Troops are moving up the slopes."

Fannon began to pace up and down, opening and closing his hands nervously. "Damn!" he said. "This is too easy."

Brosnan, thinking of the innocent French peasants who had been spared, said, "The French civilians should be happy."

Just before dawn, Farraday approached the Captain. "Colonel Walker reports the Isle of Levant secured."

Fannon stopped pacing abruptly. "What about the big guns over there?"

Farraday grinned. "He says they were dummies, made of wood."

"Damn!" Fannon said, "We really got screwed."

Brosnan said, "At least nobody got killed."

The crew's feeling of success, however, was premature. A short time later, Farraday reported again to Fannon. "Port Gros Isle is giving the landing force trouble. Colonel Walker has discovered a deeply fortified gun position, and he hasn't been able to take it."

Fannon said impatiently, "Does he want help?"

"Yes, sir, the *Augusta* is on the way." Then the TBS crackled, and the *Augusta* requested that Phelps send two destroyers to join the cruiser.

Phelps, listening carefully, responded. "Go, Fannon!" He turned to Kuberski. "Tell the *Grayston* to join us."

In the growing daylight, Fannon conned the ship toward the *Augusta*, now closing the Isle of Port Gros. The group on the bridge began to search the craggy area on the northern coast for signs of the German emplacement. Barley said, "I can see Commandos moving around that large brown area."

Fannon searched the area. "I can see them. Brill, tell Gun Control to scan the brown patch."

Before Brill could transmit the message, he said, "Sir, they're on target." The hydraulic motors of the mounts began to whine as the guns followed the director.

When Fannon was satisfied the *Lawrence*'s guns were on the target he had discovered, he picked up the TBS transmitter and called the *Augusta*. "Request permission to open fire."

The reply from the *Augusta* was swift. "Negative. My main battery is on the target designated by the shore fire control party. It says 5-inch fire will not penetrate the embrasure. I am about to open fire."

Fannon relayed the information to Gun Control and began to pace up and down, trying to control his frustration.

A tremendous crash sounded as the first salvo of eight-inch projectiles left the *Augusta*. Yellow smoke and debris rolled down wind, and the concussion in the heavy morning air shook those on the *Lawrance*'s bridge. Fannon shook his head. "We can't match that."

After several salvos, debris and smoke rose in a large column above the embrasure. The *Augusta* reported on TBS, "The Landing Force Commander reports the fortifications too deep for 8-inch fire. I am requesting the help of a British battleship."

Fannon stopped pacing and listened to the transmission. Then he said, "Glad we didn't waste any ammunition."

Phelps said, "I agree. At least the attack force has accomplished its mission. The German battery hasn't been able to fire on Romeo Force. The French Commandos report they are all ashore and that the road has been cut."

*　　*　　*

A British battleship arrived on station one-half hour later, and settled down in the water like a large hen. Soon, her crews began pouring salvos of 15-inch projectiles on the embrasure, and after fifteen minutes Colonel Walker reported, "Target destroyed."

As the last salvo was fired, Parma came running to the bridge with a decoded message. He was puffing deeply. Phelps read it quickly and passed it to Fannon. "Sounds like we're needed to the east to help Task Force CAMEL." He turned to Benson. "How far is it?"

Benson bent over the chart and picked up the metal dividers. "Thirty miles, sir."

Phelps turned to Fannon. "Let's proceed at 25 knots." Then he turned to Kuberski. "Stanley, make a visual signal to the other ships to form column at 25 knots."

Brosnan said to Fannon, "Sir, that's just enough time to feed the crew lunch."

"Do it," Fannon said. Then he grinned, "And I won't even ask you what Parma has cooked up this time."

Brosnan said, "I don't know either, but the crew will be hungry enough to eat anything."

CHAPTER THIRTY-FOUR

By 1200 on 15 August, the four ships of Destroyer Division 32 had formed a column and by 2100 were racing along the southern coast of France at 25 knots. In the pilothouse, Phelps, Fannon, and Brosnan bent over the chart showing the landing areas. Phelps poked a pencil at the SITKA area. "We just left here, and we'll pass areas ALPHA and DELTA en route to CAMEL. Should arrive about 1300." He reached for a sandwich on a tray brought up by Stevenson, and Fannon and Brosnan followed suit, taking the last ones.

Kuberski came up from CIC and joined the group. Brosnan noted that he was looking at the empty sandwich plate. "Sorry, Stanley," he said. "You were just a few seconds too late."

Kuberski's face fell, and he reached over and picked up a few of the crumbs still lying on the plate. "Wow! Good cheese," he said.

Fannon took a huge bite from his sandwich and chewed with pleasure. "Good stuff. This Stilton from your reserve, Commodore?"

Brosnan, also chewing, said, "No, sir. Pasha Parma cornered the Stilton market in Portsmouth. Even the crew is eating this today."

Kuberski moaned. "I think I'll go below and see what the crew is eating."

Phelps grinned, "A remarkable young man, that Parma. He'll go far in the Navy."

Brosnan turned toward the Commodore. "Maybe even farther when he gets out of it after the war."

Phelps's eyebrows shot up. "You have plans for him?"

"Possibly, sir. I think he'd make a good head of American and African marketing for Annette's winery."

Fannon said, "This cheese is good but a little dry. What's in the pitcher?"

Brosnan said, "Iced tea."

Phelps turned up his nose. "Probably hedge clippings."

"Oh, no, sir. Right off the boat from Ceylon," Brosnan said.

Phelps sighed. "Not another coup by Parma."

Brosnan grinned. "None other, sir."

Fannon moved the sandwich plate aside. "This is good stuff, but let's get down to business. The Intelligence Annex says the coastal waters are heavily mined and the land defenses are strong and well concealed."

Benson pointed toward the chart. "I set the course line well off shore. We will pass at least five miles from the closest land, and the 100 fathom curve is only 3,000 yards off shore."

Phelps nodded "Then we're plenty safe from mines. They can't be planted in more than 100 fathoms."

Fannon finished washing down his sandwich with iced tea, and the three walked out on the bridge wing to look at the Saint Tropez area being assaulted by Admiral Lowery's Task Force ALPHA. Fannon turned to Farraday, who was dragging his radio receiver lines behind him. "Farraday, as soon as you've finished that sandwich, shift frequencies and let us know what's happening over there."

Farraday swallowed a last bite. "Already shifted, Captain. The troops are well inland. A large group of German troops surrendered a few minutes ago at Saint Tropez. Didn't seem to want to fight much anymore."

Phelps asked, "Is it that easy?"

"No, sir, there's been a lot of heavy fighting, and many big guns have been camoulflaged or concealed. Our naval gunfire was very heavy this morning."

Fannon, remembering the details of the operation order, said, "I'm sure it was. The orders were for the landings at ALPHA and DELTA to begin at 0800, following heavy air and naval bombardment."

Benson left the pilothouse and addressed Fannon, "Sir, we're now passing by the area where the German forces are being attacked by Task Force DELTA under the command of Admiral Rodgers."

Fannon turned to Farraday expectantly. Faraday lifted one of his radio earpieces and said, "Radio Central has already shifted. The information is coming in now."

Phelps said, "While you're taking all that in, we'll get some more iced tea."

Five minutes later, Phelps and Fannon were back, and Farraday began pointing out the Bay de Bougnon in the distance. "There's the landing area. Very narrow, and the vehicles are having trouble with the rocky beach, but the infantry is well inland and moving without vehicles."

Phelps nodded. "They don't need us, either, but Admiral Lewis and the CAMEL Force do."

"They have by far the most difficult mission," Fannon said. "They have to take the territory at the head of the Golfe de Fréjus. There is an airfield there near the beach, and the roads behind it lead inland."

Phelps interrupted. "We consider it the most likely route of invasion to the north that our forces will take if they want to flank the Germans."

Fannon said, "We do, and so do the Germans. They read the same maps we do. They've concentrated their defenses there. Big guns, thousands of mines, lots of troops. That's why H-hour was delayed to 1400."

Phelps raised his binoculars and examined the area off the Rade de Gay, now only a few miles away. "There's where the first landings will take place, and I can see landing craft heading in now."

Fannon was also looking at the area. "I see them, but they're hard to make out. The smoke from the naval gunfire is very heavy. I can see the *Arkansas, Tuscaloosa,* and the

French battle cruiser *Emile Bertin*. They are really pounding the hell out of the beach."

Farraday, now busy listening to the Task Force CAMEL Landing Force circuit, said, "Maybe it looks great, but it's not doing much good. The minesweepers have been chased out by heavy German fire. Late this morning, 90 American Air Force Liberator bombers dropped bombs with little effect."

Fannon rubbed his hands together. "Maybe there's some action left for us after all."

*   *   *

Fifteen minutes later, the Division was close enough for Phelps to report to Rear Admiral Lewis for duty. The Admiral assigned the destroyers to fire support stations and gave each ship a specific target.

Benson provided Fannon a course and speed to the *Lawrence*'s assigned station, and Fannon soon maneuvered the flagship there. The squawkbox sounded. "Captain, we have a target assigned. Gun Control reports on target."

Fannon answered the squawkbox and then turned to Chief Brill. "Gun Control, commence firing when ready."

The *Lawrence*'s 5-inch guns boomed out, and the concussion pushed against Fannon's chest. He blinked his eyes to clear them of the debris in the smokeless powder gas rushing across the bridge. Fannon raised his binoculars to follow the flight of the projectiles. When they landed, he shouted, "What the hell! We're hitting a beach house."

Chief Brill heard him. "Sir, Gun Control says that's our target. The Germans have a gun concealed in it, and they've done the same thing with other guns."

The third salvo blew the roof and walls off the beach house, and the gun became visible. It was now twisted and useless, and the *Lawrence* was given another target.

Fannon laughed. "The damned thing looks like a naked bather."

Naval gunfire continued until 1400, when Farraday reported, "The Navy big shots are arguing over whether or not the landing area should be shifted to find an easier place to land. It seems they can't get in touch with the Army Landing Force Commander by radio."

Fannon, still watching the effects of the *Lawrence*'s fire, said, "Keep us informed."

*   *   *

Ten minutes later, Farraday said, "They still can't reach the General, so the Admiral has decided on his own to shift to Beach GREEN."

"Damn!" Phelps said, "That beach is close to the Golfe de Fréjus all right, but it's in a very heavily mined and defended area. The boats will have a tough time in there."

Farraday said, "I believe the Admiral knows that. He's sent in two squadrons of minesweepers to clear the mines, and the destroyer *Ordonaux* has been ordered to shepherd the landing craft in as far as she can go."

Fannon was still unhappy, his small mustache twitching nervously. "That won't be enough."

It wasn't. In a few minutes the *Lawrence* was ordered to assist the *Ordonaux*. Fannon moved the ship quickly into a position where she could fire, and the lookouts and Gun Control watched anxiously for signs of opposition from the shore. The boat waves moved forward, and the tension mounted on the bridge as the heavily loaded boats neared the beach.

For a moment, Fannon thought they might make it without opposition, but the Germans were merely waiting for a clear shot. Without warning, all hell broke loose along the shore. At first, a few scattered guns fired. Then more joined in. The flashes of gunfire became almost a continuous curtain of red flame.

With the first salvo, Fannon could hardly believe the strength of the German fire, but he paused only an instant. "Commence firing!" he bellowed, and the 5-inch and 40-millimeter guns began firing. As the projectiles from the destroyers burst ashore, the German fire slackened appreciably, not only because their guns were being destroyed, but also because smoke and dust were obscuring their view of the landing craft.

"Pour it on!" Fannon shouted. "The poor bastards in those boats are catching hell."

Gradually, as the destroyers maximized their rate of fire, the fire from the shore defenses slackened. But a few splashes began to appear around the destroyers as bigger guns inland opened up.

Fannon watched the splashes move nearer and then began to manuever the ship to throw off the German aim. Even then, the big shells came closer and closer until one showered the after decks with sea water. "Damn!" Brosnan said, "That was close!"

Fannon backed full, but it was too late. There was a loud explosion aft, and Fannon saw pieces of the whaleboat fly through the air. "Let's get out of here!" he shouted. "All ahead full! Right full rudder!"

He managed to leave the bursting projectiles behind, but the *Lawrence* was followed by a column of flames and smoke billowing from the area around the whale boat stowage. Fannon, obviously worried about the spreading fire, turned to Brosnan. "Beetle, go aft and take charge."

*   *   *

Brosnan slid down the ladders to the main deck using the handrails, hardly touching the treads, and ran aft. Even before he reached the area of the fire, he knew there was serious trouble. From the color of the flames and the nature of the smoke, he knew there had to be oil feeding the fire. When Brosnan got close enough to see the base of the flames, he saw his answer. The diesel fuel tank on the boat had ruptured, and the burning oil had run aft along the slanting deck to the area under one of the K-guns. The K-gun itself was bent outboard with the depth charge and the arbor to which it was attached still hanging to it. Compounding the danger, though, were the three depth charges normally carried in a storage rack next to the K-gun. The rack, made of heavy angle iron, had been badly bent and damaged by the whaleboat motor, which had been blown in the air and had landed on top of it. Oil-fed fires on the deck now were licking at the depth charges.

The after repair party worked frantically to rig canvas fire hoses so they could spray water on the depth charges, but the fire was increasing rapidly, and Brosnan knew he would have to find a way to get the depth charges over the side before the heat caused them to cook off. Brosnan grabbed a man on the after repair party who was wearing a telephone. "Tell sonar to send Mister Gerlach back here on the double."

Nearby two men of the repair party were being dressed in asbestos suits with matching headgear faced with tempered glass plates. Brosnan slapped the men on the shoulders and motioned them to take off their suits. The men took off their asbestos helmets and looked at him enquiringly. "Take them off!" Brosnan shouted over the noise of the flames. "Put them on Mister Gerlach when he gets here and on me."

Gerlach came pounding down the deck and skidded to a stop, slipping on the wet decks and bowling over the telephone talker. "What's up?" he asked Brosnan.

Brosnan pointed to the depth charges. "We have to get them over the side, and you and I are the only ones strong enough to lift them."

Gerlach already being stuffed into one of the asbestos suits, said, "Yes, but we'll have to pry the collapsed rack off two of them first."

Brosnan turned to the chief boatswain's mate in charge of the repair party. "Get us two six-foot lengths of galvanized iron pipe."

By the time Brosnan and Gerlach were encased in the suits, the lengths of pipe were brought to the scene, and Brosnan started to lead Gerlach toward the fire. The crews manning the hoses played salt water on the depth charges, but the burning diesel fuel clung stubbornly to the charges and the wreckage of the storage rack.

Brosnan could feel the cool water from the hoses hitting his back, and only a little heat radiated through the protective suit.

The depth charge on the K-gun was the first to go. Gripping opposite ends of the charge, Brosnan nodded at Gerlach through the faceplate, and the pair heaved until the depth charge and the arbor attached to it rose out of the k-gun. The load clanged against the scuppers on the way down and dropped into the water, leaving a trail of bubbles.

The other three depth charges were more difficult. The charges were pinned down by the whaleboat motor resting on top of the bent angle iron of the storage rack. Brosnan and Gerlach worked the ends of the pipes under the boat motor and heaved on the pipes. At first there was no movement, and Brosnan thought for a moment that they might lose the whole stern if they were not successful and one or more of the depth charges exploded. He peered at Gerlach through his face plate, raised his fist and clenched it, and Gerlach seemed to understand.

The two set their feet, gripped the pipe ends a little farther toward their ends, and heaved. Brosnan thought his gut muscles would burst, and he waited for the pain of a hernia to begin, but nothing happened to him nor to the motor. It refused to budge. He waited for a moment, gave Gerlach the thumbs up signal, and the two heaved again. This time, Brosnan felt a slight movement, and he heaved so hard he began to shake. Suddenly, he could feel the weight giving way and the motor began to slide faster until it finally slid off of the wreckage.

By hand signals, Brosnan showed Gerlach where to put the pipes under the folded angle iron, and in a few seconds the iron pieces had been lifted enough to release the depth charges. Two were freed enough to be rolled over the side, but the third had to be lifted up through the wreckage and carried over to the side. Brosnan paused for a moment, breathing in gasps as wisps of the smoke filtered into his helmet. He wondered if the two of them had the strength to do the job, but there was no alternative. They had to lift and move the 300-pound charge or face the chance that it might explode.

Brosnan bent over the depth charge, got a firm grip, set his feet, and looked at Gerlach, who was set opposite him.

Gerlach's muscles, bulging against the white asbestos suit, gave him confidence, and he nodded. The two strained, gasping and shaking from the effort. Slowly their knees straightened, and the depth charge came up. When it was high enough, Brosnan nodded again, and they began the task of inching toward the side. The movement seemed to Brosnan to take forever, but finally he could see the side of the ship out of the corner of his eye, the scuppers still running with a mixture of salt water and burning diesel oil.

Brosnan gave one last convulsive nod, and both heaved the charge toward the side and let go. It clanged loudly on the scupper and bounded into the sea. Exhausted, Brosnan and Gerlach leaned briefly on the adjacent life lines, watching the round can sink into the depths of the blue water, trailing a stream of bubbles after it. After another moment, Brosnan turned weakly to Gerlach and shook his gloved hand. He could see Gerlach grinning through the tempered face plate. Brosnan mouthed the words, "Well done," and Gerlach nodded happily.

CHAPTER THIRTY-FIVE

Brosnan took off the heavy asbestos suit and retrieved his helmet and lifejacket from the top of a nearby locker where he had heaved them before putting on the asbestos suit. He looked down at his uniform. Brosnan was soaking wet from the physical effort he had made, the confinement of the asbestos suit, and the heat of the fire. He shrugged. Cleanup would have to wait. The Captain would be anxious to hear his report.

As Brosnan trudged wearily up to the bridge, Phelps and Fannon watched his approach. Fannon grinned and said, "Ah, Beetle, you're an awful mess. Please stay downwind."

Brosnan started to say something, but before he could open his mouth, Phelps said, "A helluva fine job, Brosnan. Tell us what happened."

Brosnan shrugged. "Well, sir, there wasn't much we could do. The whaleboat is completely destroyed, and the port K-gun is out of commission. All of its depth charges are over the side, and the reloading rack looks like a pile of gray spaghetti. The diesel oil fire is out, and a lot of paintwork is badly burned. Fortunately, no one was hurt."

Fannon laughed and slapped his knee. "Beetle, that was the most no-soap report I've ever heard. I had continuous reports coming up here from the repair party talker, and I know exactly what you and young Gerlach did. Frankly, I was afraid one of those cans would cook off and take the whole stern with it. I think you and Gerlach saved us, and I'm going to recommend you for the Navy Cross and Gerlach for the Silver Star, and don't tell me you don't deserve them."

"But, Captain—."

"Don't argue. The Commodore agrees with me. Now go below and get cleaned up."

*　　*　　*

When Brosnan got back to the bridge, the *Lawrence* was back on station waiting for a firing assignment. Farraday brought him up to speed. "The troops are all ashore on GREEN Beach, but their General is still bellyaching because the decision on where to land was made without him. The Admirals are shrugging their shoulders and telling the General they wouldn't have to make those kinds of decisions if the Army's communication equipment would work. Any landings on Beach RED in the Golfe de Fréjus will have to be delayed. There are thousands of sea mines in the waters off shore, and land mines are buried in the sand on the beach. The minesweepers are taking heavy casualties."

Brosnan interrupted. "What do you think our assignment will be tonight?"

Farraday shrugged. "Stay right here, I think. I don't believe Beach RED will be opened up until at least tomorrow and maybe not until the next day."

"Good. I'll get Parma started on a good dinner. Maybe the Captain will let us go to Condition III long enough to feed the crew sitting down."

Farraday grinned and rubbed his lean belly. "I could go for that."

*　　*　　*

Brosnan got permission from the Captain to go to Condition III for dinner. "But," Fannon said, "we go to general quarters again at dusk. These Germans are tricky."

At dusk, German fire from hidden positions behind Green

Beach erupted again. Large splashes rose and fell back again in puddles of angry water. The *Lawrence* joined the cruisers in pounding the area behind the beach where other by-passed German guns were trying to irritate the Allied forces on the beach.

All of the German fire irritated Fannon, and he strode up and down, alternately cursing the Germans and encouraging Aronson to locate and destroy them. After dusk the German fire began to die out and became desultory because the German gunners couldn't see their targets. As darkness settled in over the beachhead, the firing by both sides ceased, but a peaceful night was not in the cards.

About 2200 CIC reported, "Large flight of unknown aircraft bearing zero one zero. Approximate altitude four thousand. Course one eight zero. High hills below the contact are making radar tracking difficult."

Fannon said to Brill. "Tell Gun Control to acquire a target on their radar. It may be difficult unless they come closer."

Ashore, many large flashes erupted, some from guns near the beach, and more from inland. Phelps observed, "They're dropping bombs ashore."

A few bursts of small weapon antiaircraft fire from the troops ashore laced the night with white tracers that arced across the sky and then winked out. Fannon said grimly, "That won't stop them." He turned to Brill. "Ask Gun Control if they're having any luck."

Brill said, "Gun Control says at least two aircraft have crossed the edge of land and seem to be headed for us."

Phelps said, "They don't have radar, and I don't think they can see us. They're just looking for a way home, and we are in their way."

Fannon clenched his teeth. "We'll help them out. Brill, tell Gun Control to commence firing when they are on target and ready to fire."

Below, the 5-inch mounts' hydraulic motors began to growl as they followed the director. Brosnan could hear Aronson, up above, ordering "Commence firing!" and he shut his eyes to preserve his night vision.

The guns crashed, and Brosnan opened his eyes. Four projectiles were climbing quickly toward an invisible target, their tracers looking like four huge fireflies. The first two salvos each burst in a small group of flashes, but with no result. The darkness closed in again. The third salvo hit home. First, a small flare of light appeared. Then it blossomed into a large fiery cloud, and Brosnan could plainly see the outline of a large aircraft as it nosed over rapidly and powered into the black water below.

"Ju88!" Brosnan bellowed.

Fannnon laughed. "One less Nazi!"

The remaining German aircraft observed the kill and turned north, short of the destroyers. Phelps said, "Well, that should do it for the night." The Commodore's judgement however, proved premature. An instant later, a huge flash of white light blossomed to the north. Farraday, listening intently to his radio circuit, clamped his earpieces tightly over his ears to shut out the local noise on the bridge.

Fannon approached him, cleared his throat, and looked at him impatiently. "Well?"

Farraday refused to be intimidated and said, "Sir, you'll have to wait a minute. Nobody on this circuit knows what happened yet, except that a fully loaded LST is burning and sinking."

Fannon moved away and looked at the burning hulk through his binoculars. "Poor bastards," he muttered.

Soon Farraday stepped forward. "Sir, the hit was by a glide bomber."

Fanon, still watching the flames rising from the burning ship, said to Brosnan, "Could we have countered it if we'd been close enough?"

Brosnan shook his head, "Intelligence says the Germans are no longer using the radio controlled bombs we encountered during our battles off Italy. We've found a way to defeat them, and they know it. They've developed a glider bomb that doesn't need radio control. A glider bomb is really a small aircraft carried by a mother Ju88. It is aimed and released just like a bomb but on a much shallower path. It glides along a predetermined path with no further control by the mother aircraft. If we were close enough in daytime, we could have shot it down. At night there wouldn't have been time to track it by radar before opening fire. We were just too far away."

Fannon shook his head sadly. "What will the boffins think of next?"

*   *   *

The rest of the night was quiet except for the sound of gunfire ashore, both small arms and artillery, as the troops pushed forward. At dawn, the little minesweepers entered the Golfe de Fréjus to resume their operations.

"The minesweepers look like scared seagulls that aren't able to take off from the water, but wish they could," Brosnan said.

Fannon laughed. "Speaking of seagulls, I heard one of the crew say the hardboiled eggs Parma served for breakfast tasted like seagull eggs."

Brosnan shrugged. "He can't win them all. Our egg supply is getting low, and those we have were laid in the States months ago."

Farraday interrupted. "Sir, the troops that landed on GREEN Beach have taken the Golfe de Fréjus from the rear. The remainder of the troops will land as soon as the minesweepers have finished their job."

"I guess the worst is over here," Fannon replied.

Phelps shook his head. "Not by a long shot. There are still many large guns unaccounted for ashore. I'm sure the Germans are deliberately withholding fire for a more favorable moment when they can do more damage."

*   *   *

Fifteen minutes later the TBS crackled. Admiral Lewis ordered Phelps to take the *Lawrence* and *Hanly* and report to the French Landing Force Commander. The *Grayston* and *Thatcher* were to remain on station, off the Golfe de Fréjus.

Brosnan looked at Farraday. "Do you know what this is all about?"

Farraday shrugged. "Nothing on this circuit, sir."

The mystery was soon solved. A few minutes later, Doctor Taylor came running up to the bridge with a decoded dispatch. "From Admiral Hewitt," he said.

Kuberski scanned it and began to summarize it for the others. "Two destroyers are to be detached and sent west to report to the Commander of the French Fire Support Group. It seems their cruisers are out of ammunition and their destroyers are all very low on ammunition. There isn't much activity there, but the French General wants naval gunfire to be available in case of a German counter-attack on his forces."

Fannon, listening intently, turned to Phelps. "Commodore, that's why you've been ordered to take two ships there."

Phelps nodded. "Doesn't seem like there's any urgency. The French destroyers must have enough ammunition to hold out until we can get there at reasonable speed. Let's proceed at 20 knots. Stanley, get the signals out."

*   *   *

The trip along the coast at 20 knots was almost pleasant. Brosnan, having ordered Parma to serve lunch, relaxed and watched the shore sail by. The ALPHA and DELTA beaches were busy but much more peaceful than the CAMEL beaches had been. Hundreds of landing craft scurried between the large ships lying off the beaches and the shore. Mountains of supplies crowded the narrow beachheads. Ten miles inland, Brosnan observed occasional plumes of smoke, which marked the moving battle scene as the Allied Forces pursued the Germans toward central France.

At 1300, the *Lawrence* and *Hanly* reached the French sector and glided to anchorages.

The French General sent Phelps a message of welcome and suggested that he have his ships remain at anchor on short notice.

Brosnan got permission from the Captain to set condition III and went below to set security watches to amplify condition III. He felt tired, but not exhausted. The operation had not been as demanding as the Normandy landings, and the weather was mild and even invigorating. Still, he thought, a shower and nap would be nice, and he headed below for his room.

CHAPTER THIRTY-SIX

Brosnan completed his arrangements to provide a quarter-deck watch using the members of the 40-millimeter crew. Fannon insisted on staying at condition III because he was concerned that the Germans might still have some hidden assets. "Might use swimmers," he grumbled. When Brosnan was satisfied that the ship was secure, he went below, shaved, showered, and changed into a clean uniform. Just as he was adjusting his belt, there was a knock on the door.

"Come in," Brosnan called.

A messenger entered. "Sir, there's a landing craft coming alongside."

Brosnan arrived on the quarterdeck in time to receive the boat coxswain, carrying an envelope. The man saluted the colors and said, "Permission to come aboard, sir. I have a letter for Lieutenant Commander Brosnan, and I am to wait for him."

Brosnan took the envelope and looked at it carefully. It was addressed to him in a flowing hand and on the back of the envelope was an embossed crest and the words "De Lattre de Tassigny" below it.

He opened it and unfolded a single page. The note was topped with the same crest and name that he read on the envelope. It began, "Sir, General De Lattre de Tassigny, Free

French Army, requests that you call on him immediately for a conference that will last about three hours." It was signed, "Marcel Lefrond, Lieutenant, Free French Army, Aide-de-Camp."

Brosnan sent the boat coxswain to the galley to get a cup of coffee and went to the bridge where Fannon and Phelps were leaning on the bulwark and watching the bustling activity along the beach ashore.

Fannon read the letter and grunted. "What the hell! What does the French General in command want with you?"

Brosnan shrugged. "I don't know, sir, maybe something about arranging for naval gunfire support."

Fannon handed the letter back. "You'd better go. Tell Kelly to take over your job temporarily."

*   *   *

Brosnan stood in the back of the landing craft next to the coxswain and braced himself against the rail as the boat bounced along the waves, heading for the beach. "Coxswain, do you know anything about this letter?" Brosnan shouted over the roar of the boat engine.

The coxswain shrugged. "Some Frog officer with four strands of gold around his shoulder said to take it to you. I figured I ought to."

When the boat pulled up to a small fishing pier, Brosnan could see an American-made jeep painted with French colors parked at the head of the pier. A French officer was slumped in the front passenger seat next to an enlisted driver. Both were obviously sound asleep.

Brosnan walked up to the jeep and cleared his throat. The French officer's eyes flew open and he bounded out of the jeep, clicked his heels, and saluted. "Lieutenant Lefrond at your service, sir."

Brosnan showed him the envelope with the name and the crest on it. "I'm Lieutenant Commander Brosnan. This says the General wants to see me."

Lieutenant Lefrond grinned. "I should say he does. Please get in the jeep."

*   *   *

Fifteen minutes later, the jeep pulled up at the front entrance to an imposing chateau. To one side of the building, a large tent was pitched. On the other side were other tents and a vehicle park full of jeeps and dirty, ominous-looking half-tracks, all American made, but painted with French insignia.

Brosnan followed Lefrond to the entrance of the chateau and down a long hall. The pair approached an imposing set of double doors, guarded by a French sentry standing at attention. Lefrond spoke to the sentry in French, "Is the General free?"

"*Oui*, sir."

Lefrond turned to Brosnan. "We'll go in. The General speaks excellent English, but he may want to test your French. Don't be nervous."

Brosnan shrugged, "I should be all right. I've been practicng it for a year."

Lefrond raised his eyebrows. "With a good teacher, I trust?"

"The best."

Lefrond opened the huge doors, and Brosnan followed him. Lefrond stopped, clicked his heels loudly, saluted crisply, and said in French, "Sir, may I present Lieutenant Commander Brosnan, United States Navy."

Brosnan saluted awkwardly, not used to saluting with his cap off.

The General nodded, but kept on writing. Lefrond left, and Brosnan remained standing, looking around the room. It was beautifully decorated and furnished. Brosnan looked down at the General, who was still laboring over a piece of paper. A folded piece of cardboard was perched in front of him. On it was crudely lettered, "De Lattre de Tassigny, Commanding." Brosnan noted the General's short, iron-gray hair, matching mustache, and strong features. He knew he would like the Frenchman.

As if he were reading Brosnan's thoughts, the General threw down his pen and looked up. He inspected Brosnan carefully. "Ah," he said in perfect English. "You are not quite what I expected, but I think I will like you." He gestured around the room. "Don't let this fool you. I am a soldier. I use this building for conferences, but when I'm in the field, I live in a tent. The large one you saw outside is mine. I'm about to leave for an inspection of the front, and I won't be back for at least two hours. It is yours for that time. I will speak to you further when I return."

Brosnan said, "But, General—."

The General rose and strode out of the room. "Later, Brosnan, now go to the tent and wait."

*　　*　　*

Brosnan walked out of the door after the General and watched the jeep carrying the General and Lefrond leave the courtyard in a spray of gravel.

He looked at the tent, shrugged, and walked over to it. He pulled back the door flap and walked in. Annette was seated on a folding cot. "My God!" Brosnan gasped.

Annette grinned, "I thank him for this moment."

CHAPTER THIRTY-SEVEN

Annette was dressed in her floppy black peasant's clothing, but she had removed the jacket, and Brosnan could see the outlines of her firm breasts stretching the white fabric of the singlet she was wearing. He realized how much he missed her physically as passion began to surge within him, but it was the huge smile on her face that captured his attention, and he ran across the tent floor and swept her into his arms.

Annette murmured to him, her face pressed against his chest, "Oh, Beetle, I've missed you—."

After a few minutes of increasingly passionate embraces, Brosnan reluctantly pushed her back so he could see her face. "I've missed you, too, and I want to know how all this came about, but first—."

Annette put a finger on his lips. "Later. Now help me get out of the rest of this ridiculous outfit."

Brosnan thought he would never get off his own clothing, and he compromised by leaving on his socks and shoes. Annette giggled as he pressed her to the cot. "Beetle, I think I can wait until you take off your shoes."

Brosnan kicked them off. "Maybe you can, but I'm not sure I can. We only have two hours."

Annette sighed. "Then let's make the most of them."

For Brosnan it was the most satisfying two hours of his life, and he hoped that married life would bring a sucession of such joyous moments.

* * *

Somewhere in the second hour, Brosnan said, "How did this miracle come about?"

Annette reluctantly withdrew her caressing fingers from Brosnan's hair and wrinkled her brow. "A long story, but I'll try to tell you. When we heard at my estate that the Allies had landed and that the invasion had started, we destroyed our radio transmitters, gathered our intelligence team, and started south toward where we knew the invading friendly forces would probably be."

"How did you get through the German lines?"

"We weren't in any hurry. We had an old truck and several cans of gasoline. We went south slowly to gather as much information as we could on German dispositions and troop movements. Just before we got to the van of the retreating German forces, we left the truck on a side road, buried the cans of gasoline, and hiked up the side of the river valley to a ridge on a high point of land. We were safe there, and we could see the movements of the German Army below us."

Brosnan began to kiss her, and then after the next wave of passion subsided, he said, "Go ahead. What did you do after the Germans passed?"

"We went down to the truck, dug up the cans of gasoline, and resumed our trip south until we met the vanguard of the French forces advancing along the road toward the retreating Germans. We told them what we knew about the German forces, and they sent us back to see the General."

"I guess he was glad to see you."

"Oh, yes, after I completed my debriefing, he said I had been so valuable that I could have anything I wanted. I asked if he could bring you ashore for a short visit."

"Well, he did," Brosnan said as he looked at his watch. "Damn! Our two hours is about up." He got up from the creaking cot and began to get dressed.

Annette said, "I'm to be sent to SHAEF Headquarters for about two weeks for further debriefing and then I'm to be demobilized from the Free French Forces. As soon as the Germans are clear of my estate, I will be free to go there and try to bring it back to full production. The Free French Government is looking forward to reviving the country's economy, even before the fighting is over."

"Do you know how much damage the German troops have done to your estate and the vineyards?"

"Oh, yes, when they departed, they took along all of my art collection. Otherwise the damage is repairable. The chateau is, how do you Americans say it, 'badly used,' but they didn't hurt the vineyard very much."

Brosnan laughed. "My friend, Stanley Kuberski, will put together another art collection for you."

"Lieutenant Kuberski? I didn't think he was excactly the artistic type."

Brosnan finished tying his shoes. "He is, and I hope to see a lot of him after the war is over. By the way, I'd like to take over the sales part of your operation after we're married. I already have some help lined up."

"Yes? Who?"

"A young supply officer named Parma. He can do anything, and I think he'd make a good sales representative in the States and in the Middle East and Africa."

"But what of our sales in France?"

Brosnan grinned. "Do you remember French Lieutenant Marcel Lefrond?"

"Oh, yes, that nice *Aide-de-Camp*. I liked him, and he helped us with the General."

Brosnan laughed. "I think all Frenchmen either like to make love or to help someone else do it. He arranged all this for us, and if he can sell this to the General, he can sell anything."

Annette smiled warmly. "It sounds good to me. All I want to do is raise grapes and babies. But we won't do any of that until you've lived with me for at least thirty days."

"Why? We know we love each other."

"I want to make sure you'll like being a Frenchman."

"I know I'll like it, and I've been practicing my French for almost a year."

"But, Beetle, I hear a reservation in your voice."

Brosnan sighed. "Well, of course I'll miss the Navy, and I've always wanted to command a destroyer. If I could do that, I'd leave the Navy a happy man."

"You've still got time. Finishing off the Germans may take a year, and there will still be a need for your Navy. You may have a chance."

"You think the fighting will continue that long?"

"Oh, yes, it's a long way to Berlin."

CHAPTER THIRTY-EIGHT

Brosnan stepped out of the tent, secured the flap firmly, and started toward the General's headquarters, being careful not to give the appearance of straightening his clothes. Before he reached the door, Lefrond came out and strode toward Brosnan. "Ah, Brosnan, I was beginning to think I might have to, ah, interrupt your conference." He raised his eyebrows. "I hope the General's field cot is still all right. I had to steal it from an American general."

Brosnan laughed. "It's fine and so is my fiancée. I thank you both from the bottom of my heart. This has been a day I will never forget."

Lefrond sighed. "Madame Duchamp is a charming woman. I have seen her estate near Lyon. It is a big one and it has a fine vineyard. Well known in France."

"I've never seen it."

"What! And you are her fiancée. You must see it soon. I do not understand you Americans. Marriage is more important than just an affair of the heart to us Frenchmen. We would want to learn all about our bride's financial affairs before we, how do you Americans say it, committed ourselves."

Brosnan held up his hand, "Stop, Marcel, everything will work out in due time for both of us. When the war is over and you are out of the French Army, I might even have a job for you on Madame's estate."

Lefrond beamed. "As a wine taster?"

Brosnan shook his head, "No, as a salesman."

Lefrond shrugged. "Very good. I would have to taste the wine before I knew it was good to sell, and I think I would make a very good salesman."

"What did you do before the war?"

"Ah, yes, I was a salesman."

"And what did you sell?"

Lefrond sighed. "Don't laugh. Lady's lingerie. Underwear, I think you call it."

"Do you know anything about wine?"

"Of course! Every Frenchman knows the basic facts about wine. Also I worked in a winery every summer between school terms before I left for the Sorbonne."

"What did you take there?"

Lefrond shrugged. "A little of everything. Mostly about how to be a well-educated gentleman."

Brosnan laughed. "I think you succeeded. You will do well, and I will speak to Madame Duchamp about it. Now I have to thank the General before I leave."

"Of course. Follow me."

When Lefrond knocked on the huge door, the General said firmly, "*Entre*."

Lefrond pushed the door open and said in English, "General, Lieutenant Commander Brosnan would like to see you."

The General looked up and said in French, "Ah, Brosnan, good to see you. I didn't want to ruin the surprise when I saw you before. Now sit down for a moment. I want to tell you what a remarkable woman you are engaged to be married to, in the event you do not already know."

Brosnan smiled, sat down, and declined a cigarette offered by the General. De Lattre de Tassigny lit his cigarette and leaned back. He continued the conversation in French. "Annette has been the key to our intelligence operation in Central France for some time. My forces are advancing rapidly, now, using the local intelligence she and her team furnished. Her work will save many days of fighting and hundreds of lives."

Brosnan beamed. "And I understand she will be demobilized soon."

"Yes. As valuable as she was, as soon as we pass by Central France, she won't be needed any more for intelligence purposes. She will be more valuable to our country helping to rebuild its economy. By the way, your French is surprisingly good for an American. I notice you have a Lyonnaise accent, and I can guess why."

Brosnan grinned, "Yes, General, my teacher comes from near Lyon."

*   *   *

Lefrond escorted Brosnan to the landing in the General's jeep and arranged for a landing craft to return him to the *Lawrence*.

As Brosnan jumped down into the LCVP, Lefrond saluted. "I hope to see you soon."

Brosnan returned the salute. "Thank you for arranging one of the best days of my life! I hope to repay you some day, and you will hear from me as soon as the war is over and we have been demobilized."

Lefrond reached into his inner pocket, pulled out a card, and handed it to Brosnan. "You can reach me here at any time."

"Thank you."

Lefrond grinned knowingly. "Ah, of course I know where to reach you."

CHAPTER THIRTY-NINE

As the landing craft gathered speed and turned toward the *Lawrence*, Brosnan looked and thought he was seeing double. Apparently, another ship of the division was moored to the port side of the *Lawrence*. "Coxswain, isn't that another destroyer moored to the *Lawrence*?" he asked.

"Yes, sir, the *Grayston* pulled alongside her a couple of hours ago."

*   *   *

The LCVP came alongside the *Lawrence*'s accommmodation ladder and stopped, its exhaust burbling loudly. Brosnan climbed up the ladder and saluted the colors. Kuberski was standing next to the top of the ladder. "Beetle, I've had your gear packed. The Commodore and Captain want to see you in the Commodore's cabin on the double."

Brosnan's jaw dropped. "What the hell is going on?"

"Just go. They'll tell you."

Brosnan knocked on the Commodore's door, and Phelp's voice said, "Come in."

Phelps and Fannon were bent over several dispatch forms and personnel folders spread on the table. Phelps looked up. "Ah, Beetle, you just made it. I was about to send Kuberski off in your place."

Fannon added impatiently, "Yes, you almost missed the boat, so to speak."

Brosnan said, "Would someone please tell me what this is all about?"

Phelps nodded. "Sit down. You are about to take over command of the *Grayston*. I'm sure you saw her alongside to port."

Brosnan's eyebrows shot up. "What happened to her, sir?"

"She took a shell hit on the port side of the bridge. The bridge on that side is a shambles, and the 5-inch gun director above it is also out of commission. It can't be repaired short of the yard, but the battery can operate in local control and the ship is otherwise sound."

Brosnan shook his head, thinking about his friends in the ship. "Was anybody hurt?"

Fannon nodded. "The Captain, Executive Officer, and Gunnery Officer were all badly wounded. Several men and particularly those in the signal force also were wounded. All the wounded have been sent to an APA equipped as a hospital ship."

Phelps said, "I've been ordered to furnish a destroyer to escort a dozen damaged amphibious ships to Oran. They left an hour ago, and the *Grayston* will have to catch up with them."

Brosnan was beginning to recover from his surprise. "Commodore, I'm honored to be considered for command, but I hate to leave this ship."

Fannon was grim. "Beetle, I hate to see you go, too, and I'll miss you like hell, but you deserve the chance to command. You'll take the *Grayston* to Portsmouth for repairs after dropping off the Amphibs at Oran."

Phelps interrupted. "You'll need an executive officer. I'm sending Lieutenant Raymond along with you. He'll have to double as gunnery officer. Captain Fannon has agreed to let Barley go with you, as well. Some of the lightly wounded quartermasters and signalmen on the *Grayston* will stay aboard and will be available as soon as they recover. You'll have to navigate."

Brosnan nodded. "I'll make out all right, but what about the *Lawrence*? Lieutenant Kelly is only marginally qualified as an executive officer."

Phelps said, "Captain Fannon agrees, so I'm sending Stanley Kuberski to the flagship to relieve you, and I'm ordering a young officer from the *Hanly* to relieve him."

Fannon said, "You'll have to get a move on. Kuberski has sent your belongings over to the *Grayston*, and you'll have half-an-hour to turn over your job to him."

*   *   *

Kuberski was waiting outside the Commodore's cabin. When Brosnan came out, Kuberski grinned. "Beetle, I'm happy for you. You made it."

Brosnan was pensive. "Yeah, but the hard way."

"Don't knock it. You'll get used to it, and the *Grayston* is a fine ship. Let's get on with the turnover."

Brosnan shrugged. "What's to turn over? You're well-qualified, and you know the ship."

"Okay, I relieve you. Get going. Your chariot awaits."

Brosnan poked his head back into the Commodore's cabin, and Kuberski looked over his shoulder. "Sirs, we've done the relief bit, and with your permission, Captain, I'll go to the *Grayston*."

Fannon answered, "I'd like to see you off formally, but we're all busy as hell. I wish you the best of luck, Beetle, and you have my permission to leave."

Phelps chimed in. "Yes, I second that. And I have a request. After the war, I suspect you'll be living in France, and I expect an annual visit to my, er, Lady Claudia's estate."

"I promise that, sir, and I'll also visit you, Captain, in Oklahoma."

Fannon grinned. "I'll count on it. Perhaps we can have some reunions in England. After all, I expect to be spending a lot of time there."

CHAPTER FORTY

Before Brosnan crossed the small brow to the *Grayston*, he asked for permission to leave the ship from the petty officer of the watch and saluted the *Lawrence*'s colors. Then he stepped over to the *Grayston*, saluted her colors, and turned to the petty officer of the watch on the *Grayston*. "Permission to come aboard, sir?"

The petty officer of the watch replied, "Permission granted. Welcome aboard, sir."

A fresh-faced lieutenant was standing forward of the petty officer of the watch. He saluted and said, "Lieutenant Fisher, sir, temporary commanding officer. Welcome aboard."

Brosnan turned to him, noting that his young features were marked temporarily with lines of stress. "I'm Lieutenant Commander Brosnan, and on the verbal authority of Commander Destroyer Squadron 30, I hereby assume command of the *Grayston*. My permanent orders will come later by dispatch from the Navy Department."

Lieutenant Fisher looked relieved. "I'm glad to see you, sir. Lieutenant Raymond is already aboard and has assumed duties as executive officer. He's on the bridge preparing the ship ready for getting under way."

Brosnan nodded. "What is your regular assignment?"

"CIC officer. I was in CIC when we were hit."

"Then you took over command?"

"Yes, sir, I transferred the wounded to an APA and then steamed up here to report to the Commodore."

"Looks like you did a good job. Just escort me to the bridge and then you can go back to CIC."

Fisher fell in at Brosnan's left, and they started forward. Brosnan wanted to run up to the bridge, but he restrained himself and set a moderate pace. Fisher spoke nervously, obviously trying to make conversation. "Sir, I hear you were a college wrestler at Ohio State."

Brosnan, half listening, said, "Yes, a long time ago."

"You look like you're still in pretty good shape. Could we go a few minutes sometime?"

"Ah, yes, but we'd need a mat, and destroyers don't usually have one."

Fisher brightened. "But we do. Also we have a pretty good wrestling team. Even the cruiser teams have trouble beating us."

Brosnan nodded. "Congratulations. Maybe we can work out something."

Fisher was still not satisfied. "Captain," he said. "What were you doing over on the beach?"

Brosnan pulled up short and looked at Fisher's earnest young face. "Just a conference. It lasted several hours."

Fisher beamed. "It must have been interesting, meeting all those Frogs."

Brosnan looked at Fisher's face, and he couldn't resist the temptation. "Actually I spent the time in a tent with my girlfriend."

Fisher laughed. "Aw, Captain, the officers on the *Lawrence* said you were a kidder, but that's too much."

Brosnan shrugged. "Okay, then, take your pick."

By now the pair were at the bottom of the ladder, and Brosnan grabbed the rails and bounded up the steel treads.

Fisher, following more slowly and said "Great sense of humor, sir."

Tubby Raymond and Chief Barley were waiting for Brosnan at the top of the ladder. Barley spoke first. "Congratulations, Captain, watch your step. The shipfitters are rigging a temporary platform on the port wing of the bridge. You'll have to use the starboard side for getting under way."

Brosnan replied, "Thank you, Barley." He turned to Raymond. "What about the bridge instrumentation?"

Raymond reported, "The steering gyro repeater works and the gyro repeater on the starboard wing works. The magnetic compass is undamaged but obviously off by several degrees, because of the rearrangemnt of the steel on the port side of the bridge. I think we can use it in an emergency, and we can get a temporary calibration and comparison with the gyro after we get under way."

"Sounds okay. What else?" Brosnan asked.

"The TBS and all the intra-ship communications work. The port torpedo director is a shambles, and the 5-inch director is badly damaged. We'll be okay in local control, and I think I can control both the 5-inch battery and the machine guns from the bridge level."

*   *   *

Fifteen minutes later, when Raymond reported the ship ready to get under way, Brosnan walked to the starboard wing and looked over at the *Lawrence*'s bridge. Phelps, Fannon, and Kuberski were lined up along the bridge rail. Brosnan saluted and said to Phelps, "Sir, I have assumed command in accordance with your verbal orders, and I request permission to get under way and carry out my orders."

Phelps returned his salute. "Permission granted. Good luck, Brosnan."

Fannon looked unhappy but resigned. His small mustache drew a thin black line across his tense face. He saluted. "Good luck, Captain."

Brosnan turned to the talker. "Take in all lines except two. Main Engine Control, stand by to answer all bells."

The men on deck moved swiftly to bring in the mooring lines, and soon the talker reported, "All lines in except two, sir."

Brosnan took a last look down the starboard side to make sure all was clear. "Right full rudder. Port ahead one-third. Starboard back one-third."

The ship began to vibrate as the engineers below opened the throttles. Brosnan felt the movement through the soles of his shoes. "Just like making love," he thought, remembering the time he had spent with Annette earlier that day.

He put those thoughts out of his mind and concentrated on his new love, his first command. "Rudder amidships. Take in two. All back two-thirds. Do not sound the whistle."

The vibration increased, and the ship began to move astern rapidly. When she was well clear, Brosnan ordered, "All ahead full, left 10 degrees rudder." The *Grayston* began gathering headway and turned slowly to port. She passed the *Lawrence* abeam at about two hundred yards. As they passed, Brosnan was busy looking ahead to make sure the prospective course was clear.

Barley interrupted his thoughts. "Captain, look over there. Your friends on the *Lawrence* are waving at you."

Brosnan turned to look at the bridge of the flagship. On her bridge wing were several figures waving at him. Brosnan waved back and raised his binoculars to see the faces more plainly. Phelps was pensive, Fannon was grim and unhappy, but Kuberski's pleasant face was split into a huge grin.

*   *   *

As the *Grayston* forged ahead rapidly, Brosnan gave one final wave at the *Lawrence*. He turned to Barley, who had his telescope propped on the bridge bulwark. "See anything up ahead?"

"Yes, sir, I see several masts about ten miles ahead. I guess you know we don't have any radar. All the wave guides on the mast were destroyed. You'll have to depend on my telescope."

Brosnan said, "I always have. Do you know how far it is to Oran and then to Portsmouth?"

"Sure. Eight hundred miles to Oran. Seventeen hundred more to Portsmouth."

Brosnan did some mental calculations. "I make it about three days to Oran and another five to Portsmouth, depending on what speed the amphibs can make."

Barley broke into a huge grin.

Brosnan looked at his chief. "What are you so happy about?"

"I get to see Sadie in Portsmouth, and that handsome bastard Acton won't be there to get in the way."

Brosnan suddenly realized that he might get to see Annette before she left for France and he smiled as well.

"I see you are smiling, too. Will you get to see your fiancée?" Barley asked.

"It will be close."

Barley shrugged. "What do you care? Now that you're the skipper, you can take leave and go to France to see her. Lieutenant Raymond can take over for you. It might do him some good."

"How's that?"

"He might lose some pounds worrying."

Brosnan frowned. "I like him just the way he is." Turning away, he raised his binoculars and looked back toward the *Lawrence*. She was still visible, riding to her anchor. He looked over her lines, trying to fix them in his mind. He knew how lucky he was to have a destroyer to command, and perhaps to be seeing his fiancée soon, but somehow he wasn't enjoying his good fortune. The new captain of *Grayston* knew he would miss the *Lawrence* and all her officers and men. He had fought and bled with them, and they were all his brothers, from Phelps to Jason.

Brosnan blinked his eyes and felt the moisture beginning to gather in the corners. He lowered his binoculars and wiped his eyes on his sleeve.

Barley saw what he was doing. "What's the matter, Captain, got something in your eye?"

"Yeah, stack gases, I guess."

Barley looked at him closely. "But we haven't blown tubes recently."

Brosnan sighed. "Then it must be nostalgia."

Barley nodded. "My eyes are running, too. I guess it's just something going around."